"GOOD WRITERS [...]
CAN MAKE US BEL[...]
RONALD BASS."
—*Publishers Weekly*

In Washington . . . in Moscow . . . in Paris . . .
in London . . . in Venice . . . in Switzerland . . .
in Mexico . . . in Saudi Arabia . . . in Japan . . .
in China . . . all over the globe, the world
order was trembling like a house of cards.

A new tide of terror was rising—and only one
man had a clue to who was behind it and why.

That very lone man was Harry Lime—and he
had to unmask a menace that made the Cold
War look like a lover's embrace. . . .

LIME'S CRISIS

"A PLEASURE . . . Harry Lime is a character
you won't soon forget."—*John Barkham Reviews*

Thrilling Reading from SIGNET

LIME'S CRISIS

A Novel by

RONALD BASS

A SIGNET BOOK

NEW AMERICAN LIBRARY

PUBLISHER'S NOTE

This novel is a work of fiction. Names, characters, places, and incidents either are the product of the author's imagination or are used fictitiously, and any resemblance to actual persons, living or dead, events, or locales is entirely coincidental.

For Chris and Jennifer

Acknowledgments

There were many kind friends who gave invaluable advice and support. I would particularly like to thank my good friend Paul Jordan, as well as Paul Langer and Wally Baer, for their direction, guidance and interest.

1997

ONE

Harry Lime stirred against the weight of his sleep. The weight of waking up. As always, his body would creep toward Jenny's side of the bed. A leaf turning to the sun.

He was just ending his dream of Jenny as his muscles stretched toward her. She had held him in his sleep, in his dreams, as she had always held him. Jennylime. Held him from behind as he lay curled on his side of the bed. Held him and whispered her warmth into his ear. The terrible whisper. She would leave him.

And now, the instant when his mind could wrap itself around the whisper. In the surge toward waking, his arm reached, nearly clutched, at Jenny beside him. Then, that first dead moment, the one before he would realize that she was in the john or the kitchen. The numbing moment of grasping at air and knowing she was gone. Knowing the dream was long ago and Jennylime was gone.

He almost had to hold his breath to live through those first few seconds. And as his mind cleared, he swam fitfully away from them and toward Jenny just stepping from her shower, pink and full, black hair spread across her back and shoulders. He swam toward Jenny in the kitchen, stirring Lissa's eggs.

His mind strained, as it always did, for one sound of affirmation, a pan clanging, drawer closing. And he smiled to himself, as he always did, that the silence should frighten him so. That the silence of a moment could put the lie to what he knew. Jenny was there and would always be there. She would burst from the bathroom in her pale yellow robe and dig her warm hands under him, chew at his ear and breathe her life into his face, his mouth. Jennylime, Jennylime, please just hold me one last time.

Harry's body eased and his head rolled back with its smile, and he had to catch himself to keep from calling her name. His belly was the last to unclench. It was the part of him most affected by the dream, still squeezing out its sour warning.

Something hopped lightly onto the bed and settled delicately between Harry's legs. It was Murray, the cat. And with Murray, his mind was suddenly clear.

Murray was a female, like most calicoes. Queen Murray, Jenny had named her, Queen Murray the Weird. She was a tiny, soft thing. Half of her face was black, the other half mottled white and cinnamon.

She sat on Harry's stomach, purring rhythmically, looking at him with such love. Harry wondered if Murray still loved Jenny, if a cat could remember someone it had loved very much. Harry guessed that if any cat could remember, it would be Queen Murray the Weird. Even after two years.

That had been Harry's morning.

Now it was night and Harry was driving to Malibu. The darkened beach houses slipped by to the left, past the Colony, where the very-casual-very-rich were dreaming mellow dreams.

Between morning and night, there had been lunch

with Warner Alden. Last week, Alden had phoned from New York. Good God, Harry, must be fifteen years. Great to hear your voice, Harry. Harry had to rummage around in his mind before recalling the faded distaste that went with Alden's name. They had been classmates and strangers at Harvard Law.

Harry replayed the call in his mind. Alden's voice was oily-warm, but nervous. No doubt, Alden said, Harry recalled Horace Tate, one of the class' most illustrious products.

Harry did. Tate was a disagreeable beanpole with a first-rate mind and a habit of working twenty-hour days. He washed out of two Wall Street firms on personality grounds, no small feat. Hooked up with an unknown congressman, and by the time his boss became a senator, Tate was his administrative assistant. Last January 20, the Senator had changed his address to the White House, and Tate had become Chief of Staff.

Alden explained that he and Tate had kept in contact through the years. An absurd thought. Tate had been an irritable recluse. Alden had no friends who were not both rich and mediocre, two qualities Tate conspicuously lacked.

Alden confided that Horace Tate had tapped him for help in recruiting a Special Assistant to the President. Alden had assured Tate that Harry was just the chap for the job. Harry told Alden he was surprised, flattered, grateful for the thought, but not interested. Edgy throughout the call, Alden now seemed shocked, even frightened. At least let's take a luncheon on it. He'd fly to the Coast on Monday. Harry was regretfully not interested. Alden swung into hysteria. Harry was politely not interested. Alden simply begged. Harry consented to lunch, but was most definitely not interested.

Harry was interested.

It had been nine years. Nine lifetimes. He had never once thought of going back, even in the darkest moments after Jenny left him. But somewhere in the week before lunch, through obligatory cocktails and excruciating small talk, through the clumsy guile on Alden's face as he made his stumbling offer, Harry knew he was going back. And the distant smell-taste of those acids was in his mouth.

Harry pulled off the highway and down a little path called Escondido Beach Road. He and Jenny had rented a tiny wood-frame here, the summer Lissa was six. In the early mornings, Harry would tiptoe to Lissa's room and carry the sleeping child through the tangle of brush and trees down to the beach. She would wake in her father's arms on the cool sand. They would look out to the sea, and she would tell him what she had dreamed. He would tell her of places far away. Places he promised they would see together.

Harry drove automatically to the old cottage. He tripped the lock on the gate and stepped onto the weathered redwood deck. At some near-conscious level, he assumed that no one would be using the place this early in the year. The house was dark and still.

From the deck, he looked through the blackened shapes of two large palms, out to the moonlit sea. Harry had been here only once since that summer. He had come at sunset on the night Jenny left. He had stood staring between those palms for whatever time it had taken for the sun to slip into the sea. He had watched the pink underside of the clouds begin to orange and bloom, then glow. After the last slice of the sun's rind had disappeared, Harry had stood for a long moment. As if making absolutely certain that it wasn't coming back.

Very slowly now, in the coldness of early morning, Harry picked his way down to the beach.

Harry sat on the sand, in the slacks of his nice flannel business suit, staring out at where the sun had been. Staring after all the things that weren't coming back.

There would be no sleep tonight. For a while, there would be no thinking either. All of the tactical decisions of Harry's life involved thinking. When to keep your mouth shut. Would you trust the veal in a place like this.

Turning places in Harry's life had very little to do with thinking. Join the Agency. Marry Jenny. Quit the Agency. Go on living after Jenny was gone. No thinking, no decision. There was only, finally, a realizing of whatever it was that Harry was going to do.

Harry had come to turning places alone before, before Jenny, when being alone could only be compared to dim dreams of what it might be to not be alone. There was no one to give scent or fire to that pain. For before Jenny, there was no one.

This was the first of the things that would have to wash over him tonight, to let him be ready. Harry knew that there was nothing he could do to make it easier. He would have to sit quietly and submit. He couldn't deal with the feelings all jumbled together. They would have to come to him in their own time, wash over him, fill him up and then flow past.

Jenny would have to come first. There were so many things Jenny had taught Harry. Loving Jenny taught him that he *had* been alone. Alone in his childhood. Alone in the love of his father, a love that never truly knew his heart or tried to share his feelings. Alone in the seeming warmth of college friends and later lovers who shared only time with Harry. Only time and were gone. Alone most of all in the rarefied atmosphere of the Agency. A place that subjected every feeling to thought. Where concentration, focus, was life itself. Finding Jenny had meant leaving that place, though Harry had been slow to see it.

And so, Jenny came to him as he sat on the sand, came from the moon and the sky, and told him again the truth of what she had been to him. The only one. The one who shared her life with his life until it was their life. The one who made him whole. The one who was forever.

Jenny's coming had taught Harry that nothing truly mattered unless it was forever. Jenny's leaving taught him that nothing would be forever.

Harry sat as Jenny filled him for a while. There was no sense of time or sound or the chill wind off the sea. She filled him with her eyes and her black hair. With a thousand memories, now flashing quickly through his body, now lingering exquisitely. There was too much truth. Too many truths. Jenny had existed. Had never. Was gone.

When she washed out of every cell of his body, he was sweating and shivering. Cold and wet and exhausted, he was left with Jenny's last truth. To never love like that again. To never give yourself to someone who would leave you.

And so, Harry knew why he would come to the Agency again. To be utterly self-contained, to have his very survival depend on that absorption, that commitment.

Lissa came to him next, a sweeter, simpler pain. Lissa came first at six, the summer on this beach, this spot. She came at her birth, and at the first time he saw Jenny nursing. A broken foot. A birthday party, he couldn't remember quite . . . yes, the one just after he'd left the Agency. She was three then, wise and fat and never slept.

The one that stayed the longest was the night before Jenny took her away. Jennylime hadn't come home that night, and Harry had told Lissa some ridiculous lie. It was the sickest he'd ever felt. The most alone. He and Lissa had eaten in silence. Then his nine-year-old daughter climbed into his lap and put her arms around his neck. She told him she was scared and he told her the truth. She told him she would always love him. Me too, he said. And prayed that neither of them was lying.

Harry was suddenly aware of his utter exhaustion. The sound of the surf had broken through for the first time and actually startled him. The tide was coming in the moonlight, surf now lapping gently only a few yards away.

He looked up at the sky. Harry had never learned which stars were which, and that made him feel suddenly sad.

He knew that he wasn't going to cry. Harry had finished his crying over Jenny and Lissa long ago. He was glad of that. Crying had always meant something quite different to Harry. Throughout his life, it had been his natural response when something touched him deeply, wonderfully. Such crying was no sob or sound, only wet eyes, dampness that came from some part of Harry that he liked very much. Through his weariness and his misery, Harry knew that such moments would come again. He would save his tears for them.

After Lissa, the rest was easy. His parents, friends, enemies. His past came piece by piece to pay its respects to his future.

The Agency came last. Buck and old John Knowles and all the men who had put the SIA together, after the CIA had all but unraveled. Paris, Bangkok, Vienna. The life he had dreamed of as a boy. The life he'd lived until he had "retired." At thirty-three.

It was first light. The sun was coming up behind Harry as he stared out to sea. Dawn in less than an hour, and Jenny and Lissa were gone. Buck was there, and Vienna. He could only go forward now by going back. That thin acid was in his nostrils and under his tongue. He felt the rush of it. Bitter and, there was no way to deny it, thrilling. It was first light, and Harry knew it was once again time to think.

There was no wondering about what they wanted him for. They would tell him soon enough. He would not believe them. As he had not believed Alden. It was not useful for Harry to believe. Sooner or later, he would stumble over the truth.

The wondering was about the way it was happening. And what it meant.

Harry's mind carefully sorted out the pieces.

If they had truly been after Harry, they would never have approached him through a man like Warner Alden. If it were Agency, the Director of SIA would have called in person. Ross Buckley would have shown up in Harry's living room one night, sucking his pipe and listening to Brahms and slugging down Harry's cognac before Harry could turn his own key in his own door. Buck would smile the smile of nine years ago and speak in a tone that would disappear the time between. Something's turned up, Buck would say, that might amuse.

If it were not Agency, if he were really to work for this administration, Horace Tate would have picked up the phone. Why would Tate contact him through a fool like Alden? Alden said Tate had called him, looking for a top negotiator in the private sector. Absurd. Even if Tate wanted to search the old class for names, he would never have used Alden. An outsider might think that fund-raising chairman was a good contact, but Tate had been in the class himself. He had to know Alden was an archetypal loser. The man had been an infamous pain in the ass. No one from their class, not even a loner like Tate, would have chosen Alden.

Any way Harry turned it, there was no way it could have been Warner Alden.

But it *had* been Alden. And it was too unreasonable to be without a reason.

TWO

Harry was ushered into the office by a somewhat prissy male secretary. He was seated in a hard wooden chair and told to wait.

It was the office of a workaholic. Papers and files covered every inch of available surface. The desk was dreadfully jumbled, but everything on the credenza and side tables was neatly arranged. No matter how long the workday, this was a man who cleaned his desk each night to prepare for the onslaught of the day to come.

There were no less than five aluminum filing cabinets lined up behind the desk, blocking the windows. Painted a sickly rose color, each cabinet was within reach of the swivel chair behind the desk. Three phones, each with extra-long extension cords so that files could be perused with one hand while holding the receiver in the other. The cords were tangled horribly. No one had time or interest to untangle anything nonessential in such a place.

Harry waited patiently, alone. Not knowing whether he was being observed, he remained in his chair. He looked around the room only frequently enough to appear natural.

The desk held an old coffee mug crammed with

pencils, each carefully sharpened. Harry could picture Mr. Prissy squirming under a lecture from his/
her boss if those points weren't up to snuff. Selection
of the cheapest possible felt-tip pens in all colors of
the rainbow, blotter, letter-opener, stapler, staple-
remover, paper clip holder, all tired and used. They
had followed him from place to place for years. Served
him well. No need to replace them.

The walls held a large portrait of the President of
the United States, and a larger pink map of the President's home state. Nothing else.

There was one more hard wooden chair exactly like
Harry's, and that was it. No other furniture.

There were no meetings here. This was a man who
made the journey to wait on his superiors. His inferi-
ors were dealt with by intercom and telephone. He had
no peers. A war went on daily in this room, and the
man fought it alone.

Harry smiled blandly as he waited. His eyes now
locked into middle distance.

After twenty-five minutes, Horace Tate entered his
office. Without a word, the White House Chief of
Staff seated himself behind his desk. Folded his bony
hands tightly before him.

"We've never met?" Tate asked, at last.

His face looked absurdly long and narrow, accentu-
ated by his baldness. His shoulders were hunched,
and so narrow that they seemed pointed. Like the
wings of a large bird at rest.

"No," said Harry.

Tate opened a file, glanced at the top page, then
closed it.

"I knew your name, of course," Tate said, looking at
the closed file. "At the Law School. It's . . . quite a
file."

He turned his hollow eyes toward Harry.

"No question about it," he said. "You're an interesting man. Have any notion why you're here?"

"Only what Warner Alden told me."

"And what was that?"

"Well," Harry smiled, "you know ol' Warner."

"Not really," Tate said, making no effort to hide his distaste. "In fact, not at all."

Silence followed.

"Did he . . . tell you otherwise?" Tate asked. His cheeks sucked in as he pursed his lips.

"I suppose I jumped to that conclusion," Harry said.

"Having spoken with ol' Warner myself," Tate said dryly, "I think I know what you mean. He did tell me that you and he were extremely close. His recommendation of you was most energetic."

"Kind of him," Harry observed.

Tate leaned back, spread his elbows and propped one foot up on his desk. The effect was as if the same act had been accomplished by a flamingo in a three-piece suit.

"The President," he said "has decided, quite privately, that he would like this administration to avoid the entrenched bureaucracy . . . which he considers, at best, mediocre . . ."

"And, at worst, Republican," Harry noted.

Tate laughed. An empty snort which sounded like a honk.

"End run the bureaucrats," he repeated with a frighteningly broad grin, "and look to the private sector for the really key people. And as you read the *Post*, you see the speculation that cabinet-level appointments, even State and Defense, will have minimal influence compared with the President's personal advisers. This takes place to some extent in any administration, but I think it would be accurate to say, more so in ours." Harry noted the royal "we."

Harry offered a perfunctory smile. Benign and reserved.

"As you suggest," Tate said, "the opposition has been in office for quite a while, and their strength in the departments of the executive branch of government is ... well, pretty deep. Of course, we are replacing many of these people, but that isn't the whole answer."

Tate cleared his throat. Sat upright again.

"The real problem is nonpartisan. For a long time, it's been evident that the best minds in our country avoid politics and government like the plague. For most of the people who enter government, we're talking about a lifetime of low pay, no influence, very little opportunity to make meaningful contributions. Why should someone with a superior intellect choose such a life?"

"To be of service," Harry offered, as though Tate's question had not been rhetorical.

Tate looked at Harry's eyes, and decided it was the proper moment.

"Is that why you signed on at SIA?" he asked.

In the old days, Harry had never heard anyone in government refer to the Security Intelligence Agency as SIA. It sounded too much like CIA, and, of course, the avoidance of that implication had been the very reason the Agency was formed.

"I joined the Agency," Harry said simply, "because I thought I'd like it."

"And left?" Tate said, somewhat too sharply.

"Because I didn't like it anymore."

Tate puckered into a small frown. Harry had been chosen. Tate had his orders. Still, he was hoping for some slight clearing of the air that would tip his personal feelings in Harry's favor. For the moment, that feeling eluded him.

Tate decided to go in another direction. He leaned forward, tucking his elbows inward. He wanted his smile to be confiding. A shared recognition between equals of their common task.

"I think it's fair to say that we're at the gravest crossroads this nation has faced since its birth, Harry. May I call you 'Harry'?"

Harry smiled his assent.

"Because," Tate said, "if we can't do something meaningful about this energy situation, you're going to see this nation disintegrate into anarchy and violence so squalid . . . the Civil War was North against South, this one will be every man against his neighbor. How long do *you* think we have, Harry?"

"I don't know."

"Neither do we. When do we impose martial law, Harry? When we have twenty-five major riots per day, killing five hundred people? How long will it take to get to there? We don't know when the energy's going to run out, but we do know one thing. The nerve and the patience of the people of this republic are going to run out a whole lot sooner. The press. Informative, Harry, they're very informative. You can't pick up a national news magazine without reading some grisly scenario about exactly what happens when we have to cut back fifteen percent on pharmaceuticals or twenty percent on plastics. When a guy runs out of gas at the end of some five-mile line in Cleveland, he doesn't just see the end of his job, he sees the end of the world."

Tate took out a large handkerchief and blotted the moisture from his glistening forehead and crown.

"I'm assuming that everything I've just said is exactly the reason why you're sitting here."

"It's part of it," Harry said quietly. "I don't know how much."

"My point is," Tate leaned forward as far as he could, which was very far indeed, "that if the President is going to send somebody in to buy oil from the Arabs or the Mexicans, he wants it to be the best goddam negotiator he can find in this republic. Not some asshole hack from State who I wouldn't send out to buy a used car for my Aunt Minnie."

Harry nodded thoughtfully. This was as good a time as any.

"Why me? I'm sure Warner must have recommended lots of other names." Alden had told Harry that he had given Tate more than a dozen names.

"As a matter of fact," Tate said, "he only recommended yours. Not that I gave a shit what he recommended. As I told you, I don't even know the man. From the little I've seen, he's a moron."

Harry just smiled.

Tate had no thought that he was being interrogated. As other trained interrogators, Harry leaned heavily on misdirection. Instinctively, he turned to it now. Warner Alden's body would lie unnoticed on the table, until they stumbled over it together. Surely, he was of no interest to either of them.

"Why the hell," Harry said in his most confiding tone, "would you guys want to go shopping for trouble? Must be a thousand fellas you coulda picked without my special . . . problem."

"You mean that little detail about you being a traitor to the republic?" Tate cocked his head to one side and grinned playfully. The Birdman of Pennsylvania Avenue. This looked about as intimate as he was likely to get.

"That little detail," Harry smiled in appreciation of the Birdman's wit.

"We're magnanimous enough to chalk that up as a bullshit, over-zealous, Republican witch-hunt. Willing, that is, after Ross Buckley personally put his ass on the line for you. He spent forty-five minutes alone with the President, and when he came out of the Oval Office, you had the job."

"Some of those witch-hunting Republicans are still around, Horace. I can think of two or three in the Senate."

Tate spread his wings in a gesture of reassurance. His fingers were outrageously long and most expressive. The hands of a pianist, Harry thought.

"No problem, Harry. For the same reason that America . . . for 'America,' substitute the *Times* or the *Post* . . . never heard of the affair in the first place. With the CIA blown to kingdom come, the SIA was the last chance this country was ever going to have for a functioning, effective intelligence service. If there was one secret that had bipartisan plus Pentagon support as being worth the keeping, that secret was you. Outside of the Agency, your name is known to a very short list of men trying very hard to forget they ever heard it."

Harry's eyes still held their concern.

"Why take any chance at all? Why bring me back and let some kid at the *Post* go digging around?"

Tate flapped his shoulders with an involuntary shudder. It was, of course, a question he had asked himself. He had also asked the men who could provide the answer. They did not. Instead, he sat with them as they constructed an answer to be given to Harry. An answer which Tate now patiently offered.

"Well, that's a strong question. I'm not at all sure there isn't some risk of that kind involved. On balance, we decided that if the tracks were too cold to find nine years ago, they'd be nine years colder today.

In the final analysis, the President felt that if the story were to surface at this point, how much of a scandal could they make of something nine years old? Two administrations ago. Yesterday's news."

Harry nodded thoughtfully. He understood.

"Only thing is, Horace, why bother? What's the upside?"

"You. Your name came to us by accident, but it was a terrific stroke of luck. We need a negotiator who can slip in and out of some very sensitive arenas with . . . well, experience and . . . discretion. If he can remain totally anonymous, so much the better."

"And why is that?"

"We're looking for a man who can move and deal freely, responsible only to us. This means free from State and Defense, but mostly it means free from public pressure. Press means pressure, Harry. When you're through giving the First Amendment its rightful homage, you have to face the reality that we're in a death-struggle for the survival of this country. We're dependent, yes, *goddam* dependent, on dealing with nations who are accustomed to having the security of their communications respected. Accustomed, hell, they demand it."

His head was tilted back, shaking from side to side. Hands splayed open on the desk.

"Christ, Harry, they're absolutely paranoid about the papers. *And* the networks. You find yourself in a press conference walking out of every door, misquoted shit thrown around on the nightly news, you're gonna find yourself with your balls cut off. Jesus, look at Salt IV. Incredible. We can't afford that, Harry. Not with these stakes. We need a professional. Period."

Harry continued to nod. He was clearly sympathetic.

"If it's that critical, why go for a man who's nine years rusty?"

Tate stopped cold for a very noticeable instant.

"Ross Buckley said you were extraordinary." His voice had a faint edge of pleading.

"He hasn't seen me in nine years."

Tate could think of nothing to say. This man, he'd been told.

"Get someone directly from the Agency," Harry said softly. "There's a school for negotiators. Buckley's specialty. He'll get you one with a cross-section of language skills, degrees in economics or petroleum engineering, knowledge of contemporary weapons and codes. Someone integrated into their system. Able to communicate with other Agency personnel, use their support."

"We . . . can't . . . use anyone from SIA," Tate said, almost distractedly. "We can't compromise the Agency. Can't risk bringing them into . . . any chance of a spotlight. That was the beauty of you. There's no damn record that you were even *in* the goddam Agency. An Agency man with no Agency attribution possible."

This much, of course, Harry Lime had known. Sitting on the beach at Malibu in the cold dawn, it had been the only thing he *had* known.

Tate licked his lips.

"Are you," Tate began, and stopped. "Are you still . . . the same man you used to be?"

"Yes," Harry said, very quietly.

Tate nodded slightly. They looked at each other for a long moment before Tate was fully himself again.

"You will be," Tate said, "an assistant to General Hubert Longview, one of the President's closest advisers. Since his portfolio, officially, is national security matters . . . and since he coordinates so closely with the Pentagon . . . his staff has the most immunity from media interference. You'll be one of fifteen or twenty staff. Nameless, faceless."

Tate paused, as if for questions. Harry said nothing.

"All of your negotiations will, of course, be classified at the highest level. In most cases, when there is
any public announcement, your meetings will be attributed to the General himself. As if he had conducted
the negotiations personally. Any other attribution to
you will simply be as staff or spokesperson. Without
name, even gender. The Secretaries of State and Defense have already been advised that the General will
have the burden of all meaningful negotiations on any
matter which touches national security. Also, that
some of these negotiations may be attributed to their
departments. As further insulation from press interference."

Tate stopped again. Then smiled, almost in apology.

"I'm waiting," Tate said, "for you to tell me your
conditions."

"Conditions?" Harry repeated blandly.

"Ross Buckley guessed that there might be some."

Harry smiled a friendly smile.

"And what were those?"

"You'd want to meet with the President. Establish
that you'd be working directly for him. Responsible to
him."

"No," Harry said. "I don't need to meet with anyone until they want to meet with me."

Tate leaned back and stared down his beak at Harry.
It was like talking to Buckley himself. Tate was never
comfortable with men who presented themselves as a
vacuum.

"Buckley said," Tate began, "that we could control
what you do, but never how you do it."

"Don't worry," Harry said lightly. "I won't let you
down. I'll do you and ol' Warner proud."

Tate laughed again. His short, honklike burst.

"For godsake," Tate said, "leave that asshole out of

this. My secretary will send him a polite note in the morning, thanking him for his help, telling him that you turned us down."

Harry's eyebrows raised in surprise.

"Don't tell me," Tate smiled, "that you really thought Alden was involved in this?"

"I guess it did seem a bit peculiar," Harry admitted. They grinned at each other for a moment or more, at Alden's expense.

"Ol' Warner," Tate said, "was the rarest thing in public affairs, Harry. A bona fide accident. Last month, he calls my office, tells my secretary we were classmates, somehow talks him into getting me on the line. While I'm desperately trying to ring off, he tells me that his old chum from our class is the best negotiator in the U.S. of A., and that the State Department just won't be able to function without him."

Harry was visibly amused.

"Helps to have friends in high places," Harry said, and Tate laughed again.

"Well, I did remember your name from Harvard, so I threw it over to State. You know, process through their usual channels. Next thing I know, Longview comes to me with an 'eyes only' report from the FBI. Some agent had turned up your file, and it had a cryptic instruction to send all inquiries about you directly to SIA. Of course, they're jealous as shit of SIA down there, so the Director goes straight to Longview with it."

Harry's smile remained pleasant, neutral, nonintrusive.

"By then, of course, the Big Three plus Buckley had noodled the whole thing out and realized you were the answer to their prayers. We had quite a debate over how to approach you, I must say. They were a little worried about any chance of Alden get-

ting wind of something. I told Longview that Alden
was a dolt, but he said that Buckley was paranoid
about any nonsecure person having any knowledge
whatsoever.''

Harry nodded, and now they exchanged grins about
Buckley's paranoia.

"He's a careful soul," Harry observed.

"Apparently. Anyway, we decided that I should
ring Alden back. Tell him that you were just the
ticket for a nice civilized spot on my staff. Carry the
title of Special Assistant to the President, like every
other guy on the payroll. Asked him to do me the
favor of contacting you directly. Figured you'd turn
him down cold, he'd be out of it, and I'd ring you
myself in a week. You screwed things up a bit by
being so damn polite to him."

"Well," Harry admitted, "I'm just that kind of guy."

"No harm done," Tate said. "Don't give it another
thought."

THREE

Harry strolled aimlessly down Pennsylvania Avenue toward the Capitol. It was still early morning, but the cars and electric trams had long since clogged the Avenue. It had been this way since six-thirty, when Harry had come to the Mayflower for breakfast. By now, the wet air was heating up, and the din on the street was fearful.

He bought a paper on the street and thumbed through it casually as he walked. Harry had no idea whether he was being followed this morning. There was no sign of it. He did not expect any.

He detoured to the Cannon House Office Building, a large structure with many exits. He walked briskly through the first-floor corridors, which were virtually empty. Very junior congressmen had their offices in this wing. Staff was young. Not yet rolling in from last night's parties.

Harry went directly to the southernmost of the First Street exits. He walked south a block, then cut over to Second and continued south to E Street.

The neighborhood had been upgraded. White row houses lined E for blocks, many proclaiming vacancies. All of the buildings had streetfront basement apartments, with neat white staircases leading directly down from the sidewalk. Harry had taken a tour of this neighborhood by taxi the previous day, and had noticed that many of these row houses had common rooms on the second or third floors, with large picture windows and a full view of the street.

Harry now walked the 200 block slowly, noting the five buildings with vacancies and picture windows. He then walked behind the row houses, and found that many of the buildings, including three of his prospects, had service entrances from the alley.

Returning to the street, Harry selected a large building at the east end of the block. The super was a young woman in an oversized cardigan, obviously her husband's. Despite the heat, the cardigan was fully buttoned. Perhaps concealing whatever she feared would encourage unwelcome advances. Harry explained that he wanted a room on the first floor, near the back of the building. There was one apartment, which wasn't quite suitable, and Harry took his business three doors west.

The super at 231 was an old black woman with a gold tooth. She showed Harry a small three-room flat. The apartment had two exits, each from a different room, each to a separate corridor. The back exit was only a few feet from the service door to the alley. The kitchen was tiny, and Harry had the woman demonstrate the working order of each appliance, as he talked cheerily of the insurance business in Miami and of his son, terror of the cub scout soccer league.

The super had a grandson in law school at George Washington, and she proceeded through his life story as she guided Harry's tour of the laundry room, vending machine area and, finally, the common room on the second floor. Television, card tables and three old leather reading chairs up against the curved picture window. There was a full view of the street entrances to each basement apartment on the west end of the block.

Harry rented the room for a month, under the name of Cooke. Cooke with an "e," he said carefully. He paid cash for the month, plus security deposit, and gave the super a large tip for her trouble.

He then proceeded west, inquiring at each building with an alley entrance. The manager at 217 had a vacancy in one of his streetfront basements. The flat contained five well-furnished rooms. There was an exit from the kitchen, leading into a short dark corridor, past heating pipes, to the alley service entrance. Harry rented the apartment for a month, paying by personal check and making a point of showing two pieces of identification. He politely, but obviously, avoided every question concerning his business in town or his background.

After lunch, Harry returned to the Sheraton in Georgetown and collected his things. He paid his bill through the end of the week, saying that he would be gone for a day or so, but would probably return. They could have his room if he wasn't back by Sunday night. He took a taxi to his basement apartment at 217 South E Street. He chatted with the cabbie on the street for a while, as conspicuously as possible, before the cabbie helped him bring his five pieces of luggage down the stairs to the apartment. Harry bought some groceries and disappeared from the streets of Washington. He shuttled between his two apartments, using only the alley, usually at night.

Most of his personal things were kept at 217, but the three suitcases of books and periodicals were installed in the apartment at 231. Harry had called in a chit from a friend at the Rand Corporation. Together they had gathered every public report available from the Agency, CIA or any other government department, concerning world energy supply and demand. There were books by economists and political strategists, two biographies of the nation's new President, and every article available on the careers of his two principal advisers. The material on Longview was particularly extensive.

Harry read the material slowly, methodically. Five hours for reading, one hour of language study. Harry found that his French and Italian were still serviceable. His German was not. His Russian was worst of all. This six-hour pattern was repeated three times each day.

It took Harry nine days to finish his reading. On the tenth day, he called Horace Tate.

Mr. Prissy was all aflutter, hearing Harry's voice. Mr. Tate has been trying to reach you for a week. You'll have to give me a number, he's on another line right now. Harry hung up.

Two days later, Harry called again. Tate came to the line immediately.

"Harry, how are you?" The White House Chief of Staff asked. "We were a little worried."

"About what?" Harry asked sharply.

There was silence. Harry had waited twelve days to judge the tone of this man's voice. The first sign of how badly they wanted him.

"Harry, you disappeared on me for two goddam weeks." Tate was frightened. His voice sounded uncertain as to just how angry he could afford to be. Harry did not want to leave him in doubt.

"Get used to it, Horace."

Another silence.

"What's that supposed to mean?"

"I'm an eccentric, Horace. Love me or leave me."

Horace would have to love him.

"Look, Harry, I'm not sure I appreciate your tone . . ."

"You sound cross," Harry said. "Maybe you'll be in a better mood next week. I'll call back then."

"No . . . hang on . . . Harry, really. Please. The . . . General was very upset when we couldn't find you. Very . . . worried for you."

Harry said nothing.

"We're losing time," Tate went on, now almost pleading. "Your first meeting is in five weeks. It's terribly important. You have to begin your briefings immediately. Are you here in Washington?"

"When would the General like to meet?"

Instant silence.

"He's . . . out of the country right now. You're to meet with one of his aides. One of his *top* aides."

Harry couldn't help but smile.

"Is this phone secure?" Harry asked, as if it were not the most absurd question in the world. Harry reasoned that it would not sound absurd to Tate.

"Of course," came the answer.

"Tell General Longview's top aide to come to my flat tomorrow at noon. I'll make us some lunch, so tell him to bring his appetite. His top appetite."

More silence.

"I'm at Second and E, Southeast, Horace. Number two-two-seven, Apartment A. It's a basement apartment with a staircase right on the sidewalk. Goodbye, Horace." And Harry gently placed the receiver in its cradle.

FOUR

After his conversation with Tate, Harry stayed put. He slept soundly that night at 217. The deepest sleep he could remember. None of his dreams held any pain, any fear. Harry was coming alive again.

Waking well before dawn, he left a note on his doorstep, where it could not quite be seen from the street. Back in a few minutes, it said, key under the mat.

He took his alley route to the flat at 231. It was just after four. Harry filled the tub with the hottest water his body could stand, and eased himself in.

Harry had placed a chair next to his tub, within easy reach. On the chair was a cigar and a new bottle of Martell Extra. Next to the bottle was a brandy snifter Buck had given him long ago.

Harry had always kept a special love for small pleasures. Cigars held a place of their own. They helped him think. Long, slender cigars from Holland. Black and strong and difficult to find these days. Everything difficult to find these days.

This cigar wasn't the usual black Dutchman. It was a huge sinful Cuban. He lit it in the darkness and closed his eyes. There was no sound. Only the heat reaching into every muscle and bone, and the taste of the Cuban.

An Agency man with no Agency attribution possible. They needed him. Enough to let Harry write some of the rules. Buck would have known that was the only way. Would have told them. We'll have to do a little putting up with young Harry. And young Harry will have to put up with us. Harry will understand that, gentlemen. There'll be a short period while we write the rules together.

Now it was Buck's turn. Harry was ready to listen. Harry spent an hour with the Cuban in the darkness, as the water slowly cooled around him. He felt wonderful just as he was, and the Martell remained unopened.

At first light, Harry was seated in a leather chair at the window on the second floor. A book was open in his lap, but his eyes scanned the row houses across the street. Nothing at any of the windows. Nothing Harry could see.

He sat for six hours, gazing dreamily at the windows. He watched each car that passed. Each person strolling the block. Harry knew he would find nothing, but he watched.

He first saw Taradan at three minutes before noon.

He had parked a long block away and was walking briskly toward Harry from the west. At a hundred yards, in his civilian clothes, he was clearly military. His gait, squared shoulders, the way his arms moved as he walked.

He checked his wristwatch as he crossed the street at the corner of Second and E. He strode into the 200 block and walked directly to 217. Directly to it, and down the stairs to Harry's apartment. It was the first confirmation that Harry was under surveillance, but he had been so certain of it that this was only mildly of interest.

Of greater interest was the carelessness of the man's

conduct. Of course, the mistake was probably Tate's, but this too would be confirmed momentarily.

Harry left his seat and returned to the apartment below. He picked up two full bags of groceries and left the building through the alley. He detoured for a block and emerged onto E Street at Fourth. Then, jauntily bearing his load, he strolled the two blocks to his apartment at 217, skipped down the stairs and rang the bell.

Taradan let him in.

Young and dark, with large dark eyes that made Harry think he was looking into a mirror ten years ago. Fifteen. Smiling, almost shyly, he introduced himself as Davis Taradan, and took the larger of Harry's grocery bags. He was shockingly young, which made Harry feel suddenly old. As he walked ahead of Harry toward the kitchen, Harry was struck again by the square posture and military movement of his upper body. He was lean and very fit, and well under thirty. Longview wouldn't have a lieutenant shine his shoes. The boy must be a captain.

"Just leave it on the counter, Major," Harry said brightly.

The boy turned with a slow smile.

"Captain," he said. "Mr. Tate said he hadn't mentioned I was Army. I guess the military kind of shows through."

"So does the Agency," Harry said quickly, smile easily in place.

There was a hitch in the boy's face. A fraction of a second during which the flow of movement stopped at the eyes and mouth. It was the instant that it took the boy to realize the necessity of disobeying an instruction. Denial would be impossible, could compromise him irreparably.

When the hitch had flickered past, he gave Harry his most winning smile.

"Agency?" he said easily, "now just what gave that away?"

Harry had turned away and headed to his favorite reading chair. The boy followed and perched on a sofa across the room. Respectful. Attentive. Too fucking young. Harry knew he would be stuck with this boy as his aide and part-time jailer, and he was now hoping very much that the error had been Tate's. That this boy was not going to be a serious liability. Come on, sonny, show me a little something between those ears.

They said nothing for a long moment. The boy tried an expression of momentary doubt.

"Pardon me, sir, for pushing my question. But . . . you wouldn't be in contact with Director Buckley, would you?"

The boy was reaching for intimacy by pretending to share Harry's paranoia. It was a believable ploy, something Harry might have tried in the boy's place.

"No," Harry said. "Horace told me you were the General's top aide. Longview was Pentagon's . . . liaison . . . to the Agency. Ten years ago. I never met him, but Mr. Buckley used to tell me about him. The only rising star in the military who truly appreciated the role of intelligence. I guess I've just assumed that he would staff accordingly."

Taradan nodded as if he understood.

"Actually," Taradan said, "very few of us on staff are from the Agency. I was selected for you because General Longview felt you'd be more comfortable with a professional."

Harry smiled broadly.

"The General was very wise. One more conversation with Horace Tate and I'd have packed it all in.

Talk about amateur night, Dave ... do I call you Dave?"

Taradan nodded.

"Horace was happily chattering away on an open White House line, which he assumed was toally secure. That's why. I gave my address as two-two-seven."

The boy's face stopped entirely, as he saw the trap Harry had set. It was clear to Harry now that the slip-up had been Tate's fault. Since Tate knew that SIA had already found Harry's apartment, Tate wasn't even listening when Harry gave the address. Taradan had not been given the wrong number, so he had no opportunity to plan a cover. He had walked straight to 217.

Harry looked away to reach for his pipe and tobacco. He wanted to give Taradan a moment to think. Whatever the boy's explanation would be, Harry would have to appear to believe it.

"I'm sorry," Harry said, eyes on the tobacco pouch, "I wasn't back in time to spot you on the street. Hope you didn't have too much trouble."

When he looked up, the boy was smiling easily.

"Goddam Tate," he said, "didn't give me a number at all. The man's an idiot. All he caught was two-hundred-something. I walked the block, hoping you'd spot me. Luckily, I saw the note on your door."

Harry graded that B-plus. Acceptable.

"No more Tate," Harry said quickly. "From now on, just family. Okay, Dave?"

"I'll see to it," the boy answered.

FIVE

Harry stepped into the elevator behind Taradan. The computerized door closed soundlessly. They were in Virginia, the Pentagon's newly finished Annex. As if in a vacuum, they stood in the sudden silence, Taradan methodically examining each of the keys on a large ring.

Taradan had found the first key quickly, but the second eluded him for some time. Finding it, he removed both keys from the ring and inserted them into the first and fourth keyholes of the panel before him.

He smiled briefly at Harry, in apology for the delay, and turned the first key. Instantly, the elevator slipped down into the earth. There was no way to calculate the speed or the distance. It felt deep. As soon as they had stopped, Taradan turned the second key. They slipped deeper.

The door slid open to reveal a long corridor, not unlike those at the surface. The uniforms were only Army now, none below the rank of captain. They did not exchange salutes with Taradan or each other, as Harry was led through the maze of corridors in a bewildering series of turns.

Suddenly, Taradan stepped into a cul-de-sac, at the

end of which stood an unmarked door. Another wait, as Taradan produced two keys for the double lock.

The room could not have presented a more startling contrast to its antiseptic military surroundings. It was a library, a private study. The appointments were Victorian and meticulous. Soft leather reading chairs, dim lighting, wall lined with books from floor to ceiling. An enormous Persian rug of maroon and pale blue. The silence of the study was comforting, warm.

Taradan motioned for Harry to be seated, but said nothing. He stood, legs apart, strong hands clasped behind him. Taradan looked younger than ever in his crisply starched uniform, a fact that Harry seemed unable to ignore. Young and straight and beautiful, in a way that Harry could not match against the memories of his own youth. Whenever that had been.

Harry sank into his huge leather armchair. Taradan now looming before him as if he were indeed Harry's keeper. The younger man smiled, but remained motionless.

At last there was a sound, and a man appeared in the doorway's light.

"Gentlemen!" said a tired voice. It was the voice of an executive trying to clear his head for one last meeting. The smile was weary, Harry could see that through the shadows. With the light pouring in around him, Harry could see little else.

Longview was not in uniform. He wore slippers and a heavy flannel shirt, with sleeves rolled up over strong forearms. He carried a slim folder in one hand, a large pipe in the other. There was an athlete's spring to his step, a compactness of muscle and movement that made him, for a moment, seem lithe and small.

As he crossed the room, the General held Harry's eyes. He ignored Taradan as though he were less than the lampstand. As Harry started to rise, Longview stopped him with the slightest movement of his hand.

The smile was warm, almost self-effacing, as he slipped into the reading chair across from Harry. It was widely known that the President of the United States listened to only two voices. This man's was one of them.

"Thank you for coming," he said softly. "Godawful hour." It was 2:45 in the morning.

The General was now in the full light of the reading lamp. He was not a small man at all. His shoulders and chest were full, his hands seemed unusually thick and strong. Everything about the man seemed to speak to Harry of compact efficiency. As if there were endless time and strength for work. None for waste.

The man's head was far older than his body. To be more accurate, it was his skin that had browned and toughened and aged around the rest of him. The eyes were small and alive, set very deep in the tan and blotch of the weathered face. The hair was thinned almost to vanishing, though somehow there was just enough left to define the crisp outlines of a military cut. Against the rules, against the odds, he was still a handsome man. There was too much force and too much life for this man not to stand apart at any age, in any company.

He sat, completely at his ease, looking at Harry's eyes.

"Young Davis Taradan treating you proper?" Sounded too much like Buck.

"Young Davis get you everything you require?" he said in an even softer voice, since there had been no answer.

Harry permitted the slightest hesitation before he nodded.

"Captain," the General said with a smile, but slow

enough to hint of menace, "wanna tell me exactly where you fucked up?" Longview still riveted on Harry's eyes.

"Sir, Mr. Lime has requested current photos, bio and psychological profile of key intelligence, military, energy and administration personnel of selected countries. And of the chief personal aide to each such individual."

"Selected countries?"

"Twenty-six countries."

Longview nodded as if it were the most natural thing in the world.

"And when did Mr. Lime make this request, Captain?"

"Yesterday, sir."

Longview nodded again. A very small smile.

"And why hasn't his request been complied with?"

"No excuse, sir." Taradan could scarcely keep a straight face.

Longview turned his head slowly and rolled his eyes up to Taradan.

"Mr. Lime is in a hurry, Captain. He's in a hurry to help his country. I'm in a hurry. Are you in a hurry?"

Taradan's smirk was gone. He had been certain that Longview was joking. He wasn't certain any longer.

"Sir. Mr. Lime's request involves detailed information concerning more than eight hundred individuals Not all of that data is . . ."

"Old age," Longview interrupted, "must finally be attacking my hearing. Could have sworn I heard someone say 'no excuse, sir.'"

Taradan was sweating.

"Yes, sir."

A slow smile crossed the General's face.

"Just when," Longview said, "did you first notice that you were losing it?"

Taradan shifted his weight.

"Losing it, sir?"

"Your sense of humor."

The Captain's tension burst in a boy's giggle. The General watched with pleasure.

"Jesus, Dave, if I didn't love you like a son, I'd bust your ass all the way down to major."

"Have to promote me to colonel first," the boy beamed.

The General looked at his charge not as a father would, but perhaps more as a football coach. Building character and loyalty was a constant process of alternating deprivation with reward. There was no reward to equal a sudden glint of pride. The more understated, the more precious.

"That thought has crossed my mind," Longview said, and turned slowly back to his guest. "Eight hundred profiles, Harry?"

"The opposition," Harry said simply.

Longview thought for a moment. "Captain," he said, still fixed on Harry's eyes, "how much material did Mr. Lime request on world energy production, resources, potential?"

"None, sir."

Longview's small smile had returned.

"Did you ask why, Captain?"

"Sir. Mr. Lime said he was here to execute policy. Not make it."

The General's eyes rolled back up to Taradan. "Not so dumb, eh, Captain?"

"No, sir. It'll be a privilege to service his assignment."

"Yes," Longview said to the hands folded in his lap, "I was in the Oval Office when Mr. Buckley told us just what kind of individual we were adding to the team. We're blessed, Dave. Blessed to have Harry aboard. You take care of him with everything you've got."

Harry watched as the exchange between General and Captain came to its preordained conclusion. Watched as the Captain took his leave so that Harry could have the honor of a completely private audience. Harry settled in for such meat as there might be to this meeting.

After Taradan was gone, Harry politely declined cognac, cigar and, most politely, small talk.

The General fondled the curved pipe in his lap. Watched it for a moment. He was calm through the silence. Not simply at ease, but able to actually draw strength from it. In Harry's world, this was one of the major divisions through which creatures were classified. Sharks were comfortable in water, falcons in air. Professionals in silence.

"So," the General said at last, "to why you're here."

Longview glanced up and locked Harry's eyes again.

"Twenty years ago, Harry, 1977. Where were you?"

"Law School," Harry said on cue. "Harvard," as if that might help.

"What did they tell us then about the energy crisis. That's what they used to call it, Harry. Crisis. Seems there ought to be a different word for the unraveling of civilization. What did they tell us was going to ride in on its white horse and solve our pesky crisis?"

And it was clear to Harry that the General would be supplying his own answers from this point on.

"Well, synthetic fuel, for one," the General said to some point in space where the ceiling met a wall. "We have all this goddam coal. Turn it into oil. Even gas. And all that shale in Colorado. Why import eight million barrels of OPEC ransom a day, when we can squeeze it out of coal and shale?"

He let out a deep breath and shook his shoulders.

"Of course, we were producing about 130 million tons of coal a year, and if we used *all* of that for oil, it wouldn't come close to a million barrels a day. Forget what it would cost to pull the shale out of the ground, every barrel of shale-oil would take almost three barrels of water. Where was that going to come from? Forget raping the land, the carbon dioxide buildup. Jesus, twenty years ago they were projecting that coal-oil would cost forty, forty-five dollars a barrel, and even that was bullshit. They were scared, Harry. There was a lie under it all. We all shared in it."

He found Harry's eyes again.

"Fission. What about fission, Harry? All we need is enough nuclear fission plants happily churning out the electricity. It was dirty and it was dangerous. And they couldn't control it. And they fucking knew it. They just had nothin' else, so the, stumbled on. Breeder reactors will feed on themselves and we'll have inexhaustable, renewable energy. If we can just handle the waste ... and the politics. Then comes 1985, and if it hadn't been Clinch River it would have been ten other places. Our lie was still there, Harry. What was the lie?"

Harry would wait for the General to tell him.

"Conservation. That was the funniest. The saddest. We'll use less. More people, more jobs, more technology. Expand the economy. Get this country producing again. Pull that standard of living, that was our holy grail, pull that standard of living out of the mudhole and be America again. Through private enterprise, of course, through our god-blessed free market economy. Just use a lot less energy while you do it. What was the lie, Harry? Your lie. Mine. Have you spotted it yet?"

The General clasped his strong hands together.

"What have we got here, Harry? Economy in ruins.

Dollar gone from a joke to something, well, unspeakable. Twenty years ago, we were pumping 10.2 million barrels of oil a day. Now it's 7.4. Twenty years ago, we were importing 7.7 million barrels a day. Today it's 9.5, and that's only because it's all they'll give us. I need eleven, Harry, maybe more. Where am I going to get it? What's our savior today, Harry? What's going to ride in on the white horse and slay our dragon?"

Harry watched the deep eyes of the General. Steady and strong. He could not remember the eyes blinking once.

"Thermonuclear fusion," Longview said with mock reverence. "That's how the sun makes its energy. Just throw a deuterium nucleus in with a tritium, and we have all of these lovely, fourteen-million-volt neutrons. Control it, compress it. Use lasers. All we need is something to turn billions of microexplosions into something usable, economic. Twenty years ago, it was twenty years away. Today it's thirty years away. Where's our lie, Harry? The one at the bottom of it all. The one we've never been able to face."

The General smiled. Almost tenderly.

"The lie is," he said, "that everything is going to be all right. That somewhere there *is* an answer. That there *has* to be an answer."

The smile was gone.

"Rage," the General said. "Rage against the dying of the light. Do not go gentle into that good night, Harry. I'm not. The President isn't either. We're going to rage a while longer. Will you rage with us? Will you?"

Harry nodded that he would.

"We're buying time here, Harry. Time for physicists and engineers. Time for us. Time is oil. The oil is in OPEC's ground. I'll cheat, lie, steal and kill to get it out. Am I speaking plainly enough?"

He was.

"OPEC's reserves are about 320 billion barrels. Twenty years ago, they were producing about eleven billion a year. New discoveries replaced maybe five or six on the average. Discoveries are slowing, Harry. They don't want to run out in forty years. They're shooting for another century. Twenty years ago, the Saudis were pumping 9.5 million a day. Next year, they'll be down to eight. They're hoarding it, Harry. They're saving their ass by kicking mine."

"They're frightened," Harry said.

The General's face stopped dead for an instant.

"Ghawar," Harry said, speaking of the largest oil field the world had ever known, "had seventy billion in reserve in 1980. Thirty-four today. Safaniya-Khafji had twenty-five, now it's seventeen. Abqaiq is gone. They're not going to let that happen to Manifa or Zuluf or the others."

Longview nodded. He thought for a moment.

"What," he asked, "is your appreciation of circumstances in the Soviet Union?"

"They've got problems," Harry said evenly. "The Siberian motherlode was smaller than they thought, and a lot tougher to recover. They once relied on the Samotlor field for twenty-five percent of their needs. It's been horribly overproduced. Eastern Europe has drained them for thirty years. The old fields like Romashinko are used up. Until they can really get Siberia on track, their other fields just can't carry the load."

"Other, meaning?"

"Arian, Uzen, Mamontovo. Bolshoye-Chernogur. Pokachev."

"Your data," the General said slowly, "is CIA, three

years old. I'll have Dave give you some SIA materials. Nothing startling, but they may be of interest."

Harry thought again how much the man could sound like Buck. A connection he needed to know more about.

Longview smiled with a trace of something new. Perhaps closeness.

"Thank you," the General said at last, "for revealing your familiarity with these matters. I know that disclosure is not simple for someone with your training. I want you to know that I understand that, and that I appreciate the gesture. You took a step. There will come a time when I'll respond."

Longview leaned forward, resting his elbows on his knees.

"Tell me about Dave," the General asked.

"He's acceptable."

"You know that he's your jailer," the General smiled.

The one I can see, Harry thought. Why don't you start "responding" by introducing me to the rest of them.

"It doesn't matter," Harry said.

"In other words," the General was smiling broadly now, "you feel you can handle him."

"My life," Harry said with his warmest smile, "is an open and well-thumbed book."

"I rely on Dave for information about you, no more or less than I'll rely on you for information about him. You know this whole part of the spiel, so I'll skip it. What you don't know yet is Dave. You think you know him because you think you've seen dozens of him coming through Buck's tender hands. They are all ambitious, they are all disciplined. Dave is smarter than most and quicker than most, and Dave . . ."

Here Longview stopped and surveyed Harry for a moment.

"Dave," he went on, "is ideal for protective custody, both by instinct and disposition."

This meant that Dave was an assassin. Longview's pause was not lost on Harry, who was already thinking of Vienna and of Buck's mentor, old John Knowles. And protective custody.

"My kind of guy," Harry said.

The General was slightly amused.

"He'll protect you. He'll service everything you need. When he gets too close, tell him to bugger off, General's orders. The instant you want him out, I replace him for you. I want you comfortable and free. I mean that."

And always, Buck had taught, when someone adds that he "means" something, he is either telling the perfect truth or its precise opposite. Never in-between.

"So," the General said at last, "to why you're here."

They had come again to that.

"Mr. Horace Tate has told you that you have been engaged to serve as a negotiator. It is true that negotiating is a sub-set of your training, and a valuable one. I have nothing against negotiating, mind you. If you see the chance to do any of it, go right ahead. God's speed."

Harry smiled.

"What excites me about you, Harry, is the broader aspect of your training. You are an interrogator. You observe and you obtain information. That is why you are here. An Agency interrogator with no Agency attribution possible. Without generosity, without distortion, Buck told the President that you are the best he'd ever trained. The best."

And I mean that, Harry added silently.

Now it was Harry's turn to bask in the proud gaze. It lasted a long moment. It could have been sincere, thought Harry, and knew that he might never even scratch the surface of General Hubert O. Longview.

At last Longview reached to the floor and picked up the slim folder Harry had noticed when the General entered the room. He offered it silently to Harry.

There were eleven sheets, each with a color photograph and words. Vital statistics, education, psychological evaluation. A final entry titled "intangibles."

Longview was silent for several minutes as Harry's eyes moved over the sheets.

Finally, he said, "In four weeks, you'll be in Mexico City. Their principal negotiator will be Miguel Robles Fraga. As you see, he's head of Pemex, the national oil monopoly."

Harry's eyes continued to move across the profiles.

"You might choose to pay some attention to the material on the silver-haired gentleman. Guzmán. Forty years in their foreign service. Urbane, extremely intelligent. He also happens to be related to President Morín Calero. I've met Guzmán. He'll be there as an observer. Robles Fraga may do the talking. Guzmán will be the man."

Harry was already staring at the patrician features of Luis Guzmán Silva.

"What," Harry said, "would you like me to know." Always a statement, not a question. Indication of readiness. Consent to proceed.

"Mexico is producing 3.2 million barrels a day, Harry. They export 1.5. We've been getting 900,000 barrels, and every drop is life's blood. The rest goes to Japan, Canada, France and Israel, under contracts that have years to run. Our contract is up."

The General ran his hand back over his wispy hair. It was a gesture of impatience, perhaps even anxiety, which had not surfaced before.

"The problem," Longview dropped his voice, "is

that they want to cut back production. Prices keep going up, the stuff's not going to last forever. It's better all 'round for them to leave it in the ground."

"Cut back . . ." Harry said quietly.

"Are you ready for this? Half a million barrels. Since we're the only expiring contract, it all comes out of our share."

Harry thought for a moment.

"The price?" Harry said.

"Right now it's one-sixty-five a barrel. I'd go to anything if I could reduce that cutback by even 100,000 barrels. I'd pay one-eighty. They're absolutely adamant. They're just like the Saudis these days, Harry. They all are. Arrogant little . . ."

His voice trailed off. His eyes were strong, and still they were pleading.

"I think I understand," Harry said.

A long silence followed.

"Anything I can do for you?" Longview asked.

"I'd like," Harry said, "for you to switch the show to San Francisco."

"Why?"

"For this particular approach, I'll be more comfortable on home soil."

The General thought briefly.

"You've got it."

They sat in silence again, until Longview was certain that there was more.

"Any last questions?" he asked.

"Will I have a free hand?"

"That depends," Longview smiled, "on what you're going to do with it."

Harry nodded.

"Well," Harry said slowly, "if I don't have a free hand, I'll see what I can do."

"And if you do . . . ?"

"Well, then I'll kick their butts for you."

The General just beamed. "The beginning," he said, "of a beautiful relationship."

SIX

Taradan drove Harry back to his apartment, chattering as the dark avenues slipped past. Harry tried to be pleasant, but to communicate exhaustion. After all, it was nearly 4:30 in the morning.

Once alone, Harry sat quietly in the light of his living room for twenty minutes. Then he extinguished the light and sat for another thirty.

In the darkness, he found his small travel bag, hiked the strap over his shoulder and let himself silently out the kitchen exit.

Harry walked through alleys for more than a mile, then doubled back and headed for Pennsylvania Avenue. He found his taxi on the way. It always seemed miraculous to Harry that Washington could produce taxis at any hour, in any quarter of the city.

All the way to Dulles, Harry and the cabbie shared confidences. The cabbie had seen it all in this town, of course. He knew which senator was screwing which young thing from State or Treasury. About the only bed-partner he really hadn't identified yet was the one his old lady had taken up with Tuesday nights. He'd find the sucker when the time was right, though. Waste him good.

Harry, the insurance broker from Miami, didn't have

much to share beyond his son's triumphs in the cub scout soccer league. The cabbie wisely counseled that Harry had best look to his own old lady when he got back down South. Treat her right. That's where it all starts, when you don't treat 'em right at home. Harry knew what he meant.

At Dulles, Harry found a comfortable spot. Ticket lines were open, but the airport was pretty deserted, and Harry preferred to buy his ticket in a crowd.

At seven o'clock, he joined the longest queue he could find and bought two round-trip tickets to Minneapolis. He could have purchased one ticket all the way to his true destination, and since he had no identification other than his own, he gave this a moment's thought. Harry disliked multiplying transactions. He disliked even more, however, sharing more than the minimum data with any one ticket-seller. The tickets were purchased for cash for Mr. and Mrs. Walter Clarke. Clarke with an "e," he said most particularly. If identification had been requested, Mrs. Clarke would have his wallet and other things in her overnight bag in the ladies room. It was not.

On the flight to Minneapolis, Harry settled back and let his mind run to Andy Maclennon. Andy was the only man from Harry's life at the Agency whom Harry knew was a friend. It had been nine very long years since they had spent an evening alone with a bottle of Dewar's. Andy had been, well, fifty-nine. He must be retired three years now. Nine Christmas cards, nine quarts of Dewar's. The stuff was still in the basement somewhere.

In Minneapolis, Harry bought two round-trip tickets to Green Bay. Mr. and Mrs. Terrence Wilkes. With an "e." It was a sleek little jet which stopped first at the Central Wisconsin Airport, servicing Steven's Point, Wausau and Wisconsin Rapids. The tiny airport was practically empty. As if by rote, Harry's eyes deftly probed the few available faces, looking for a wrong one.

In Green Bay, Harry hired a car and driver for the short trip up the peninsula of Door County. He told the driver that he'd been flying all night from Denver, with the aid of four martinis, and needed some shut-eye. The driver understood.

Harry hunkered down in the back seat and stared dumbly as the blight of Highway 57 began to pass slowly in review. His mind was as blank as he could make it, but sleep would not come.

They crossed the bridge at Sturgeon Bay, and they were in Door County. Highway 42 was green, and in an instant it was the green of Cape Cod. The green of one small, incredibly clear moment from very long ago.

It was a moment that shocked Harry with its clarity and, more, its unimportance. He had married Jenny four days earlier. They had driven a distance and Harry was tired. They were walking, fingers loosely coupled on a cold, quiet beach. He wanted only to fall onto the sand and lie there, motionless, holding her forever. And in that moment, she told him that she wanted a hot dog. Big and gooey with chili. He had stopped in his tracks and looked into those huge eyes. He had thrown his arm around her shoulders, and as they stomped off through the sand to find her hot dog, she had clutched him like she could never bear to let him go. That was the moment. There was nothing more. It was not one of Harry's treasures, carefully taken out and held to light so many times. In fact, he had never recalled that moment once before. And now it was frozen before his eyes.

"Egg Harbor," the driver said after a long time had

passed. It occurred to Harry that the driver had no instructions.

"Never been here," Harry said. "What's up the road?"

He saw the driver's smile in the mirror.

"Egg Harbor's nice," the man said. "Then comes Fish Creek." He said "crik" for "creek," as though it were indeed New England. "Then Ephraim. Big cookout there today. It's nice. Then Sister Bay. After that, no place much to stay."

Harry nodded as though he were thinking it over. The driver's eyes watched from the mirror.

"Well," Harry said at last, "let's go to the last one then, so we can see them all."

The shoreline was lovely in the way of clear water and dense wood. It could have been Italy, or anywhere. Then there were small boats and wood-frame cottages, and it was New England once again. As they passed through Ephraim, half the village was massed at cookstoves in front of the old town hall. They were cold and happy. There was a restaurant with grass on its roof, and two goats grazing. There were gas stations with shorter lines than Harry had seen in years.

When they reached Sister Bay, Harry saw the gallery. The first hotel after the gallery was called Hotel du Nord. It was pseudo-Swiss-or-Danish and looked very pleasant. He let the driver go on about a mile, and told him to pull into a motel court. Harry asked the driver to wait, while he checked whether a room was available.

Harry reappeared after a few minutes, paid the driver and included a generous tip. He returned to the motel lobby and sat for twenty minutes. Then, hiking his bag over his shoulder, Harry trudged the mile back to the Hotel du Nord.

At the desk, Harry said that his wallet had been left

with his family in Green Bay. Luckily, there was enough cash in his silver money clip to pay the night in advance. He entered his room half expecting to see Davis Taradan sitting on the bed with a cold stare for a welcome. When Taradan did not materialize, and when the pine-walled room reminded him not at all of any room he had shared with Jenny, Harry permitted himself a fitful sleep.

When Harry entered the gallery in the morning, the artist/owner was in deep discussion with two patrons. The husband was a porcine fellow, expensively dressed. His voice was too loud and flaunted a constant timbre of irritation. His wife, a hard, rich-looking woman, stared appraisingly at the object of the dickering. It was a large, innocuous watercolor. At the lower corner of the painting was a tiny card on which appeared the legend $1800 in the smallest print imaginable. The card seemed an apology. Harry was pleased that he was reasonably well-dressed this morning, and that his shoes were clearly quite expensive. He buttoned his jacket.

"I don't haggle," the fat man haggled, "it just isn't my style. I said twelve hundred dollars, and I mean what I say. If that doesn't suit you, I'll take my business down the road."

The owner seemed unperturbed. His eyes were clear and open, his smile calm. Only his enormous Adam's apple displayed his distress by bobbing up over the neck of his sweater. He was a pale man, with thinning red hair and sharp features. His voice seemed sympathetic to his customer's distress.

"I hate to lose the sale," he said sweetly, "but I've had a policy for years against cutting any of my prices. You really have me in a quandry here on this."

Harry had sidled up behind the perfume of the man's wife. He stared over her shoulder at the treasure. The fat man glared at Harry and the insolence of his intrusion.

Without taking his eyes from the painting, Harry said, "You want eighteen hundred for this piece, friend?"

Harry turned slowly to the owner, past the infuriated gaze of his tormentor. The owner was speechless.

"Eighteen hundred?" Harry said again, loud and flat.

The owner managed a nod.

"You got it," Harry said. "Closed."

The fat man exploded. "Just who the hell do you think you are?" Shrill, threatened.

Harry looked at him as though he were a five-foot cockroach. "I'm the guy," Harry said softly, "who just bought this painting. You're the guy who's taking his business down the road."

The fat man wheeled on the owner, demanding a shred of decency and fair play. "Were we or were we not concluding a transaction when this ... this ... person ..." He was bouncing up and down. His wife was staring at Harry from top to bottom.

The owner held up his hands. "Gentlemen, I really ..."

"All I want to know," the fat man shrieked, "is who was here first."

"Does that mean," Harry said with a nasty smile, "that you're willing to buy this painting for eighteen hundred?"

The fat man was near to a stroke. "You bet your sweet ass, you sonofabitch."

Harry smiled at the man for a long moment. "In that case," Harry said very quietly. "I'll bid twenty-five." And as an afterthought, "Lard-belly."

The rich-looking woman tugged at the fat man's elbow, but was far too late.

"Three fucking thousand."

"Is that your final offer?" Harry grinned.

"It's the highest fucking offer so far, you sonofa-bitch."

Harry thought another moment, looked at the painting. Then he held up his hand to silence the owner. "I'll go forty-five hundred," he said slowly.

"Five," the fat man shouted.

His wife finally gasped a "Herbert," and the man's eyes watered. He was through.

"I'll pay cash, though," Harry said to the owner, "you won't have to worry about getting stiffed."

More than the fat man could bear.

"You will have the personal check of Herbert Sloan, Mr. Maclennon. I am a banker, for godsake. No one has ever questioned . . ."

The owner's hands were raised in a plea for peace. The Adam's apple was going wild.

"Are you gonna take this guy's check?" Harry demanded.

"Of course I will," the owner said protectively, and moved half a step closer to the fat man, as if to add physical confirmation of his trust.

Harry reached into his pocket and found his wallet. He took out a card from some Italian restaurant and handed it to the owner.

"Stephen Ridder," Harry said. "Ridder Galleries, New York. When this jerk's check bounces, you give me a call."

Harry stood watchfully as the fat man wrote his check, waited for his painting to be meticulously wrapped and, glaring with triumph and rage, bounced out the door.

One beat after the fat man had disappeared, Andy Maclennon grabbed Harry by both ears, and kissed him full on the mouth.

SEVEN

They sat in a dinghy. Fishlines in the water, with nothing on the hooks. There were no other boats, and they were too far from shore to be reached by directional microphone. As if there were such a device within a thousand miles.

The years had slipped off Andy easily. Always had. "Same with you," Andy noted, popping open a local beer and handing it across, uninvited. Harry took a long dutiful swallow, as he would with the Dewar's that night. "Ten years, twelve, not a trace," Andy said. He had that way of speaking so clean, so open, no one could ever question. Andy just said what was true.

"I'm back into it," Harry said, finding his eyes. They were never hard to find. Always there waiting for you. Pale and clear and patient.

"Why?"

"I don't know."

Andy thought about that for a long while.

"What's the best lie you've told yourself so far?" he said with an Andy smile.

"Goes like this. What is there really, in your life? Your wife, your child, your work. When you're down to the last one, it's got to be enough to fill up a whole life."

Andy hadn't known about Jenny's leaving. His eyes showed that he shared the pain. He wouldn't add to that pain with words of sympathy.

"Sounds like real Foreign Legion stuff," Andy said.

"Sounds like real bullshit," Harry agreed.

They let the boat bob up and down on the bay for a while.

"Whatever it is," Andy said quietly, "you know you've got it. Just give me the shopping list."

For Andy was a master painter, in Agency terms. Andy was a forger. The best there had ever been. He had been old John Knowles' personal forger in the salad days, in the first years after Knowles had formed the SIA. He had done other things for Knowles as well. Andy could lay his hands on the best of any equipment. But forging was his genius. He'd been too close to Knowles, though, and after Knowles' fall, Buck kept Andy at arm's length. Andy had never shown that he noticed. He let them use him as they would, and slipped away to his watercolors and his pension when the time came.

"Four passports," Harry said easily, as if it were a dozen eggs. "Philip Cooke. With an 'e.' Born Miami. Married. Sells insurance. Samuel Allen. A-l-l-e-n. Born Denver. Single. Teaches American literature, secondary level. Walter Clarke, With an 'e.' Born San Francisco. Art dealer. Terrence Wilkes. With an 'e.' Born Wilmette, Illinois. Married. Writes free-lance."

Andy nodded. He would not need any of it repeated.

"Birthdates," he said mildly.

"May 20, 1955. May 1, 1956. April 12, 1957. April 8, 1958." The years, of course, were random. The dates belonged to people Harry loved. They could not be forgotten.

Andy digested for a moment, then repeated all of

the information, with correct dates for each. Harry smiled his approval.

"Let's take the years down," Andy said, "maybe five years. You just don't look that old."

"I'm aging fast. Take them down three."

Andy nodded.

Harry reached in his coat pocket and presented Andy with an envelope. Four sets of photos, each with a different expression, each undeniably Harry.

"Driver's licenses," Harry said, "state of birth. Major credit cards, two for each. Let's give Cooke something from an insurance association of Dade County. Allen teaches school in Boulder, maybe some ski association. Clarke will need . . ."

Harry stopped, as Andy's grin had broadened.

"Will you forgive me," Harry said, "for sounding like I'm telling you your business?"

"There's a national association of art dealers," Andy said. "Two of them. Clarke just joined both. Mr. Wilkes will have two or three sets of press credentials from the suburban Chicago area. There'll be a few other pieces. I think you'll be satisfied."

Harry was certain he would be. "Need some cash in advance?" Harry said finally.

"From you?" He looked genuinely hurt.

"I meant, you know, Santa's helpers."

Andy knitted his brow. "I think," he said, "if you'll trust me on it, well, I'll just muddle through on this one all by myself."

Harry was very grateful for that.

The boat bobbed for a while longer.

"Whatever else you need . . ." Andy said finally.

Harry felt the jolt of facing up to it at last. "I just mean," Andy was apologizing, "I mean, if you're not going to Buck for your paper, then . . . look, I know you never used to carry anything."

Harry stared down at his hands. His palms were damp. "The smallest you've got," Harry said, "so long as it carries six rounds and has some stopping power. I don't know much about these things, you know that. Some kind of harness, a spring that would come down my arm."

"It's a very good idea," Andy said soothingly. "You'll have it in a week. I'll work with you for one hour and you'll be comfortable with it. Maybe practice a little, once a week or so."

Harry just kept nodding down at his hands.

"Just the one piece?" Andy asked.

Harry kept nodding.

"Need anything else, you can buy it off the rack. I'll give you some model numbers. Rifles, other stuff. Look, it's like taking the umbrella along to make sure it never rains."

Harry looked up at his friend. He thought of the nine quarts of Dewar's in his basement in Los Angeles.

"Thanks," he said.

Andy watched his face for a while.

"Take maybe ten days to pull everything together. You could probably use a little something to tide you over. How 'bout a nice Wisconsin license for Mr. Stephen Ridder? I owe him a quick favor anyway. Get you half a dozen supporting pieces to go along with it. No trouble at all."

No harm in asking, Harry thought.

"What if Mr. Ridder would rather be a free-lance journalist than an art dealer. By, say, next Tuesday or Wednesday?"

Andy's smile wrapped around Harry. "Think I'll close up shop for a couple days. Drive you to my place up in Cable. All my stuff's up there. Do some fishing, paint some stuff for you. Service while you wait."

It took six hours for them to cover the distance.

Andy driving effortlessly, never seeming to watch the
road, let alone his back. But Harry caught the signs.
The extra flicker of a glance at the mirror. The steady
speed of fifty, so that anything could pass that wanted
to. The pulling over to the side for a snapshot or a
breather or a leak when any vehicle took more than
twenty minutes to pass. Harry doubted that Andy had
any film in the camera. Harry did not doubt that Andy's
place up in Cable was a very private matter.

Endless farmland, with cows and sky and even silos
in their proper place. Harry tried to stay with the
conversation, to really be with Andy. After Andy, he
didn't know when he'd be talking with a friend again.

He thought of the day they met. They had been at
an SIA briefing where everyone addressed Andy simply as "Mac." Harry offered to buy him a drink, and
when they were alone, he asked Andy what he liked
to be called. Andy said that everyone called him Mac.
Harry said it didn't seem Andy much liked that. Andy
said his folks had called him Red. Watching his face,
Harry said it didn't seem he much liked that either.
"I like 'Andy,'" Andy said. "Just nobody ever asks."

It was night when they pulled up to Andy's cabin
by the lake. The stars were brilliant and the air was
very cold.

Andy fished two enormous steaks out of a freezer,
and cooked them over wood. They sat by the fireplace
and traded happy stories over the inevitable quart of
Dewar's. Happy stories only. Old days, new days,
whatever.

Finally, Andy pulled himself to his feet. "I'm going
somewhere to get you a little bedtime reading," he
said. "It'll take forty minutes, and I want you to stay
right where you are. Is that okay?"

It was okay. When Andy left, he took a shovel with
him.

Harry sat for forty minutes and wondered what could be so precious that Andy would bury it twenty minutes' walk from the cabin.

Andy returned with what looked like an old family album. He sat next to Harry in front of the fire, and gave him a hard look of strictly business. Not a look Andy normally wore.

Harry opened the album and was staring at a dossier profile. A mild, forgettable face. Poor quality black and white print. A name. Very limited background. The final entry was called "tools of preference." Harry knew what he was reading. There were eleven profiles in the album, and Harry knew that he would stare at them through the night, until each face was burned forever into his mind.

"Collectors," Andy said needlessly. "Complete till the day of my retirement, July the first, three years ago. There'll be some new ones since. But this kinda stuff is hard to update."

Hard to update was a fact. The very possession of this material was a death sentence. Andy had just trusted Harry with his life.

The collectors were not killers in the sense of Dave Taradan, or the other boys from protective custody. Those guys were merely experts, and there were dozens of them. You could toss the word "assassin" around pretty lightly, until you came to the collectors.

"Interesting faces," Andy said distractedly, peering over Harry's shoulder as the pages slowly turned. "The kind of faces you'd like to remember if you see them again."

Harry looked at Andy, wishing for all the world that he had some confidence to share that was half worth the trade.

"Do you know," Andy asked lightly, "what's really up?"

"No," Harry said. "I'm not working for Buck. It's not Agency they tell me. I'm negotiating for oil with Mexicans and Arabs. Go to Europe and feel out our treasured allies. Watch their eyes. Buck told everyone I'm good at watching eyes."

Andy nodded ever so slightly.

"They picked you because you're so good at watching eyes. And they expect you to buy that shit?"

Harry's eyes drifted back to the album in his lap. "Don't know who they are," Harry said, "or what kind of fall they have in mind."

He found Andy's eyes again. They were there, waiting.

"You do know it's a fall," Andy said, so simple, so true. "Lots of retired questioners out there. No one else took his records with him. No one else they can call traitor quite so easy. You gonna let 'em use you, maybe kill you, because your wife left you? You were the brightest boy in the shop, Harry. I know you fifteen years, I never gave you one piece of advice. You tell 'em to fuck off. Okay?"

Harry tried the bravest smile he could find. "I'll be careful, okay?"

Andy had to smile back. "Who you tracking next Tuesday or Wednesday?" Andy said, just to back off for a moment. "Stephen Ridder, investigative reporter. Top secret?"

Always been their favorite expression. Andy would look over from his barstool and ask what Harry was drinking. Top secret, Harry would say. You having the lamb or the veal? Top secret.

"Ithaca, New York," Harry said. "Guy named Steingart on the Cornell faculty."

Andy's eyebrows raised. He knew the name.

"Jesus," Harry said, "you're a pretty well-read Scotsman in your later years."

"Norris Steingart. Microwaves. I keep track of who's number one in anything. This is for Buck?"

"Just for me," Harry said. "Something I read last week. Few questions came to mind. I figure, go to the best. That's what I'm doing up here, letting mosquitoes eat my ass."

Andy laughed. Then the look returned to his face. He would take one last shot. "You know it's a fall," he said. "Tell 'em no thanks. Harry, it's their own religion."

It had been his first briefing at SIA. It was everyone's first briefing. Whether it was John Knowles coming down from the sixth floor, or Buck or whoever inherits the sixth floor when Buck is dead and gone. It is always the same. "Gentlemen. The first words you will hear in this service should be the last ones you forget. You join a religion today. Devout and fanatic. Our religion says that all things exist in this universe, perhaps even God. All things exist, that is, except one. Coincidence. Believe with all your souls that coincidence does not exist. Or walk through that door this moment and never come back."

EIGHT

Harry stepped from the doors of San Francisco's Hotel St. Francis, onto Powell Street. The doorman, in his crisp livery, waved as always. His name was Douglas, and in other days he would have blown his magic plastic whistle, and presented Harry with a taxi. Taxis were a rarity these days in the golden triangle of downtown. The few that existed inched along with the rest of the traffic. Motion was so infrequent that Powell Street seemed a linear parking lot, stretching up Nob to the Fairmont.

The movement was on the sidewalk and Harry joined it.

The air of San Francisco always held a special taste for Harry. Each breath crisp and singing with excitement. He spent his college years at Stanford. Each weekend meant the thrill of probing and exploring the city as a boy would do only with a first love. San Francisco had been Harry's first city, and nothing could change that.

He was walking slower than the crowd as he headed up Nob, almost strolling. The stale smell from a diner took him back to breakfasts at the old Buena Vista, hunkered over his bloody mary. The walk through the Wharf to the ferry for a picnic on Angel Island in the

71

clearest sunshine ever. Tiburon, the drives to Sausalito and, suddenly, a thousand distinct images flashing past so quickly and yet so clearly that his eyes couldn't help but be damp from the love of those moments. And the distance from them.

Eighteen, nineteen, twenty. Dangerous and distant years. Maybe it was just the years that Harry had loved, and San Francisco had simply been there.

He had reached Pine now, and the city was gone. Bending his body further into the climb up Nob, he was back in Cable with Andy Maclennon. Fishing together in hours of silence on that still, empty lake. And the crazy thought that kept replaying endlessly. This might be his last time alone with someone who was truly his friend.

Harry had stayed with Andy for two weeks, leaving only briefly for his journey to Cornell and his interview with Dr. Norris Steingart. Harry had not known any physicists in his academic years, and had always fantasized that they were brilliant and colorful old ducks. Steingart turned out to be a kindly soul, whose brilliance was focused on a single obsession. Harry had charmed him instantly, and was never asked to present the credentials which Andy had so carefully prepared. The old man was thrilled by Harry's knowledge of his newest book, and they walked alone for hours in a small garden. What sets microwave apart, he had said, is that the technology already exists. The knowledge is there. Only the politics are impossible.

When Harry returned to Wisconsin, the pistol and its harness had arrived. Andy had fetched them from Minneapolis and displayed them for Harry with the simplicity of a man demonstrating a kitchen appliance. The holster, the spring inside the right sleeve. The certain subtle pressure on the inner arm which brought the pistol silently to hand. For half an hour, the gun leapt from its spring, past his clutching fingers and onto the ground. By the end of the first day, he was catching the weapon neatly, in position to fire. Most of the time.

Harry could not believe the size of the tiny weapon. It seemed lost even in his own small hand. And when they walked deep into the woods to test it, he truly could not believe the force and the sound that something so small could create. The harness was incredibly uncomfortable, and despite his constant scrutiny in the mirror, Harry was certain that any professional could spot the device in a moment. He told Andy that he would wear it always, until it became part of him. He promised himself that, out of Andy's sight, he would never wear it again. It would remain forever in its concealed compartment in his luggage. An insurance policy which had expired.

When Harry returned to Washington, he took a cab to the front door of his apartment at 217 South E Street. He lingered, chatting with the cabbie, then skipped down the stairs and turned on all the lights. The apartment had been dusted, in Agency terms. Very neatly. My compliments to the chef, Harry thought. Papers inside jumbled drawers were replaced at almost the precise angles at which Harry had carefully laid and measured them. Almost. If Taradan had done this, Harry's respect increased.

Harry did not call Taradan, or anyone else, for three days. It must have been excruciating for Taradan, knowing that Harry had returned, and holding his discipline. The more excruciating because Taradan had unquestionably been reamed inside and out and inside again over Harry's disappearance. More than two weeks without a trace. If you're not a tracker, you're not a jailer. It's half the job and the bigger half by far. Harry was certain that Longview would not replace Taradan, since he would want Harry to have the confidence that he could slip the leash at will. It would mean more and better trackers, though. Harry didn't like that, but his visit with Andy required such a sacrifice. He would try to appear accessible from now on.

On the fourth day, Harry called Taradan and received a warm and relaxed welcome. No questions were asked. Harry apologized. He had to get away to his little place in the Caribbean. Think through his approach to the Mexicans. Walk on a deserted beach. Come up with something fresh. He was sorry. He should have called. Not a bit of it, Taradan assured him.

For the next ten days, Harry made Taradan his constant companion. He let Taradan conduct all briefing sessions, and listened with attention and appreciation. Harry made it clear that he wanted no third party around. He probed into the boy's personal life as gently and warmly as he could. They went to basketball games at Landover. Junk food raids after midnight. Taradan moved into Harry's apartment and slept on the couch.

Harry told Taradan that he wanted him to sit at the bargaining table alongside him. How's your Spanish, Dave? Serviceable, was the answer. That meant fluent. "Good" would have meant perfect. Then you're my translator. No one else in the room. You and me and the Mexicans. The boy seemed honored. Harry sent him on ahead to San Francisco, to welcome their guests and personally supervise all arrangements.

Arriving in San Francisco, Harry phoned Luis Guzmán Silva at the Stanford Court. Longview had identified Guzmán as the real power in the Mexican delegation. As Longview was the President's senior adviser on national security matters, his name would be the only introduction Harry would need. "General Longview has asked me to personally present his compliments. He spoke to me so warmly of the time you spent together. Could I impose an invitation to a late supper?"

They had walked up California Street to L'Etoile, and dined elegantly at a late hour. Guzmán would remember the young man as charming and most intelligent. He would also remember something else about Harry. And in the maelstrom of those next few days, as Guzmán would sit alone with his cousin, President Morín Calero, he would try to call up that quality that he had sensed from the beginning. This Harry Lime, Guzmán would tell his President, was reaching out to me that night. He wanted to warn me.

And now Harry had strolled Pine down its steep length to Montgomery Street, in the crisp morning air. And now he had entered the huge building of glass and steel and found his elevator. And as he stepped out onto the twenty-seventh floor, he walked into the silence of an anteroom cleared of all personnel save military guards.

"Harry Lime," he said to the wide-eyed lieutenant. "I believe I'm expected."

He had been expected for an hour and twenty minutes. The leadership of Pemex, Mexico's national oil monopoly, was waiting.

In a moment, Taradan appeared. He betrayed none of his inner terror that Harry was simply never going to show. That Harry was in Timbuktu. He looked calm, and concerned only for Harry's well-being.

"You're all right?" he said.

"Everything is all right," Harry said to him. "You just sit next to me and do what your training tells you. Whatever happens. I'm relying on you, Dave."

Taradan ushered Harry into a large conference room.

A massive cherrywood table with five men seated. They all stood. Beyond, a wall of glass, and below, the Embarcadero and the Bay. The sunshine was suddenly blinding.

Harry was introduced in turn to the Director of Pemex, Miguel Robles Fraga, and his two aides, economic and political. Their faces had appeared among those in the dossier Longview had provided. Then, their translator. Finally, not knowing of their meeting the night before, Taradan introduced Harry to Guzmán.

Politely explaining to Taradan, Guzmán watched Harry's direct gaze. Watching for a further scent of what he had experienced the night before. It was there. Guzmán would later recall it almost as a pleading. Not born of fear, but of compassion.

Robles was plainly furious. Whatever tactic this lunatic intended by keeping him waiting for eighty minutes, he did not know. It would cost him dearly. Obviously, Mr. Harry Lime had miscalculated grievously. The Pemex Director had been humiliated in front of his subordinates, and most importantly, in front of Guzmán.

Harry failed to offer a word of apology or explanation. As they took their seats, Harry's gaze became cold and flat, and rested squarely on Robles' eyes. Guzmán quietly left his seat at the table and took a chair by the glass window. He would watch Harry unobserved.

The silence became thunderous. Became murderous.

At last Robles cleared his throat. "Perhaps," he said in English, "if I could offer the courtesy of speaking in your language, we might alter the situation. Perhaps we could find a way of dealing in the . . . mutual courtesies that our situation . . . commends."

But Harry said nothing.

Robles was a small man. His face was thin and

sharp and sported a tiny moustache. The effort to control his rage was visible in every muscle. Harry had no opinion of the man's ability or character, and needed none.

Harry simply waited.

Robles cleared his throat again, and its sound was an embarrassing squeak against the silence.

"Where, Señor Lime," Robles managed, "would you suggest we begin?"

"Our contract with Pemex," Harry said tonelessly, "is expiring. My country needs to renew. We need Mexico's oil, Señor Robles. Desperately. And at reasonable prices."

Need, he had said. Desperately, he had said. Robles' shoulders lowered very slowly. He did not understand this man who sat before him, who had insulted his honor, who had stared at him in arrogance and who now spoke of desperation.

"We have considered," Robles said finally, "the needs of your country. Understandably, we have also to consider the needs of our own. You speak of renewing our present contract. Regrettably, that will not be possible. We have, however, prepared an alternative proposal for your consideration."

Harry said nothing.

Robles had not intended to discuss terms for hours. In the face of Harry's silence, however, he felt that there was no course but to administer the death blow immediately. He regretted this with some irritation, for he had spent the fury of his waiting time plotting the revenge of a slower torture.

"To come to the point, then," he said, "my government would be prepared to enter into a new arrangement for two years only. Rather than the 900,000 barrels per day under our existing agreement, we will be able to make available only 400,000."

Harry's face remained lifeless. His eyes never wavered from Robles'. Never blinked. This was not the satisfaction Robles had longed for. He decided to press the point.

"We are sincerely regretful of any inconvenience which may come to the people of your great nation. But to provide even this much oil will be a considerable sacrifice for my people. I am afraid that this will require an increase in the price as well. The current agreement stipulates one hundred and sixty-five dollars per barrel. Under the new arrangement, that price must become two hundred and ten dollars for the first year, and two-forty for the second."

Harry's eyes grew somehow colder. Robles could finally not resist the trace of a smile.

"After the two years, we can have another pleasant meeting, Mr. Lime. Just like this one. And discuss the matter further."

Harry's face took on a smile of its own. Grim, but almost pleased. His eyes returned to life, and they held Robles' more strongly than ever.

"If your government wishes to enter into a contract with mine," Harry said quietly, "these will be the terms. Five years. One million five hundred thousand barrels per day. One hundred twenty dollars per barrel for the life of the contract. You will have two weeks within which to accept."

The air had been sucked from the room. There was no sound of astonishment, but Robles' eyes could scarcely be wider. His little body was trembling with rage and surprise.

"I do not," he said with great difficulty, "require two seconds to respond to such a . . ." and his voice trailed off, as his head shook slowly atop his narrow shoulders.

Harry stood. "Two weeks," he said to Robles. And turned and left.

NINE

Harry had driven Taradan to the airport, and had put him on the plane. "I'll be in Washington on Sunday," he had said. "Tell the General that he made me a promise. Tell him not to do anything for two days. We'll have a nice chat then."

And now Harry sat in his darkened room at the St. Francis and watched the telephone. He did not know how long he could afford to wait before placing the call himself. He only knew that it would be better if Guzmán called him.

Harry sat through the evening for more than five hours. It was very late when Guzmán called.

Luis Guzmán Silva arrived to find a room in darkness but for a single lamp. Beneath the lamp, a table held brandy glasses and a fresh bottle of Martell Extra. Harry led him to the chairs beneath the light.

They said nothing as Harry poured two very stiff portions, and Guzmán contented himself to stare down into the liquid as he warmed the glass with his hands. His fingers were long and golden and seemed perfectly at peace with their task.

"Thank you, my friend," Guzmán said at last, "for receiving me at this hour."

"Do you understand?" Harry asked, with a kind voice.

"No, I know only that there is something *to* understand."

Harry's gaze was sympathetic. He said nothing.

"Miguel Robles," Guzmán said, "is not a stupid man. I have calmed him considerably. I told him this man is eighty-two minutes late to a meeting where he is to plead for the life's blood of his country. Miguel, there is a reason. In our world, everything is intended to communicate. And so I tell Miguel, this man's voice, his eyes, his preposterous demand. All there to tell us something."

Harry looked down into his own brandy. "Perhaps, Luis, there is something, something I cannot say."

Guzmán ran his hand back through the dusky silver of his hair. He had sagged back in his seat, and there was deep concern in his features now. It was not pretense. It was not confusion. For Guzmán had come that evening with one great absurd fear in his heart.

"Your proposal," Guzmán said slowly, "was so outrageous. It was obviously never intended to be accepted."

Harry's eyes were straight and clear.

"For myself," Harry said, "I want with all my heart for that offer to be accepted. But you are wise. It might appear that those who formulated the offer were counting on its rejection."

Guzmán's brandy sat atop the table. His fingers were now slowly rubbing together. He had lost awareness of them.

"Luis. Analyze the proposal on its merits. There will be enough oil left to meet the needs of your people and your contracts with others. There will also be a profit. Is it a disgrace to the honor of Mexico to take only a modest profit to help a neighbor in its hour of need?"

Guzmán's eyes were locked to Harry's, but his voice seemed far away. "Our oil is our national treasure. It is imperative that we make the best decision for its use."

Harry nodded his head slowly. "Imperative," Harry said, "that it be used in the best interests of your people. And what are those interests?"

The tension had become unbearable for Guzmán. He could no longer speak.

Harry smiled gently. "Luis. Say your worst fear. Say it now."

The muscles of Guzmán's face became hard and set. "Military ..." came the one word, shaking his own head knowingly, against the absurdity of what he had said.

But Harry's eyes never wavered. At last Harry too sagged back in his seat. He did not nod, even imperceptibly. He would not confirm. Only his silence spoke.

"Our government," Harry said at last, "is nothing more than a collection of men. Very different men. With different ideas. Some are men of reason. Some of action. Our present circumstances, Luis, are very grave. We tremble at the edge of anarchy. We come to our neighbor for help. And if our neighbor turns away from us, in such an hour ..."

Guzmán had regained his composure fully. His eyes were now playing back the sympathy Harry had shared.

"This from Hubert Longview?" he said, disbelieving.

"No," Harry said. "He is a man of reason. But there are other men ..."

"How," Guzmán asked, his voice now a whisper, "could you possibly hope to get away with any form of military intervention?"

"Speaking theoretically?" Harry asked.

Guzmán nodded. "Our military strength," Harry said, "is the only strength we have left. When you're down to your last card, you play it. Win or lose."

Harry's eyes softened. "I have to say this with all of its weight, Luis. You have to hear."

Guzmán nodded for Harry to continue.

"Speaking theoretically," Harry went on, "our one strategic concern would be the response of the Soviet Union. The Reforma are the only oil fields America could seize without directly affecting Soviet interests. The Soviets have their sphere, we have ours, and the Persian Gulf is World War III. In the sphere they've permitted us . . . you're all we've got."

Guzmán's fingertips were pressed together. "You are so sure," he said, "of Soviet support."

"Someone is. Perhaps he knows something."

Guzmán's mind clicked through each of the questions it had become pointless to ask.

"There is more to the Persian Gulf," Guzmán offered, "than Soviet opposition. The Arabs have threatened to destroy their fields. To contaminate them with radioactivity. Are you certain that we do not have the same ability? The same will?"

Harry smiled slowly.

"At four hundred thousand barrels, Luis, what's the difference? Play the card. There's nothing to lose. At one million-five, at a reasonable price, you give the men of reason on my team something to work with."

Guzmán drew himself up in his chair. "You are threatening war against my country," he said. His voice was strong.

"I'm asking," Harry said, "for your help in a time of need. Help us, Luis, we will be grateful."

"You are threatening war," Guzmán repeated. "What do you expect me to do in the face of such a threat?"

Harry studied the situation for a long moment, as if

gathering his thoughts. His face was very sad, very wise.

"I would counsel," he said, "only the obvious. I have threatened nothing, Luis. We have engaged in a theoretical discussion. There is no headstrong response demanded to defend your national honor. You have made your own interpretation of the situation. If you go public with such an interpretation, you will paint yourself into a corner."

"A corner?"

"If you tell your people that you are threatened, you will have no choice but to stand firm. Your people would see any other course as humiliation. You would lose the option of ultimately accepting our offer. If you deem that to be the wisest course after . . . thoroughly reviewing the situation . . ."

Guzmán's eyes agreed. "And your counsel, then . . ."

"Well," Harry said slowly, "you would need to test the validity of your interpretation before coming to a decision. Yet, to do so in a private manner, so as to keep your options open. I could make a suggestion."

Guzmán nodded.

"Go to my government. Tell them what you fear I have threatened. Tell them you assume it was the unauthorized ravings of a madman. Demand that I be relieved of my post immediately. Failing that, state clearly that there will be no Mexican oil for America on any terms. When my government responds, you will draw your conclusions."

TEN

It was evening of the following day as Harry began his walk up San Francisco's Russian Hill. The case banging softly, rhythmically, against his leg as he climbed.

He had spent the morning slipping into and out of Los Angeles to collect the case and its contents. He smiled to himself at the wonderment of Taradan's trackers, if any there were, as they pondered what the hell he was doing on the trip down and back.

Harry now turned up Jones Street, and in a moment was at the garden gate that signaled the entrance to Macondray Lane. For a shagetz scumbag, Stu had class, Harry was forced to admit. Macondray Lane, with its tangle of vines and trees, was one of the most secret and precious hideaways of the city. Only a few steps above Broadway to a cottage hidden from the world, with a clear view of blue water through the enfolding green.

And now Harry stopped, hidden in the darkness, and put the case gently down beside him. And tried to deal with the fear of walking those last few steps. Who would answer the door. What would the place look like. Would his first sight of her be a majestic descent down a spiral staircase. And when he looked into her face, what would be there.

Harry knew that the worst would be there.

The best, of course, would be the faintest glint of what Harry could only call love. The glimmer of that secret that would give him hope. It had been there long ago. But in his most recent lifetime, of two years' duration, it had not. Of that there was not the slightest doubt.

What would be there was indifference. Friendly, kindly, honest indifference. And Harry would have to bear that one more time.

Harry picked up the case and slowly walked Macondray Lane. The numbers were hidden in the foliage, and he found the place with difficulty.

He pressed the bell, which did not seem to ring, or was lost in the pounding of his chest and his throat. Blood thumped in his ears and he stood motionless, case clutched uselessly in his hand, held so tightly that his fingers had lost all feeling.

There was a sound of scuffling at the peephole. The door swung open.

And there was Jennylime. She was dressed for the theater in something black and cut cruelly low. Her breasts were brown and full, and Harry's first panic was that he could not keep his eyes from moving to them. Her black hair was swept back, and she was still fastening an earring. Diamonds, long and dangling, something from a man who would buy pink roses.

"Hullo," was all he could say.

Her expression was not of anger, but consternation. Harry had not been expected to fetch Lissa until tomorrow at noon.

Her expression mattered not a damn to Harry. He was looking only to her eyes as they started to register what Harry meant to them. There was respect, there was friendship. There was a wisp of almost nostalgia.

Through her impatience at the surprise, she was clearly glad to see him.

"I'm sorry," Harry said uselessly. "Got to take a red-eye tomorrow. Thought I could keep Lissa at the hotel with me tonight. Give us a few more hours."

Jenny was nodding, her hands still fastening the earring. Her eyes were softening, and she offered her first smile. It was only half-power, but it was more than enough.

"Sure," she said. "That would be just fine."

Then her eyes moved over his face and lost themselves in his eyes for that fraction of a second. It had happened before. It meant nothing, and yet had always set his pulse to racing.

"God," she said as her smile faded, "you look absolutely great. You really do."

He had heard that before as well. And each word held its separate little sting of pain.

"You too," he said. Master of the snappy response. Golden-tongued devil. No wonder she can't resist you.

"Thanks," she said, and the smile blossomed again.

They were still standing at the door.

"Can I come in?"

Instant flicker of her eye to the stairwell. "Sure. I'm sorry. We're a little late for the Geary. Let me just run up and tell Lissa."

She headed up the staircase quickly enough to make certain that the master of the house was amply warned of the intrusion.

Harry found himself a chair in a small den off the hall. Fireplace with fresh logs, neatly stacked. Large pipe in the ashtray. A goddam trophy on top of a television set. A big bronze golfer in the midst of a murderous backswing. Harry sat and simply hated himself. It was easier than hating her.

Jenny returned alone, and perched on a sofa. Hands

clasped on her knees. Her eyes found the case on the floor beside Harry's foot.

"Is that . . . ?" she asked, rhetorically.

Harry opened the case, and Murray hopped delicately onto the rug.

Queen Murray took one long look at her former mistress and slowly turned her tiny hindquarters. She sprang to Harry's lap, purring softly as he stroked her. Her tail flicking lazily in Jenny's direction.

"I'm going away for a while," Harry said. "I thought . . ."

Jenny rubbed her palms together. She seemed very uncomfortable.

"The thing is . . . see . . . Stu is allergic to cats."

Since she would not meet his eyes, this was a lie.

"Allergic," Harry said simply.

Her face was flushed. "He just doesn't like animals," she said.

Harry nodded. He thought of Lissa's dog. A shaggy Puli puppy, two years ago. Full of love and life.

"Where's Hector?"

"Out back. We keep Hector in his . . . run."

"Out back?" Harry asked. "In a cage?" Stu was obviously a sadist. There was no other word for it.

"We keep him locked up," she said angrily, "in a little box. We feed him on dried lizards and drive a stake through his little heart every day. At high noon. Okay?"

Harry was sorry.

"Look," she said softly, "Stu has a house full of nice things. He just likes to keep it neat. That's all."

In his imagination, Harry watched Hector desecrating the bronze golf trophy. Watched Jenny stifle a giggle as Stu's back was turned.

"Sounds like a fun guy," Harry said. But his voice was very gentle.

"No," she said, in the same tone. "You're the fun guy. I haven't forgotten. You're the romantic. You've got the biggest, darkest eyes. You're the number one catch out there in the civilized world. And I don't have the guts to tell that big blond asshole that I want Murray to stay with me."

She stood and pulled Murray from his lap and knelt before him. Caressing the furry ball as Murray purred madly, and shed all over her evening gown.

"You're still weird, Murray," she purred back. Jenny retreated to the couch and took Murray with her.

"Your mother is a heartless bitch, Murray," she whispered. "So your daddy will have to feed you to the sharks. Okay, my love? To the sharks?"

Melissa Lime appeared. She was eleven, and seemed to have aged years in the last two months. Harry stood and clapped his hands, and his daughter vaulted across the room and into his arms. She strangled him and kissed his lips. She looked nothing like her mother, but there was beauty all the same.

Harry was holding her tightly as Stu appeared in the doorway. Lissa followed Harry's eyes to the intruder, and Harry set her down.

"Stuart Hagen," Lissa said brightly, "this is Harry Lime."

They had never met. Harry had never seen so much as a snapshot.

The big man strode forward, smile in place. He held out a hand that was simply enormous. Harry took it, returning the pressure as firmly as he could.

Stu's face was not gorgeous. Worse. It was interesting. Worse. It was intelligent.

"It's good to meet you, Harry." The rich voice was warm and easy. "I've got two women raving on about you night and day. I was hoping we could spend some time together. All of us. Maybe tomorrow evening?"

"No way," came Lissa's quick reply. "Mom says he's leaving tomorrow night, and I've got him all for myself."

Her eyes had focused on Murray.

"Look who's come for a visit," Jenny announced, holding the cat out to her daughter.

"I'm going away for a while," Harry said in Stu's direction. "I was hoping that maybe . . ."

Lissa turned her shining brown eyes on her father. "You were hoping," she said, "that I would take care of your silly old cat for you. Well, that's going to be up to me and Stu. Stu and I will have to discuss this. And we'll let you know."

Lissa turned the eyes on Stu, and the ballgame was over. Murray had escaped the sharks.

ELEVEN

They sat at the very lip of the pond. Bare feet buried in the slimy cool. The sun smacked off the water, warming their cheeks.

"Well, he's not Jewish, you know," Lissa said out of the blue.

"No!" Harry was aghast. Lissa giggled at his dramatic reading.

"Sorry to be the one to tell you," she said through the last of her laughter.

He looked at her with great solemnity. "Someone had to," he said. "Thank God it was a loved one."

It had been a perfect visit. They had left Macondray Lane and walked to an ice cream parlor and bought honey ice cream and hot fudge and almonds. A taxi, could you believe it, was found, and whisked the happy couple to the Hotel St. Francis, where the ice cream was brought safely upstairs inside the case formerly inhabited by Murray the Weird.

Morning was breakfast at the Buena Vista. They were first in line, in the chill off the Bay, when the doors opened. Lissa sipped his bloody mary and had two orders of bacon.

They had rattled around Golden Gate Park in the warm sun. His daughter was eleven, which meant that she was alternately five and sixteen. She remained the marvel and the riddle she had always been for Harry. As always, she was the most intelligent person he had ever loved.

The visit had passed without a word about Stu, or Jenny, for that matter, until now.

"So not being Jewish," she said, looking far across the pond, "makes a difference. It explains things."

"What?" he asked.

She turned to him and squinted her eyes against the sun. "Didn't you ever know a shagetz?" she asked, using the Yiddish as though she used it all the time.

"Once," Harry said. "He had horns."

Lissa laughed again. Throaty and sixteen, at least.

"Well, I'll tell you all about him," she offered. "What's the most important thing you want to hear about him?"

Harry thought for a moment. "The only thing I want to hear," Harry said, "is that somewhere deep inside you really don't like him all that much."

Lissa smiled up at him. And now she was twenty-six.

"The only thing," she said, "that you *really* want to hear is that Mommy doesn't like him all that much."

Harry loved being outsmarted by this child. It was a common occurrence.

Her eyes were so straight and clear. "She likes him a lot," Lissa said. "I can't tell how much. He's a good guy. He's good to us."

Harry didn't know how to thank her for how much she cared, and how wonderful she was. They lay back on the grass, at arm's length, fingers squeezed tight.

"I want to live with you sometime," she said. It was something she had waited all this time to say.

"Just sometime before I grow up. Okay?"

Let's do it before I grow up too, Harry thought. But his only answer was a tighter squeeze.

"All those places we were going to go," she said. "London and Paris. Sometime." She was almost crying now, at least that's what he thought he heard.

"I promise," he heard himself say. "I promise you, and I promise me."

TWELVE

William Parkens settled himself more deeply into the leather folds of his swivel chair. Languidly, he stretched his long legs out across the top of the desk.

It was a warm Sunday afternoon in Washington, and the window of the Oval Office was open full to the breeze and the sounds of the garden. Birds of several varieties were busily singing and squawking their approval of the afternoon, but William Parkens was not listening.

Parkens was a man who wore elegance as naturally and closely as skin. Even in casual attire for this very urgent moment, he was impeccable. From his moccasins, to his Cartier watch, to the golden mane swept straight back from his forehead, William Parkens was a man with everything in place. His features were as close to beauty as a man could come without shading toward something feminine. His eyes were clear and calm. It was a face that never appeared troubled, that never gave up the secrets of the mind behind the eyes, a mind that had been described as the finest of its generation.

Across the room, another man lay sprawled along a sofa. Robert Cole was as compact and square as his friend was lean. His hair was dark and very thick. A strong jaw jutted out toward the world, making his thin-lipped mouth seem oddly small. The eyes were deep blue, and the lashes uncommonly full. There was beauty in this face as well, the beauty of a man's quiet strength.

For all of the differences in the faces of the two men, there was an identity of expression that would startle any observer. From their earliest manhood, these two had interlocked their lives and their wills in one of those curious pairings which had become commonplace to American political history. Twenty-two years of shared ambitions and triumphs had forged these two men into a single mind. The symbiotic elements of a single entity, comprising the President of the United States and his alter ego.

There was a brief knock at a side door. It opened, followed by the familiar sound of the perfunctory, "Gentlemen." General Hubert Longview entered the room, and the Big Three, as the press referred to them, was complete.

Longview moved directly to the tweed armchair that had become his accustomed corner of the inner sanctum. No pleasantries were exchanged. None were necessary.

"Brian's been on ice for an hour," Longview said, referring to the Secretary of State. "I've had him in Horace's office. He's storming around, bouncing off the file cabinets."

The others offered smiles of gentle amusement.

"Horace," Longview went on, "is hovering over him. Kissing his ass, bringing him tea. Horace would love to be included in the meeting. He practically begged."

Parkens' eyes drifted off for a moment, in contemplation.

"I don't think so," Parkens said. "Where's Mr. Lime?"

"Other side," Longview said, "locked up tight."

Parkens' eyelids dropped in what passed for a nod of approval.

Longview cleared his throat. He was at ease in almost any situation. But the combined silence of these two men was very powerful. He had known them deeply, but for a relatively short time. When they were quiet together, like this, he felt excluded. More, almost under suspicion.

"I've given you the bare bones," he said. "Shall we flesh them out a bit?"

Parkens looked at Cole, who might have been asleep.

"After," Parkens said. "Hear them out first."

"Together?" Longview asked.

"Brian first, I think."

Longview left the room. In a moment, he returned with a large, florid man in a blue suit and maroon tie. Against the casual dress of the others, he seemed oddly formal for a quiet spring afternoon.

"Mr. President," said Brian Jaynace as he entered. He was sweating at his waist, his armpits, everywhere, in heat and distress.

Robert Manders Cole did not rise to greet his Secretary of State. He barely turned his head. The bottomless blue eyes fixed on the man.

"Sit down, Brian, please," the President said so softly. "You seem upset."

Jaynace pulled out a large damp handkerchief and dabbed at his face. He perched on a hard-back chair in the center of the room, directly in the crossfire of the Big Three. He could not escape the insane momentary feeling that *he* was under interrogation.

"Hasn't anyone told you . . . ?" Jaynace began.

Cole watched the man without expression.

"Suppose," Parkens said calmly, "you tell us. Just what has spoiled your Sunday, Brian?"

The man wheeled on Parkens, his face incredulous. "Do you know who the hell this Harry Lime is?"

Parkens traced his finger along the desk blotter. "Special Assistant to the President of the United States. Came highly recommended."

The man's large hands were gripping his knees. He could feel his fury rising, and knew he must put it in check. Parkens could make a fool of him without half trying.

"Billy," the man said to Parkens, "this is the guy who almost destroyed the Security Intelligence Agency. Single-handed. Nine years ago. Nobody mentioned that little fact to you?"

The President's aide looked up at Brian with a lazy smile. Parkens' smile might have said, Can't believe everything you hear. It might have said, I'll ask the questions, thank you very much.

A small stab of something cold was working its way through the intestines of Brian Jaynace. Parkens wasn't ridiculing him for pleasure, he wouldn't waste the time. Parkens was warning him to go slow.

Parkens' face slipped easily to another mode. There was no longer the maddening scent of upper-class derision. With a small adjustment at the corners of his mouth, Parkens was at once utterly sincere. Without moving, he seemed to actually lean toward Brian in his concern.

"Brian, we know a great deal about Mr. Lime. That's why the President chose to see you privately, before we brought Mr. Lime into the room. So that we could reassure you of just that fact. Ross Buckley can document every time this guy's gone out for a pizza for the last nine years. He's clean, Brian."

Parkens' eyes were kind. His hands rested easily together. He was not angry with the Secretary of State, and therefore, neither was the President. Jaynace

had caught his breath. He was feeling a surge of gratitude to Parkens for slowing him down.

"If you sensed a certain tension in the room," Parkens
said solicitously, "a certain ... questioning ... directed at you, the President did have one concern, a
concern *for* you, Brian. We need the clarity of your
judgment on this one."

"Concern ... ?"

"There's nothing more testing, Brian, of a dedicated, disciplined member of the team, than being
passed over. This is the General's operation. That
was the President's decision. No cabinet member was
to be involved, even yourself. You wouldn't be human, Brian, if it didn't sting just a bit."

Jaynace squared his big shoulders, and fought the
impulse to adjust the broad knot in his tie. Damn
straight, it stung. He had spent the previous hour
rehearsing his resignation speech. He had even de-
luded himself into believing there was the tiniest
chance he might use it. Longview and Buckley off on
some dim-witted romp. He was Secretary of goddam
State, after all.

"I have no personal feelings, Billy," Jaynace said
royally. "Just that I have the old-fashioned notion
that a team functions best when the full leadership
has a chance to make its input." Quite a mouthful, he
decided. Maybe too much.

He spread his large hands, regretfully.

"Look," Jaynace said, "it's a fiasco, sure, but it's not
war. I soothed the sonofabitch down off the ceiling. I
mean the goddam ceiling. The point here is not to
assess blame. Point is to take care of the thing. Then
maybe we put our heads together and ..."

He wasn't sure whether the look was in Parkens'
eyes or not. The look that said stop right there. Anyway, there was no need to overplay the hand. This

was unquestionably the instant demise of General Hubert O. Longview. Not a goddam moment too soon for this republic.

"I think," Parkens said into the silence, "that this incident may help us all see things a bit more clearly."

The silence resumed.

"Hubert," Parkens said at last, "why don't you bring Mr. Lime in for a visit?"

In a few moments, Longview ushered Harry into the room. None of the three men waiting had ever met Harry, but there was no introduction, no sound acknowledging his presence.

Harry took a seat near Jaynace in the center of the room.

"Secretary Jaynace," Parkens said, in a tone of deep regard, "would you please recount for us the events of the last several hours?"

Jaynace looked over at Harry as if he were a lunatic or a cockroach. Harry returned the man's gaze and slowly, deliberately, smiled. He could see the big man's color rise.

"Last night," Jaynace said, his voice under strictest control, "I received a call from Foreign Minister Villegas. The hour was late, but he begged to see me immediately. It seems that he and President Morín Calero, and certain other senior advisers, had been meeting around the clock for the last two days."

"This," Parkens said, guiding gently, "with respect to Mr. Lime's meeting with Pemex representatives in San Francisco."

Jaynace was looking only at Harry, and trying to convey his incredulity in the most dignified manner possible.

"Señor Villegas informed me," Jaynace said, extra-slowly, "that a Mr. Harry Lime had been authorized by General Longview to conduct the preliminary negotiations on the new Pemex agreement."

Jaynace pulled his handkerchief slowly from his breast pocket and dabbed at his forehead. This was purely for dramatic effect, as his perspiration had ceased entirely. Parkens had given him centerstage, and he was beginning to warm to his task.

"At his meeting with Director Robles Fraga in San Francisco," Jaynace went on, looking only at Harry, "Mr. Lime arrived nearly two hours late. He calmly informed Director Robles that the United States would accept nothing less than an annual *increase* in supply of some 220 million barrels a year. At a forty-five dollars a barrel *decrease* in price. Fixed for *five* years."

"And, this," Parkens said, "was of some concern to President Morín?"

Jaynace had never before suspected Parkens of wanting to get rid of the General. He had always thought Parkens too secure. Clearly, he had been wrong. Parkens' wry Greek chorus seemed an eager participant in Longview's destruction. Jaynace had never sensed this kind of support from Parkens. It was heady stuff.

"I would say," Jaynace responded with a dull smile of his own, "that 'concern' would not be an overstatement."

He lowered his eyes while he carefully folded the handkerchief and replaced it at his breast pocket. He wanted to build the silence mercilessly, to increase the impact of his coup de grace.

"Of course," he said in a casual tone, "that 'concern' was somewhat heightened, when Mr. Lime met with Senor Guzmán . . ."

At this moment, Jaynace looked up at Harry with all the drama he could command.

"A meeting at which he simply advised Señor

Guzmán that, if Mexico failed to comply with his demands, our government would declare war."

Jaynace, shaking his head in disbelief, continued to gape at Harry.

"A masterstroke," Jaynace said, voice saturated with irony. "A masterstroke of foreign policy."

"And what," Parkens asked lightly, "did Minister Villegas convey of his country's response?"

Jaynace's eyes hardened. He was now nodding his head grimly in Harry's direction. *I pulled you out of this one, you sonofabitch. Thank God for me.*

"I had," Jaynace said, "to scrape him off the ceiling. I go way back with Ramón. He knew he could trust me."

Thank God for me. Very much indeed.

"Ramón told me that they figured Lime was loony. Still, he came right out of the blue as the personal representative of General Longview. Let me tell you, President Morín was described as hysterical. He'd told Ramón, in no uncertain terms, there'd never be one drop of Mexican oil for America at any price. He wanted a full public airing of this catastrophe at the United Nations. Immediately."

Silence again.

"But . . ." Parkens offered, helpfully.

"But," Jaynace said, "I reasoned with him. We're professionals. Go way back together. As of ten o'clock this morning, the Mexican Government has agreed to keep the entire matter a private one. Moreover, they will consent to sell us oil on the same terms Robles proposed in San Francisco."

"All they want . . ." Parkens said.

"All they want is a personal apology from the President to President Morín. Which will remain absolutely private. Just a personal statement that this was the mad act of a deeply disturbed individual. I can leave immediately for Mexico City, and wrap up the details with Señor Robles and his team."

Robert Manders Cole lifted his heavy lids toward Harry Lime. His eyes regarding Harry with surpassing disinterest.

"Mr. Lime," the President said. "What do you think?"

"I think," Harry said quietly, "that I got 'em."

"You what?" came the reply of the Secretary of goddam State. "You what?"

Harry turned his calm eyes on Jaynace.

"Got 'em," Harry repeated. "As in 'kicked their ass.'"

The big man's jaw went simply slack.

"Because ..." Parkens' voice wafted lightly from afar.

"Because," Harry said quietly, "we're just desperate enough to mean it. They don't have the guts to try us. They were afraid to take it public, because they knew they were going to back down. They've already offered to come back to Robles' original proposal. They're scared pissless."

"Do you have any idea," Jaynace shouted, "of the risk you've put this country through?"

"None at all," Harry answered. "To this point, you can repudiate me as a nut. The risk doesn't start till now. I got you a free look at their hole card. And there's nothing there. If you want a million and a half barrels of oil a day for five years at a fixed price of a hundred and twenty dollars, it's sitting right there on the table."

"Your suggestion then is ..." Parkens again.

"General Longview calls Villegas. He says Mexico has ten days left to respond to Harry Lime on his terms. Period. Hang up the phone."

"What," Cole asked, "if you're wrong?"

"I'm not wrong. They did just what I told Guzmán to do."

"What," Cole repeated patiently, "if you're wrong?"

Harry took a deep breath. "You're still okay," Harry said. "You fly personally to Morín Calero in Mexico City. You kiss his ass from the inside. You tell him Longview was the madman. You tell him Longview is gone."

Cole's lips formed a very real smile. "Longview is gone?" the President said.

"First the pawn," Harry said slowly. "The rook, if you must. Never the queen."

Cole pulled himself up and his full voice sallied across the room.

"And how does the rook feel about that one?"

The General was looking at Harry, and wearing a tight smile of his own. Whether it was admiration or a mask, Harry couldn't say.

"I think," the General said slowly, "that Harry's got 'em."

Cole, suddenly much amused, turned over his shoulder. "Billy?"

Parkens met the President's eyes.

"I'm afraid," Parkens said, "that I have to agree with Brian."

"You do?"

"As Brian said. It's a masterstroke of foreign policy."

Jaynace twitched as Parkens' harpoon passed through his flesh. He was a dead man.

Robert Manders Cole allowed his eyes to travel up and down over the seated figure of Harry Lime. As an art collector who has bought a piece with which he is mightily satisfied.

"Can't pull this trick with the Europeans, Harry," he said at last. "Or the Arabs. So you'll just have to think up another one."

THIRTEEN

The three men took late supper on the terrace. The President's steward had prepared the cold poached salmon personally, had served it unassisted and had withdrawn for the night.

Two silver ice buckets stood at Parkens' elbow, chilling reserve bottles of Montrachet. The garden below was entirely still. They were alone in the world.

"You know," the President said, "I listened so patiently to Buckley's whole story. On and on about *how* Lime did it. Surprisingly little about *why*. Yes, nine years ago, he's young. Ideals. Still, he had to know he might pull that whole place down behind him."

Silence followed. Three men eating. Sipping their burgundy.

"If you're wondering," Cole said, "whether I'm waiting. I'm waiting."

The General looked across the table.

"You want to know why," Longview said. "What did Buck tell you?"

The President's voice dropped a notch.

"Hubert. What did he tell *you*?"

Longview ran his palm back over his scalp.

"Old John Knowles was a cold warrior," Longview said. "Maybe the coldest warrior. Harry Lime was his pride and joy, Personal Assistant to the Executive Director at twenty-nine. Buck was officially Knowles' second-in-command. He did half of Knowles' thinking for him, the half that went on in public. But the private half, the half everyone figured Knowles did for himself, that was Harry Lime from the inner office."

Parkens silently refilled their glasses. At this point, Longview's story would spin itself best without prodding.

"John Knowles was a man obsessed," the General continued. "He saw the SIA not as a tool for the retrieval and analysis of information. He saw it as a quite secret, loaded gun. Of course, he knew that was the very avalanche that buried the CIA. Accordingly, his most significant personnel priorities were loyalty, and shall we say, a shared point of view about how we needed to deal with the Bolshies."

The General took a deep swallow of the burgundy. His eyes invited comment. There was none.

"Well, he had Buck to run the Agency for him. And he had bright young Harry to whisper in his ear. The rest of the place was a sorry lot. Since Knowles retained control of staffing, Buck found dry rot under every beam. Third-rate thugs, young and old. Security control was nonexistent. Appalling. Lime didn't need to be a genius, he could've backed a truck up to the place and hauled its guts away in broad daylight."

Another swallow. This was the part he wasn't quite sure Buck had explained completely.

"Then," he said slowly, "there were the collectors. You're familiar with that term?"

The President said nothing.

"Lots of personnel are trained in techniques of killing," Longview volunteered. "The collectors are somewhat apart. With these men, it's a calling more than a training. Not a dozen people know who they are. They don't even know each other."

The General was nodding his head slightly as he searched the eyes across the table.

"When Lime decided to quit, sacrifice himself so that Knowles could be pulled down—because that was the only way to truly save the Agency—everybody woke up on a Monday morning to find some very interesting records disappeared. Files, microfilm. Even the computer programming had been changed. The stuff that scared the shit out of Congress was the assassinations in Pakistan and Iraq. But what scared Knowles wasn't the stuff the *Post* might discover. It was what the Russkis could do with every shred of data on two hundred agents in the field. And, of course, his precious collectors. That went beyond sacred."

The President cleared his throat. "You're stressing these collectors . . ."

"You want to know why he did it," Longview said. "Buck told you that Lime was a youngster with some ideals. John Knowles and his collectors were an unholy marriage, Mr. President."

It was impossible to judge whether Cole was buying any of it. The blue eyes just stared patiently across the table.

"You aren't saying," Parkens said so softly, "that these collectors have been disbanded?"

"No. Just used differently. Reduced in number. In scope. I think everyone concedes that you need a couple of these guys on the payroll. The question is what you do with them."

Longview looked over at Parkens. Eyes cast down thoughtfully into his glass. Man could have been anything, Longview thought of Parkens, as he often did. The best agent, the best soldier, best of anything.

The General was wondering why Parkens had asked that question. But Parkens was silent. The real question would come later, and Longview was always slightly off-balance waiting for it.

"Anyway," Longview forced himself ahead, "everybody woke up on a Monday to find the family jewels were missing. Hysteria, simple and pure. Then, three days later, everything back in its place. Even the computer programming. All the information on incidents, agents, everything neatly returned. With a minor exception. Every tape, every word, every system that carried the name Harry Lime had been altered to excise that one name. The Agency was back in place, but Harry Lime was gone. Had never been there."

Silence again. They were waiting.

"So," Parkens said at last, "the Pentagon and the White House and the Senate Oversight Committee all put their pointed heads together. And all the king's horses and all the king's men decide that they'd better damn well keep Humpty together, or they'll never get another."

Parkens was looking at Longview now. That flat, straight look that you could never read. There was no anger, no guile, no anything. By the time you finished counting all the things that weren't there, you'd been chewed up, maybe, and left for dead.

"John Knowles," Parkens went on, "retires. Ross Buckley assumes the wheel and builds the SIA into what it always could have been. Much more. Perhaps none of us knows how much more. Harry Lime is a traitor, an eccentric or even a hero, depending on what you ate for breakfast that morning. He is, however, gone to the blessed peace of Private Life."

During the silence that followed, Longview waited for the question Parkens had been saving.

"It just seems," Parkens said at long last, "that this all turned out rather well for Ross Buckley."

Hubert Longview nodded his agreement. He even forced a smile.

"Turned out rather well for this republic," he added. "Rather damn well. You're not the first curious soul, Billy, to wonder whether Buck greased the skids for the old man."

After all, big fish eat little fish, Longview thought. A lesson not to be ignored when you're in the same tank with William Parkens.

"I was wondering," Parkens corrected, "about the relationship between Mr. Buckley and Mr. Lime."

FOURTEEN

It could have been a perfect morning to amble down the Champs Elysées after breakfast. Perfect for the mind to play its lazy trick of wondering whether it had been three years or five, or whether he had ever really left at all.

For Harry, each moment in Paris would always trace its way back to the first. His train had entered Gare De Lyon, just ahead of the evening. He had pulled his student bags through the tangle of the station and down the street to Place Mazas. And, there, at the edge of the Pont D'Austerlitz, he had looked up.

What Harry truly saw and felt was lost to him by now, and of no concern. The moment had been re-shaped and textured by the endless replaying of it through the rest of his life. It was his best-told story, told only to himself. In the story, Harry had stood at the edge of a bridge and looked up to the west. The sun was moments above the horizon and just past the shoulder of the Cathedral of Notre Dame. The Seine was quietly slipping from gray-green to purple toward black. All of Paris lay along that river and before his eyes, eyes filled with tears of the most unexplainable feeling.

Harry Lime had stood at that bridge in his half-buttoned overcoat, his baggage forgotten at his side. He stood and cried as the sun slid into the Bois de Boulogne. He cried for minutes before he understood. The day had ended and Harry's childhood had ended with it. It was something he simply and suddenly knew. The knowing had come into his mind and never left. The lights of Paris had come up, and Harry's real life had begun.

Once again, Harry had come to Paris alone. The cabbie had not understood why the distinguished passenger had asked to be driven slowly to the Pont D'Austerlitz. Why he had been given a princely tip to drive away, while a man stared off at quite an ordinary sunset. Americans were, of course, a peculiar lot.

Harry's eyes were dry as he left the bridge. He slung the strap of his leather bag across his shoulder, and headed up the Quai. Past St. Louis and Cité. Past the Louvre and the Tuileries. Past the Grand Palais, and finally to Avenue Montaigne. Into the warmth and light of the Plaza-Athénée, where Taradan had so thoughtfully booked him into a majestic suite.

Harry's luggage was waiting. Also flowers and champagne, in the name of the President of the United States. Taradan had sent a slightly obsequious note of national gratitude. He enclosed a clipping from the *Post*, announcing the Treaty of Commerce and Friendship between Mexico and the United States. Swift Congressional approval was a certainty. Taradan closed by mentioning that he had reserved a table for Harry at Taillevent for nine o'clock. He hoped that Harry was thus well set up for his first night in Paris.

Harry was somewhat better set up in Paris than Taradan had realized. As Walter Clarke, he had already reserved a room at a small hotel called the Regentsgarden, near Place Des Ternes. Samuel Allen, on the other hand, had taken a discreet short-term lease on a flat in Neuilly. The key for the flat was already pressed tightly into the appropriate passport. Harry took a long hot bath with his magnum of Mumm's. Then he dressed, and strolled off to collect his supper.

In Paris, Harry always slept with the window open, and always slept magnificently. There were no dreams, no thoughts, no Jennylime at all.

The morning was clear. Sun and rolling Paris clouds. He had walked to the Champs Elysées for his breakfast, Café Georges V, table on the street, three croissants and cocoa.

It could have been a perfect morning, except for the trackers.

He had counted five already. The distracted businessman whose eyes had barely followed Harry's progress from elevator to front desk and across the lobby to the door. The first team of two was on the street. Young husband and wife with baby carriage, fifty meters toward the river. Their quiet conversation began as he walked toward them. After a few steps, Harry turned and headed back toward the Champs Elysées. In a moment, the man was pushing the pram along behind him. Harry stopped at windows and a newsstand. The pram never closed nearer than forty meters.

As Harry took his seat in the café, the couple innocently strolled by. Within minutes, the second team appeared at the café across the Champs. Young tourists, very much in love. They never seemed to glance in Harry's direction. As he stood to pay his check, they did the same. He took forty minutes to stroll to Avenue Franklin Roosevelt, peering in windows, stopping at a sleek establishment to try on a cashmere coat. The couple remained across the wide boulevard, holding hands, laughing and pointing into windows of their own.

Harry knew this was only the beginning. Probably a three-team relay. It was the minimum coverage. It could only increase. There was no way to know for certain when he would be free of it. Harry would have to share the warm Paris morning with the Beta Team. Until Charlie Team relieved them. Until Alpha Team returned. Until one of them saw him safely to his supper and home to bed. Every day. For as far into the future as it made any sense to look.

Harry had seen such surveillance continue for years, if the fish were big enough.

Harry came to the Carré and sat on a bench under broad green leaves. He spread his arms along the back of the bench and turned a lazy smile to the sun. His eyes were nearly closed.

Beta Team had passed and taken a bench of their own, eighty meters down toward Place de la Concorde. Harry's face turned a little further away from them. He was more than curious. Longview, or Buck, would have said this was routine precaution. It was not. If the leash were this tight already, there was a reason. Now it was time for a tug on the leash, time to measure the slack.

Harry kept his face to the sun for forty minutes. He rose very slowly, smile in place, and set off toward Place de la Concorde. Beta Team was there, lost in each other's eyes. Harry was not watching them, however. Harry was looking for some help.

Fifty meters past Beta Team, Harry saw a young girl slouched on a bench. She was tearing small pieces of bread, tossing them to a coterie of sparrows. She wore a light trenchcoat, too warm for the morning. A tourist, afraid of an unpredictable shower somewhere on her day's excursion. A compact umbrella and a canvas bag beside her on the bench, both American.

Her legs were slim and bare. Sand-colored hair hung limply past her shoulders. The hair was clean, but shapeless. Her nails were short and without polish. Harry could not see her face very well in the shadow.

Harry sat on her bench, close, but definitely out of reach. His hands folded themselves humbly on his knees. She was clearly aware of him, but her eyes fixed on the sparrows. Her jaw set slightly, a first line of defense. He could see her face now. She was not as young as he might have guessed. Mid-twenties, perhaps. Small, simple features.

After a couple of minutes, Harry said, "Hi," in a gentle tone.

She looked up sharply, pretending surprise. As she saw his face, and most particularly the large brown eyes, she smiled, the smile of a girl unaccustomed to the attentions of an attractive man. Harry waited to see if one of her hands would involuntarily adjust her hair, and sure enough. The smile was shy, and really rather pretty. She was attracted.

"I'm Harry Lime," he said, offering his last name as a gesture of openness. If he looked any more friendly and harmless, his face would break.

"Cassie," she said.

She was clearly American.

"I need a favor, Cassie. Is it okay if I just ask? I'll sure understand if you say no. Okay?"

The smile went away, but she nodded.

Harry's smile never wavered. His eyes looked down at his folded hands, a little embarrassed.

"See, the thing is," he said, "when I tell you about this, you have to just look me straight in the eye. Is that okay?"

She looked a bit curious, and nodded again. His eyes found hers and held them.

"I know that you say you'll keep looking at me," he went on, "most people would say that. But most people can't do it. But you can, can't you?"

"Yes," she said, "of course."

His disarming smile blazed away, disarming for all it was worth.

"I know this sounds very strange," he said. "I have to get you to promise to keep looking straight at me through what I'm about to say next. Will you promise?"

"I promise," she said, and the smile returned. A little confused, but it was back. "I swear," she grinned, "on my mother's grave. Okay?"

"Okay," he said, "I'm gonna trust you. So, thinking all the time about just looking at my eyes, and thinking that you're not gonna look away if hell freezes over ... what I want to tell you is ... that there's a nice young couple seated near us ... and it's very important that you don't look at them."

Her eyes locked dutifully onto his.

"Where are they?" she whispered.

"The place where they are, the place you're never going to look, is about forty yards over my right shoulder. On the other side of the path."

The girl nodded very seriously. "Why can't we look at them?" she whispered.

"I have to ask you a question first," he whispered.

She nodded, staring resolutely at his eyes.

"Why," he asked, "are we whispering?"

She laughed out loud. And immediately covered her mouth with both hands.

"Now," he said, "we can't look at them because they're following me. And they don't know I know it."

"Are you a spy?" with obvious delight.

"Yes. But I'm a good spy."

She nodded. "And they're the bad spies?"

"No. They're good, too. The bad spies are all in the Kremlin, drinking vodka. Neat. Without so much as a twist."

They looked at each other.

"Look," he said, "this is definitely a pickup. I'm definitely going to ask you for a very proper date at the end of what may be a long conversation. But I am definitely also serious about being a spy, and about your not looking at that nice young couple. Okay?"

"Okay," she said. "Okay to the part about not looking." The date part was apparently okay, as well.

"Cassie, for as long as we know each other, which may be five minutes, I'll never lie to you. Can you believe such a thing?"

"I'll try."

"You have a pretty smile. And your eyes remind me of someone I care about."

"Your girlfriend," she said. And the hand adjusted her hair again.

"It's a man. He lives in Wisconsin. His eyes are blue and very honest."

She did not know what to say.

"We have to sit here," he said, "and talk for a while. Is that okay?"

She curled her legs underneath her and settled her shoulder into the bench.

"What shall we talk about?" she said.

'My choice?"

She nodded.

"I want to hear everything about you that you'd feel comfortable telling a spy. Be very careful, because I never forget anything. If I'm captured and tortured, I'll probably spill my guts, and everybody in the Kremlin will end up knowing your dress size."

She smiled again. "Size three," she said.

He gave a slight shrug. "Your funeral," he said.

She took a deep breath. "I'm from Montclair, New Jersey. I'm single, as a good spy would note from my conspicuous lack of a wedding ring. I've been in Paris for exactly six days. In two weeks, I start teaching at the Lycée Montaigne. I have a degree from Radcliffe in Modern European Languages. Two degrees, actually. Still working on the doctorate."

Harry felt a little uncomfortable. She was selling her intelligence in the uneasy way of a woman trying to compensate for her looks. The scent was there. She was apologizing for being plain.

Harry had learned never to reinforce that insecurity. The more he would compliment her intellect, the more he would confirm it was all she really had to offer.

She pulled the strand behind her ear again. A clip could keep it there. Just as liner and shadow could make the small blue eyes a little larger. She didn't like being plain. Harry wondered why she had done nothing about it.

"That the kind of thing you want to hear?" she asked. Insecurity was flowing over the dam and into the muscles around her eyes.

"Not really."

"What, then?"

"I wanted to hear about *you*," he said gently. "What you're like on the inside."

Both hands pulled hair behind both ears.

"Isn't this very short acquaintance for that kind of thing?" she asked.

"Very short," he said. "And I'm very interested."

She relaxed. Visibly. Smiled the nice smile again.

"I'm shy," she said. "That's a euphemism. What I am is frightened. I guess you can see that."

"I'm frightened by a lot of things," he said. 'But I'm not frightened now. Not with you. I like you."

"Me too," she said. Her eyes were even a little damp. "I mean, I like you."

Harry stood up and held out his hand.

"Go for a walk?"

FIFTEEN

They walked to the Tuileries. They sat on a bench. Beta Team was at the far end of the gardens.

"Are they still there?" she asked, the conspiratorial whisper returning.

"Sure."

"This may surprise you," she said, "but I believe every word of it. I believe you're a spy, and I believe this nice young couple is chasing you. Am I just gullible?"

He looked at her. "No," he said. "You checked them out. You looked at them in the Carré. Twice. You found them again at the other end of the garden when we sat down. When I helped you off with your coat. When you thought I wasn't looking."

She seemed paralyzed with guilt. "I'm sorry," she said. "I'm so sorry."

"No problem. You were very discreet. Very clever."

Her eyes narrowed. Harry could not remember a look of more honest regret.

"I mean," she said, "I'm sorry I lied to you."

"It's okay," he said, and squeezed her fingers. "I promised not to lie. You didn't."

"I do now," she said. "I'll never lie to you again. You can count on that. For whatever it's worth," she

117

added, in such self-deprecation that he was uncomfortable again.

"Thanks," he said. "It's worth plenty."

They walked slowly back through the gardens and up the Champs Elysées. This time on the river side. He said things to make her laugh. They popped in and out of men's shops, as he tried on hats.

As they passed Rue Galilée, he casually asked, "How good is your eyesight?"

"Very good."

"As we walk along," he said, "could you look at the movie theaters across the Boulevard and pick out the show times on the billboards?"

She tried for a moment. "Easy," she said.

"It's noon in three minutes. Can you find a show on the other side of the street with a noon start? And no ticket line. Very important. We have to walk right up and buy our tickets with no wait."

They walked a bit farther.

"How's a twelve-fifteen start?" she said quietly. "No line at all."

"Great. Now tug on my arm and point across the street to show me the theater."

She did.

"Look insistent," he said, "talk me into it."

She did. Very well.

"Okay. Don't let go," he said.

He held her hand tightly and, laughing, they plunged into the street. Once on the other side, he gave her a little hug, plunked down his money at the window and, looking at his watch, calmly entered the theater.

As the usher took their tickets, Harry asked to be shown to the nearest exit. The confused usher pointed to the door they had just entered through. "An exit to the back," Harry said. "To the alley. Quick, we're playing a joke on our friends."

The usher pointed them down the stairs toward the WC. Harry dragged Cassie off, giggling and gasping for breath.

"Your French is pretty good," she said, trying mightily to take two stairs at a time. "Very colloquial. I'm impressed."

Harry was just looking for the exit. Unmarked, but he found it.

Into the alley, he wrapped an arm tightly around her waist. They ran a few steps, and her umbrella clattered to the pavement. He stopped dead and smiled at her. Bending slowly to retrieve it, he handed it to her with a slight bow. Then grabbed her waist and they took off again. She snuggled as close as she could, cheek against his shoulder.

At Rue de Balzac, their jiggling dash became a decorous, if fast-paced, walk. He led her through a maze of streets and alleys to Avenue Hoche. Once on the Avenue, they completed their stroll to Parc Monceau in a grand and leisurely manner.

They sat under a large tree. The grass was fresh and the smell was very rich.

"That was the favor?" she said at last.

He looked at her curiously.

"When you sat down on my bench, you said you needed a favor."

He smiled and shook his head. "I can lose them anytime I want. Only we can't lose them too often, or for too long. If we do, they'll suspect we're on to them. So, we have a couple of hours. Then we'll show up back on the Champs Elysées, near the theater. Let them follow us around to their heart's content."

She looked so serious.

"Then what was the favor?"

"Two favors," he said. "Sometimes it's good to be with someone like you when they follow me. You're cover. They're certain I'd never tell you anything about business. No professional would. If I'm with you, the day must be strictly pleasure. They relax."

"Are we going to do some spying?"

"I'm training them today. I want them to get used to you."

She leaned back against the trunk of the elm. "Sounds like you figure I'm going to be around," she said. She watched her fingers twisting in her lap.

"If you want to."

"And if I don't, you'll just find someone else."

"I don't want to find someone else, I like you."

She looked down at her lap for a while. Her hands were still now. "What was the second favor?" she said at last.

"I'm lonely," he said.

She looked up at him with Andy Maclennon's eyes.

"All my business," he said, "is lies. Makes me feel alone. I need to be with someone I can tell the truth to."

"I'm just a stranger," she said.

"You are a stranger," he agreed. "And a friend."

"Telling me the truth," she said, "is that . . . professional?"

"No," he said. "It's weakness. Any trust at all is weakness. Forbidden. It's the second rule."

She sat and watched his eyes.

"Can I ask a question?" she said in her small voice.

"Always. And there'll be times I won't answer."

"Is that your real name? Harry Lime?"

"Sure. Why not?"

She smiled. "You don't look much like Orson Welles," she said.

She had found the softest place inside him. He was beaming.

"I'll bet all the girls ask you that," she said, obviously pleased with herself.

"Nobody asks me that. That film is fifty years old."

She shook her head disapprovingly. "Very famous movie," she said. "All the girls are missing out on a good line."

Not all the girls, he thought. And for a moment, Cassie was a black-haired girl in the damp night of a Washington summer. She was Jenny Steinberg on a first date, coyly asking the riddle of his name.

"My father was a cabinet-maker," Harry said to Jenny/Cassie. "He was an artist in wood. A poet. He was born in the Ukraine. In a village by a river called the Dnieper. He was a carver as a boy. He learned cabinets in Kiev."

Harry reached into his pocket for a black cigar.

"His name was Pytor Limnokov."

"He changed it on Ellis Island?" she said. And she was Cassie again, a plain, lonely girl he didn't know.

Harry shook his head. "My father was an artisan in Kiev for years. He lived alone. He worked for a wealthy Jew, a lovely old man named Nezhnayev. Gave him the best of everything. In 1935, the old man's grandson was killed by some Jew-baiting thug. Somehow, he arranged for his family to emigrate. Cost a fortune in bribes. He took my father along."

Harry found a match. He lit the slender cigar very carefully.

"My father," Harry said, "was a very serious man. All his life, he only knew work. He saved his money. He was honest and loyal. He had no dreams. That's hard to understand, I know. No dreams of beauty or romance. Of anything more to life than hard, honest work."

The girl was lost now in Harry's eyes. Lost as Jennylime had been that summer night in Georgetown.

"The old man died in 1942. My father was alone. He took the old man's name, Vassily, as his own, to keep some part of him. He moved to Chicago and he lived and worked alone. If you can believe it, he had never been inside of a motion picture theater in his life. Never had so much as a thought of doing anything so frivolous."

The girl nodded. She could believe it.

"He was walking in the Loop on a Sunday. It was cold and he was feeling particularly alone. He passed a theater showing *The Third Man*. The billboards of Vienna reminded him of Kiev somehow, and he went in. Do you remember the music from that movie?"

"Of course," she said. "It was the best part of the movie. It was a dulcimer?"

"A zither," he said. "Played by a man named Anton Karas. To my father, it sounded like a balalaika. I don't think my father really understood what was happening in the film. But the music, the joy and the mystery of it, and Vienna. It was the first romantic experience of his life. A world of feelings and dreams and beauty tore through him. As if the whole locked-up part of him were suddenly released. He sat through the film three times every night until it went away. Then he found a recording of the music and bought himself a little record player."

Harry had to stop for a second.

"My father sat in his room every night with that music. He wished for things he'd never had. He wanted to fall in love."

The girl was nodding her understanding. Her eyes were shining.

"He went to court," Harry said, "and changed his name. He didn't care that Harry Lime had been the villain of the film, a criminal. He just thought the name Lime was like his own, only beautiful and exciting. He could be the same man, but different. But he couldn't take the name Harry, because that would be too much. That name he would save for his son. And his son would truly be the man he could only dream of being."

The girl's face was Jenny's once again. Stranger and friend, eyes that Pytor Limnokov had touched.

"It took him six years," Harry said, "to find my mother. I knew she was the one, he said, because I didn't have to try to love her. I just loved her. She was young and shy and very frail. She seemed to be dying from the day I met her, he used to tell me. She gave him his son. He loved her with all his heart for three more years. Then she died."

"Do you remember her?"

"I looked at her picture, and I would try so hard to remember. And I would lie to him and tell him I remembered her and loved her. I told him that lie on his deathbed."

Harry saw that her eyes were wet now. Slowly, he put an arm around her.

SIXTEEN

They walked Rue François Prémier heading back toward the Plaza-Athénée. Charlie Team was firmly in tow.

A middle-aged couple, French and squat. He wore a black beret and an enormous nose, streaked with tiny veins. He thrust his hands deeply into his pockets. She wore rimless spectacles and carried a large net shopping bag. They were easily the best. On the Champs Elysées, it had taken Harry forty minutes of constant subtle maneuvers to spot them.

"Frontal assault," Cassie said brightly. "Exactly whom are we spying on?"

"No one."

"No one?"

Shadows were lengthening now, and the day smelled suddenly like Paris again. Harry was thinking of his time as a tracker. For Knowles himself, in Vienna. Eight men, twenty-four hours. With a special assignment waiting at the end. Tracker with a stinger. And his world changing course. Fighting off the certainty in Knowles' eyes.

"I'm in Paris negotiating a petroleum treaty," Harry said. "I'm a special bloody counsel to the President of the United States."

She squeezed his hand a little tighter and tried to appear unimpressed.

"You said you'd never lie to me. So, first you're a spy. Now you're a diplomat. What do you call that?"

"Versatility."

She stifled a giggle. "How long have you been a diplomat?"

"About three weeks."

"You like to start at the top, huh?"

"And work my way down," he said. "It's a lifelong career pattern."

She now had his hand wrapped tightly in both of hers. "And you work for the CIA at the same time."

"I never worked for the CIA. I worked for another agency. But that was a while ago."

"A while ago," she repeated.

"Nine years."

She nodded, her little features locked in a very professional deadpan. She wasn't about to grin, at any cost.

"So, you've only been a diplomat for three weeks?"

"Maybe four."

"And you haven't been a spy for nine years?"

"Seems like yesterday."

"Do anything in-between?"

"Pretty nosy for a stranger," he said, and gently returned the pressure of her fingers. They walked in silence for a while.

"If you haven't been a spy for nine years, why are these people following you?"

"They're afraid of me," he said simply. "Once a spy, always a spy."

They had come to the Plaza-Athénée. There were two messages at the front desk.

"I'll bet," Harry said, "you don't believe I'm really a big deal diplomat."

"Bet I do," she said.

He showed her the messages. Each bore the name of Claude Mairet, Minister of Energy.

She gave an impish smile. "You paid the desk clerk to set this up," she said.

Harry led her by the hand to the telephone cabinets at the far side of the lobby. He pulled her into one and sat her on his lap.

As he fumbled for his coins, Harry's eyes absently wandered the lobby. Seated far to their right, engrossed in the evening's *France-Soir*, was the tired businessman who had traced Harry's journey through the lobby that morning.

As if reassured by his presence, Harry turned to the telephone. He dialed carefully, then held the receiver so Cassie could press her ear to it as well. He told her softly about the businessman, and asked her to smile.

Harry waited patiently through three levels of screening before reaching the Minister's private secretary.

"Ah, Monsieur Lime, we have been trying to reach you all the day. The Minister must regretfully postpone your appointment of Tuesday afternoon. He has asked me to convey his apologies to you and to your government for the inconvenience."

"No apology necessary," Harry said. "I hope that all is well with the Minister and *his* government."

There was a slight pause.

"Yes," the voice came back, "there are no problems of any kind. Actually, he is leaving Monday for a little holiday he had promised his family at their country home in Provence. A scheduling mistake, really it was my fault. But the Minister did not want to disappoint his children. I hope you will understand."

"Of course. How long will the Minister be gone?"

"Only six days. Could I reschedule you for the following Monday? At the same time of day?"

"Perfect. Tell the Minister I wish him a good holiday."

Cassie had her slender arms draped around his neck. She looked very young, and once again rather pretty. "What now?"

"Well," he said, "we big deal diplomats have friends in high places all over. Just sit tight."

She did. He pulled out an address book, and playfully keeping its pages from her gaze, found another number. He jiggled the dial for the house operator.

"I'd like to place a call to Bonn, please. The number is 65-3867. I would like to speak to the appointment secretary of Minister Hoch. H-o-c-h, please. This is Monsieur Lime. Room 305."

The hotel operator reached the Ministry almost immediately. She spoke only in French, the operator in Bonn spoke only in German, but they clearly understood one another.

Cassie had leaned back now, away from the receiver. She was smiling, and concentrating on not looking out through the glass of the booth. She did not want to risk meeting the eyes of the businessman.

"Yes, please, this is Frau Tauber. Go ahead please." The voice was confident and authoritative.

"This is Harry Lime. I'm calling from Paris. I've had a scheduling problem, and I wondered if the Minister could move my appointment up to next week? Any day, of course, at his convenience."

"I am so sorry," the voice shot back without a trace of anything resembling sorrow. "The Minister is leaving Monday for a short holiday at his chalet in Bavaria. So I am afraid that would be quite impossible."

Harry's face had gone very still, very quiet. Cassie watched the face of this strange man. The face that had charmed her with its openness now stared lifelessly at the blank wall of the booth. Striking, she thought, that any change could be so instantaneous, so complete. Cassie had been told to smile, and she kept smiling all the harder. She bent forward to nuzzle Harry's ear, still playing out her role to the unseen eyes across the lobby.

"So," Frau Tauber continued, "I see we have you scheduled for the twenty-seventh. We shall then leave the schedule as it is."

"No," Harry said softly, almost in apology. "I'm afraid that won't be possible. How long will the Minister be on holiday?"

"Six days," came the rather annoyed response. "The Minister returns Sunday. Perhaps we can find something for you that week." It was clear that change was not Frau Tauber's favorite aspect of life. Harry could feel her resentment, but at the moment, her attitude was not the focus of his thoughts.

"Yes," he said distractedly. "Let me ring you back. Listen, in case you're out of the office, is there anyone else I would ask for?"

The silence was eloquent with indignation. "I *am* Minister Hoch's administrative assistant. I am the only one in authority to set his schedule."

"Yes, of course." His tone sounded embarrassed, but Harry's eyes remained behind their cloud. "What time does your office close tonight?"

"This is Friday, Mr. Lime. We close at five o'clock. Precisely. For the weekend."

"Ah, yes. I will have to ring you next week. If I call and you are indisposed, I would leave a message for you . . ."

Another pause.

"Fräulein Grümbar is my assistant. You could leave such a message with her. I do think you would do best, Herr Lime, to arrange your thoughts clearly concerning your schedule before you call again."

"Yes," he said. "Sorry for . . ." but Frau Tauber had already rung off to turn her attention to more important matters.

When Harry turned to the girl, he was struck at once by the concern in her eyes. By the honesty of it, yes. But to his fascination and alarm, more by the intellect of it. There was more intelligence in those eyes than you could pick up by chance on a park bench. Not one try in a thousand.

And in the stark paranoia of this particular moment, Harry's mind clicked back through the details of how he had found the girl on the bench. This shy and sympathetic creature he had chosen for a day's cover. Could she have chosen? His mind flashed through those moments of the morning. He replayed the finding of her, the honesty he had seen in those eyes, almost as clearly as the intellect.

Her smile was dutifully fixed in place as Harry watched her eyes. Not to trust this girl, in this moment, meant to Harry that he would never trust again. It was a simple choice.

"What on earth did they tell you?" she said through the bright smile. "Your face turned off like a light bulb."

"They told me," he said, "that Minister Hoch is leaving Monday for a holiday with his family. He'll be gone for six days."

"That's quite a coincidence, isn't it?" She had lost the smile.

"Coincidence," he said, "is meeting someone nice on a bench in the park. Two Ministers of Energy, taking identical six-day holidays . . ."

"And leaving on a Monday," she said. "If you were taking a holiday, wouldn't you start on the weekend?"

Harry nodded, with a smile.

"You think they're going to the same place," she said. "Is that important?"

"Probably not."

"But you're curious?"

"*You're* curious," he said, "and you're not even involved."

She looked almost hurt. "I'm involved with you," she said softly.

Suddenly, the girl looked very frail and very lovely. It was the first moment he could honestly tell her he found her very attractive.

"I'm looking at you," he said, "and I'm thinking how pretty you look just now. I mean that. And I mean something else. It's the least important part of you, Cassie. Of anyone. You should learn how to learn that."

She blushed deeply, and the last smoke wisps of doubt left his mind.

It was nearly five o'clock as they approached the public telephone on Avenue Franklin Roosevelt. Alpha Team was back on duty, their costumes carefully altered to a different station of life.

How is your German, he had asked her. Better than yours. Can you speak German with a French accent. Yes, she had said, with a Parisian accent, or a southern one.

You will ask for Fräulein Grümbar just before five, he had said. There is no way Frau Tauber would let her assistant off one minute early. Let's hope that Fräulein Grümbar is eager to leave on her weekend. You are calling from the Ministry. You have been asked by someone on Minister Mairet's staff to send a basket to Minister Hoch on his arrival. You've got to get the order out before everything closes for the weekend.

"So the Minister arrives, then, before or after noon?"

Harry said flatly, using the tone Cassie would mimic. "When she gives the answer, you say simply, 'and he will be staying at the . . .' Just let it hang there. No matter how long the silence. She won't be able to resist the silence. She'll fill it in with the name of the hotel. As soon as you have it, 'thank you, dear,' and ring off."

"What if she gives me the hotel, but we still can't find the city?" Cassie had asked. "A Hilton or a Grand could be almost anywhere."

"Can't be helped. Any hint that you don't know the city, the slightest, slightest hint, is out of the question."

Cassie pressed her lips together and gave a grim little nod.

"What if she sounds suspicious? Asks questions?"

"Never press it. Not the tiniest fraction. Any sign of trouble, just sound very annoyed with the bureaucrats at your end. They must have garbled your instructions upstairs, the cretins. And just as you're closing for your weekend. Always the way. Sorry for the inconvenience, dear, and just hang up the phone."

"What if she gives the phone to Tauber?"

"Don't risk any questions to Tauber at all. Start some harmless sentence and ring off in the middle of a word. As if the connection had been cut off."

"You're on your own," Harry told her. "I won't be in the booth, I won't be in your line of sight. Just stare straight at the phone box and concentrate only on what you're doing. I know you can handle it. Easily. Or I wouldn't be letting you do it."

And so, Harry stood leaning against the booth, at Cassie's back, and carefully lit a black Dutch cigar. He smiled and breathed the Paris of late afternoon, as Alpha Team lingered at a store window some fifty meters off to his left.

Cassie was at his side so quickly, he thought she

must have missed her connection. But she was smiling, very slightly.

"Danielli," she said. "Must be somewhere in Italy."

"Venice," he said, and then wondered for a moment why he'd said it. "Do you like champagne?"

"Couldn't have gone any smoother," she answered, her eyes very bright. "The fräulein told me to remind Minister Mairet that the first meeting is for luncheon at one o'clock."

"That means you don't like champagne?" he grinned.

"Well, if you don't want to know where the meeting is . . ."

"Caviar? Good caviar."

Her eyes narrowed. The girl was thinking again. She was smiling, but she was thinking. Harry knew all about the people who thought too much.

"I don't . . ." she said, and brushed the hair from her cheek, "I don't understand you."

"You're not paying attention," he said. "I skillfully changed the subject. So deft, you hardly noticed."

"Deftly," she corrected, the smile warming. "I hardly noticed."

SEVENTEEN

They arrived at Le Beluga just after ten. Cassie had never seen anything quite like it. At each table, a quiet couple stared at each other past the candle flame. Before them, only wine, a plate stacked with blinis. And large bowls over ice, heaped glistening black.

The maître d' seemed to know Harry. He led them proudly through the darkened room to a table at the far corner. He slipped Cassie's coat from her shoulders and folded it over his arm protectively. He smiled at Cassie as if he were offering her a gift, then left without a word.

Cassie was wearing the best she had. Expensive, conservative, sexless. Her eyes glowed with excitement. Sadly, though, they were not exciting.

Harry told himself that she was a chameleon. There had been beauty there, he had seen it. But so fragile, so halting, that in the wrong light, angle, he had totally lost it. He was struggling to find it again.

Harry watched himself struggling as they talked, and began to dislike himself. The struggle to find a feeling, force the feeling. He thought of giving it up. Letting it die here, at this supper. For to see her again, he would have to find a connection, an honest

one, at a level he could call beauty. Nothing else
would satisfy this girl in the end.

There was a stubborn little strength. A weed that
could poke its way through stone. There was character and honesty. There was much to suggest that
Cassie could be loved as a person. She would need,
however, to be loved as a woman. She would not need
the disappointment of another man who could not do
just that one simple, awesome thing.

The caviar had arrived. Crystal bowls of ice and
gleaming black beluga. Fifty grams in all its glory,
with its small silver spoon. The blinis, the chopped
egg and onion. A bottle of Laurent Perrier. Harry was
frightened. He was cheating this girl. It was all just
the slightest, most elusive, connection away. And he
would never find it.

She poked at the slimy black mound before her.
Rather bravely, really. Small fingers delicately probed,
then plunged the spoon. She thrust a pile into her
tiny mouth. Her eyes widened in delight. Harry did
not hear what she said. Smallness, he said to himself.
Delicate hands, features. His mind flashed to women
of that type he had admired. Feminine creatures of
soft motion and quiet strength. There was a girl at
college, Elisabeth. Small and quiet, with short hair,
cut like a young boy's. There was something in his
excitement for Elisabeth that Harry could use here. If
he didn't push it too hard, it might be a beginning.

"Tell me a story," he said.

She sucked on her spoon and thought a moment. "I
don't have a story like yours," she said. "A beautiful
story like your father."

He said nothing.

"My father is an investment banker," she said. "We
don't love each other. Actually, I suppose he loves me,
all right. Actually . . . he really doesn't."

"Tell me a story," he said again. He smiled so easy, holding her eyes.

"What kind of story? Wrong question, I guess."

He held his champagne glass to toast her. They both swallowed.

"Tell me a small story about someone who loved you."

Her eyes showed that the right story had come instantly to her, showed her deciding whether to tell it.

"Just the first someone that crosses your mind," he said. And looked away to make it easier for her to start.

"There was a boy named Charles. We were freshmen. We were together summer quarter in Boston."

She seemed sorry she had begun.

"Now what?" she said.

"Now tell me the story of Charles. Okay?"

"Not much of a story," as she peered down into her glass.

"My favorite kind," he said.

She told the story without once meeting his eyes. "Charles was very beautiful. He was small, but very athletic. He had beautiful dark eyes. We fell in love in the summer. We drove through New England. We went to the beach. We had picnics. He was very sensitive. He told me the truth."

Harry waited. He kept waiting.

"There's no more," she said.

Harry waited for more.

"He loved me until . . . until he stopped. I never knew why he stopped. He didn't know either. He stopped. So then I stopped."

Harry smiled at her. He filled his own spoon and held it out to her. Obediently, she sucked the fish eggs into her mouth. Only then did her eyes begin to glisten.

"I'm sorry," she said through the fish eggs. "Sorry it wasn't more of a story."

Harry found her eyes. "It was the biggest disappointment of your life," he said.

"I just . . . didn't know it was going to stop."

Harry's voice became very soft. "The best thing in all of life is having something that you don't want ever to stop. So, feel very good about Charles. We don't get that many of them."

She ate for a few minutes, as if gathering strength. "The beluga is magnificent," she said at last. "Translated, that means I'm almost getting used to it. You're married, aren't you?"

"Separated," he said, wondering whāt the hell that word actually meant.

"What does that mean?" she said matter-of-factly.

"It means Jenny stopped a while ago, and then she left. Beating you to your next question, I haven't quite stopped yet."

She put down her spoon and looked straight into his eyes. Pretty again in that moment. There was no fear, no shyness even.

"Give me a chance," she said. "Give me a real chance. Maybe . . . maybe I'll surprise you."

Harry really didn't know what to say. Her face was reddening, but she kept looking so strong through it all, he just had to smile.

"What makes you think I'm such a goddamned bargain?" he whispered.

"I don't know that you're a bargain," she said with a tiny smile. "I don't know you at all. I just don't want it to stop."

She reached over and put her hand on his.

"I mean," she said, "first there was my father. And

then there was Charles. You're Harry Lime. Who knows, you could be the third man."

When the supper was over, and they stood outside waiting for her taxi, Cassie told him very firmly that she was coming home with him. Her little jaw was set and her eyes were clear.

EIGHTEEN

Harry took Cassie to bed along with assorted distractions.

Making love had always been a complicated activity before Jenny. It was complicated again.

When the door shut behind them, Cassie had wound her arms around his neck, closed her eyes and kissed him. The kiss was very tender. Almost loving. There was a distant hunger in it that Harry did not share.

As he began to undress Cassie, Harry tried to build his first problem. He started in his fantasy of the sweet, plain little stranger who deserved something more. More than the rejection that would surely come when Harry couldn't find, force, the feeling. The resonance of that honest, distant hunger.

Harry's mind tumbled into the past, to other women with the hunger he hadn't shared. The uneasy ringing in his brain next morning, the hope that she would have sensed his distance and, in self-protection, pulled back herself. But she didn't. They didn't. It seemed to sharpen their hunger. As if more, only more, would make it right. And the ringing would become retreat, repulsion, even for the nice ones. It was saddest of all with the nicest ones.

And in Harry's thoughts in the darkened suite was

the lie that always came to him. If it didn't feel right at the very first, it never could. Harry had known those moments when it had felt very right from the first touch, first kiss. There had been some before Jenny. Maybe there had been ten or a dozen. And Jenny had been the last. Would be the last. Something letting go in the pit of him at the very start. This would be right. That feeling wasn't here for Cassie.

Fantasy was not the only distraction. There was also reality. For all of Harry's problem-building, he could not ignore the woman's body slowly emerging from cloth and nylon. There were gentle curves Harry hadn't expected. Most of all, there was Cassie's skin. Her skin was tight and firm and smoother than he could remember skin being. Any skin. Jenny's skin. It was the first young skin Harry had touched this way since Jenny was young. It was exciting and there was no getting around it. But Harry would try.

And as Cassie slithered as close to him as she could get, as she pressed that skin against him and wound her slender legs through his, Harry found the next problem in his growing excitement. She was so young. Not very much older than a daughter might have been if he had married Elisabeth. It was like sleeping with Lissa's older sister.

And then there was Elisabeth herself. She was from Texas. Her mouth so small and playful. Cardigans too large were rolled back at the wrists. And tiny hands played with her tea cup, with his chest, with his shoulders, as he buried his hands in her golden soft little boy's head of hair. She knew every way to make him feel larger and proud and strong. Harry had thought that he loved her. He thought it long before he knew that Elisabeth from Texas had never loved him at all. And after that, he thought he loved her all the harder.

Cassie was not Elisabeth. That was for certain. But there were flashes. The play of her small hands across his bare chest, the way her mouth opened first, but so soft and so yielding that it was more surrender than aggression.

Harry wasn't sure just how much Elisabeth he wanted in Cassie. While he was struggling with this one, Cassie slipped on top of him and drew him inside her.

Harry was shocked, and more than a little delighted. Cassie leaned back to get her choice of angles, and came up with a very good one indeed. Harry struggled to see her in the dark, struggled to know it was Cassie who was slipping up and back with those short, sweet thrusts.

He fought to enjoy the moment and not to think of Elisabeth. He reached for Cassie's hips and held them, offering help and tenderness, anything to show that she was not alone as she rocked slowly above him. Harry fought the fight to feel what was happening and to keep Elisabeth away. Winning, winning, winning until the very last, when Jenny appeared above him, breasts quivering as her orgasm began. Neither Cassie's voice nor her fingers digging into his ribs could drive the image of Jenny away, and it was into Jennylime that Harry throbbed, and it was Jenny's arms he gripped so tightly the bones would surely shatter.

Harry lay beneath Cassie's body, spent and grateful and guilty, a bittersweet mixture Harry remembered all too well. He lay with his arms gently cradling her, and submitted to the confusion of whether he had cheated Cassie or Jenny the worst.

Then he lay a while longer and laughed to himself about how fucked he was, and always had been and always would be. Then he thought of how good he felt, and how he liked the girl sleeping in his arms.

And then he slept.

When Harry awoke, Cassie was gone. There was a note inviting him to breakfast at the Meurice.

Harry arrived to find her waiting for him, sipping an orange juice. She was wearing tight little jeans, and looked, simply, the best she had ever looked in the twenty-some hours of their acquaintance. She was the kitten who had swallowed the canary. And then some.

They grinned at each other like children. They said very little.

After they had ordered, Cassie cleared her throat. "Maybe I shouldn't," she began with a little smile, "but I thought something was missing last night."

"Barnyard animals?" he suggested innocently.

She giggled. "Music," she said. "I kept waiting to hear your song. You know, coming out of the woodwork. From secret spy speakers. That's hard to say, secret spy speakers."

"My song?"

"Mr. Anton Karas and his zither. *The Third Man Theme.*"

"That record," Harry said, "is totally out of print. You can't find it anywhere."

"But you must have one saved."

"You figured I just carried the record around with me?"

She nodded very slightly. "I figured," she said, "that you're a pretty sentimental kind of guy. It's practically your only appealing quality."

Harry wondered if getting laid did as much for his looks as it had for hers. She just looked little and cute enough to pull right across the table and ravish in the middle of the lobby at high noon.

"His records," Harry said, "my father's records, were all worn out. Nothing lasts, you know. I saved them. They're in a secret spy place. But you can't play them anymore."

She just smiled at him and said nothing for a long time. "I'm waiting," she said at last, "for you to tell me the story."

"What story?"

"The story of the record *you* bought. The one that's still new enough to play."

One smart little girl.

"No story," he said.

"My favorite kind," she answered.

One smart little girl indeed. "Why isn't it sitting at my house," he asked, "next to my record player?"

"Because," she said, "when Jenny left, she took it. Or you gave it to her later. You figured that as long as she kept the record, she hadn't really stopped. You figure she sits there and plays the record, and that's your string to her. Maybe someday she'll pull the string and try again."

Harry shook his head in disbelief. "Just a lucky guess," he smiled very broadly.

She was blushing slightly and looked down at her grapefruit. "A shot in the dark," she said to the grapefruit.

He just kept waiting and kept beaming. "So?" he said at last.

"So what?"

"Well," he asked, "does she play the record? I mean, you know so goddam much. Does she sit there and play the goddam record and think about me?"

She looked up very matter-of-factly. "That's one of the two things in the world," she said, "I'd like most to know. Because if she sits there and plays that record, she's got you. But if she doesn't, I've got a chance."

"What's the other thing?"

"The other thing in the world I'd like most to know?"

"Yes."

"When we're leaving for Venice."

"Venice?"

"The Hotel Danielli. You said it's in Venice. Minister Mairet, Minister Hoch. You're a spy, remember?"

He nodded. He vaguely remembered. "Let me rephrase that," he said. "When *we're* leaving for Venice?"

"Sure. I'm cover, remember? A romantic holiday with your new girlfriend. Alpha, Beta and Gamma won't suspect a thing."

"Alpha, Beta and Charlie. There's only one thing I wanna know."

"Shoot," she said.

"When are you gonna come out of your shell?"

NINETEEN

Andrei Ilyich Voslov entered the room, and it was as he always found it. As she had always prepared it for him.

The mahogany side table held the decanter of port. French crystal. They had found it in Burgundy, on their slow drive. Thirty-six, no, thirty-seven, years, October. He could remember every day, each night, truly as if it were yesterday. The walks in each village, the love. And the meals, my God, the luncheons. Troisgros and Lameloise and Pyramide. The wines. And the love. And the talks. As they drove, as they strolled with her slender arm stretching to reach around his waist. As they lay at night.

By the decanter was a single goblet. From the set that his friend had given them on the occasion of his twentieth wedding anniversary. Eleven remained from that set. Voslov remembered her tears when the twelfth was broken. She had taught him everything he really knew about beauty. And about the sadness when something of beauty was gone forever.

Next to the goblet was the cigar she had selected for this evening, a fat Havana, moist and pungent. The silver matchbox, the deep leather chair with its easy folds.

Slowly, he settled his bulk into the friendly old leather. His pudgy fingers clutched the documents that would be his evening's reading.

For the first time, he was aware of the piano concerto which had begun softly in the background.

Mozart, the twenty-sixth, he thought. He stared at his fingers clutching the documents. He wanted to leave them, burn them, spend these next hours with her.

Of course, he could not shirk his duty to his great and good friend. More, he could never justify such a breach of ritual to his wife.

His eyes were wet now. He was old. She was not. That was the mystery of it. He had fought these past weeks to avoid any show of unusual attentiveness. He guessed that he had failed and that she had seen. He would never know.

The second movement of the Mozart had begun, and the papers were still gripped in his frozen fingers. He heard her knock. Her face appeared at the doorway. The bones, the eyes, so lovely and proud. Tatiana Serafinovna would never be old. He smiled just to see her.

"Sorry to disturb," she said. "Yuri Mikhailovich is at the door. He apologizes and assures me that it is nothing urgent."

She smiled, and there passed between them the understanding that she had observed an urgency, notwithstanding the disclaimer. She liked the young man at the door. He would most certainly give his life to protect her husband.

She disappeared, and Voslov heard her steps at the corridor. The apartment was a very large one, even for Kutuzovsky Prospekt. Eight rooms, as befit Voslov's station. More, as befit the station of his great and good friend.

With relief, he stacked the papers neatly on the side table, and waited to hear the double footsteps approaching on the parquet. Hers as firm and sure as ever.

Tatiana appeared with Yuri. His embarrassment and apologies were repeated as she fixed him a very dry British gin. She touched his hand as she left, and he smiled up at her. Seemed to relax.

Voslov offered the young man a pleasant smile. "Can we get you something to eat?"

A half-shake of the head. The embarrassed smile, now edging with the eagerness to get on with it.

Voslov could clear his mind now of Burgundy and sadness. Rarely had Yuri presented himself unannounced in this way. With an internal sigh, Voslov noted the boy's excitement. This enthusiasm always had a tendency to leach the detail from the soil of Yuri's reports. Clear now of all else, Voslov nodded slightly. Yuri was thus commanded to begin, slowly, carefully, from the first instant of conceivable relevance. With every possible detail intact.

"This is my day for the First," Yuri began.

He was speaking of the First Chief Directorate of the Komitet Gosudarstvennoy Bezopasnosti. The First Chief Directorate being the arm of the KGB responsible for all foreign clandestine activities.

"First," he said, "Third, Fourth and Fifth."

He was speaking now of departments. The First Department staffed and controlled operations in the United States and Canada. The Third, in Britain, Scandinavia, Australia and New Zealand. The Fourth, West Germany and Austria. The Fifth, Italy, France, the Benelux countries, Spain and Ireland.

"I began my rounds in the usual way at ten o'clock."

Yuri had been placed in the key Personnel Directorate. It was his official function to periodically gather data from each directorate and department. Officially, the data was to be transmitted to the Administrative Organs Department of the Party's Central Committee. This was the arm of the Party charged with protecting and nurturing the KGB. More critically, its charge was to protect the State and the Party *from* the KGB.

"I met first with Gresko. His demeanor was tense, as I usually find it, and I took this to be nothing more than his customary display of respect for you."

This meant that Gresko, risen ever so slowly through the ranks to his pinnacle atop the Third Department, appeared to be steadily pissing in his pants throughout each of his periodic chats with Yuri. For there had been no attempt to conceal from the KGB's ruling Collegium that young Yuri reported his data personally to a very particular member of the Politburo.

"Gresko gave his report with precision. As you know, he is ... meticulous ... in questions of his staff."

Yuri offered a slight smile to his mentor to confirm his thorough disgust for this groveling worm. Gresko would inform on his wife, mistress (of whom he had no idea Yuri was aware) and his children by either lady, if it could buy him a moment's respite from the chilling, constant judgment of Andrei Ilyich Voslov. For Gresko knew what every official of the KGB had suspected, then feared, then known for these past six years—that through his varied and well-chosen experience within the KGB itself, through the undeniable brilliance of his intellect, and, of far more import, through a uniquely intimate relationship with his great and good friend, Voslov possessed the tools, the will and the authority to derail careers.

There had been twenty-three such incidents in these past six years. Auspiciously, Voslov had begun with Voldemar Tselyayev, a man who had consummated a meteoric rise within the First Chief Directorate by assuming the position of second-in-command of Department V, the Executive Action Department. This was the department in charge of sabotage and assassination, and Tselyayev had distinguished himself, even in this fast company, as one of the most resourceful and merciless killers the KGB had produced. His taste for blood was evident in each operation, but planning, personnel selection and execution were always flawless. The man was undeniably effective, feared, on the rise.

Until, one morning, Voldemar Tselyayev found himself reassigned. Second Chief Directorate, Seventh Department, Third Section. One of the newest members of the Politburo had made a recommendation to the Personnel Directorate of the KGB. Voldemar Tselyayev was suddenly supervising, more accurately assisting in the oversight of, Intourist hotel facilities in Kiev.

The Chairman of the KGB, a huge man of boundless energy named Lepeshkin, in his fury, demanded a personal confrontation with the new General Secretary of the Party. He was accommodated.

And so it was that pudgy little Andrei Voslov was ushered that late evening into the inner office of Vladimir Cherny, the man who for so many years had been his "great and good friend," as Tatiana had always phrased it, with more affection than cynicism. Cherny had assumed control of the Communist Party, and with it, control of the Union of Soviet Socialist Republics, only eleven weeks before. The strain of these last months was there in his eyes in full measure.

Lepeshkin was a maddened bull. He clutched the arms of his chair with such rage that Voslov expected to see sawdust spilling from between his fingers. They knew each other, of course. Before Voslov's "retirement" some five years earlier, they had shared membership in the KGB's Collegium under the reign of the master, Anatoli Gorbatov.

Secretary Cherny peered down the full patrician length of his nose toward Voslov. In those days, they met twice each week. Tuesday morning breakfast. Friday evening supper. The Secretary had never relinquished the cord of intimacy which had bound them since young manhood. But Voslov knew that things would never be as they had been. The Secretary had many Voslovs now. Two meals a week. An occasional holiday shared by the families. Counsel honestly sought, thoughtfully received, to be weighed with the counsel of others. And Voslov had never told him of his plans for the "transfer" of Voldemar Tselyayev. He had simply done it.

"Comrade Lepeshkin," the Secretary began, "comes to us, Andrei, with an interesting tale concerning a personnel transfer. He feels that you are the author of the recommendation which has effected this transfer."

At this point, Lepeshkin's rage spilled from him. Curses, threats, bellowed forth in a nearly incomprehensible avalanche.

Through it all, Cherny noted that Voslov's round little face registered only weariness. The eyelids drooped, at one point threatening to close completely. When at last Lepeshkin's tirade had ceased, Voslov carefully began to polish the glass of his round rimless spectacles with the fine silk handkerchief Tatiana had given him for just that purpose.

"Andrei," the Secretary said, "you authorized this transfer?"

"I thought it best," Voslov said mildly.

"Best?"

"Under the circumstances," Voslov added, as if it were an explanation.

Voslov turned the tired, puffy eyes to Lepeshkin. "Nikolai," Voslov said with the warmth of a gently scolding schoolteacher, "the man Tselyayev is a killer."

The rage washed from Lepeshkin's eyes. He had, in an instant, found his senses. For something in the sound of Voslov's voice reminded him of the formidable adversary the soft little man could truly be.

"A brilliant one," Lepeshkin agreed.

Voslov shook his head slightly. "In six months," Voslov said, "this man would have been chief of Department V."

"In three," Lespeshkin agreed.

"Don't you agree, Nikolai, that the role of leadership in that department is to focus not on *how* to act, but on *when*."

Voslov turned slowly to the Secretary. "Too much . . . killing," he said. And shook his head sadly.

The Secretary studied his friend for a moment, the slumped shoulders, the sad eyes. Then he turned to Lepeshkin, looking at Lepeshkin's eyes, but speaking to Voslov.

"Of course, Andrei, you realize that Nikolai will now feel that honor compels him to offer his resignation to the Council of Ministers. Would you recommend that his resignation be accepted?"

Through a supreme effort of his will, Lepeshkin sat immobile through the shock. Dimly, he heard Voslov's voice rolling toward him through the mist of his rage and panic.

"We could not," Voslov said quietly, "accept such a resignation. Despite our every wish to respect Nikolai's feelings in the matter, the loss to the State, the Party, would be too great. We need his leadership."

Lepeshkin turned with the eyes of a dog who had been whipped so brutally, so suddenly, that he could not decide whether to tear at the little man's throat or lick his hand.

There was widespread speculation in the days that followed that Voldemar Tselyayev would show up some wet evening at Kutuzovsky Prospekt and put a bullet through the little man's head. The talk continued until the evening that Tselyayev solved his shame and fury by putting the bullet into his own ear instead.

Twenty-two such "transfers" had followed. They spanned each directorate, all levels of staff below the Collegium itself.

And as young Yuri sat before him, relaying the details of his morning meeting with Gresko, chief of the Third Department, Voslov's eyelids began to grow heavy. Far from disconcerting Yuri, this only assured him that his master was at full attention.

"At three o'clock," Yuri said at last, "I began my meeting with Strelbitsky. I could see at once that something was wrong."

Pavel Strelbitsky was chief of the Fifth Department. He was a ferret-like man, with a washed-out complexion and hair of straw. His only noticeable human emotion was envy, and this was shamelessly displayed at every public and private moment as if it were a badge of martyrdom. Yuri held a special dislike for this man, which Voslov knew to be strong enough to perhaps affect his judgment.

"He was too cordial by half," Yuri began. "He had gone to particular trouble to dig up some extra filth for me on half a dozen of his staff. Clearly, he wanted to fill my plate. Naturally, I suspected that something was being withheld."

Inwardly, Voslov sighed. He would, of course, let the boy come to his point in his own way. There was no help for that. He could return to mine the detail of

Strelbitsky's statements and demeanor, if closer examination were indicated.

"Accordingly, I had a private supper with Konstantin Dolya."

Dolya was Voslov's man in the Fifth Department. A ruddy-cheeked boy with a clear eye and a mischievous grin, Dolya had been spawned in the Illegals Directorate. Eighteen months ago, he had been moved into the Fifth Department at a slightly lower level, supposedly a demotion for lack of aggressiveness. Dolya had groused just enough, to just the right combination of flunkies, that his transfer was because he had not played ball with the coterie at the Personnel Directorate. He had no taste, he said, for the ass-kissers who prized their relationships with the Central Committee (meaning, of course, with Voslov) above true service to the State. He agonized whether he should leave the service, rather than submit to a career of frustration.

It was not an unusually imaginative ploy. But, so far as Voslov had been able to see, the boy had played it very well, meaning very slowly. Over time, Dolya's resentments came to the attention of Strelbitsky himself. Rather than reporting the boy to Yuri as a malcontent, Strelbitsky took him to his bosom. Slowly increasing his authority and, more importantly, his access to Strelbitsky's personal files and thoughts.

Accordingly, the news that Yuri had dared a private supper with Dolya was something of a shock. Voslov believed that both youngsters had been trained well enough to avoid detection. Still, it had taken so long to set Dolya in place. In the last analysis, however, if Yuri had asked permission for such a contact, Voslov would have certainly granted it. Yuri had known this, and felt that the asking was unnecessary and would evidence lack of initiative. Yuri was wrong and something would have to be said, in a gentle way, in a proper moment.

"Again," Yuri said, "I knew from the first moment that my instincts were correct. Dolya was agitated, because he had wanted to present this to you himself. He was waiting for one last piece of information to make you a gift of the entire package."

Voslov's eyes grew heavier. The boredom of his countenance was ominous to Yuri.

"He was very much in error to wait," Yuri assured his master, "and I told him so quite directly. Time is very much of the . . ."

Voslov's eyes opened wide. He smiled only slightly, but enough to make Yuri laugh aloud with embarrassment.

"So why don't I cease my babbling and come to the point," Yuri said. "Strelbitsky is involved with something which he has withheld from Dolya, from everyone. Apparently, Strelbitsky's instructions come directly from someone in the Collegium. He is working on it alone, at least alone within the Fifth Department."

Voslov's fingertips met each other across the breadth of his belly.

"Dolya says," Yuri announced, "that this is related to the Marco Polo Alliance."

A slight frown.

"Certainly," Voslov said slowly, "Marco Polo has been a matter of intensive and cooperative scrutiny among many departments. I've reviewed the file personally on several occasions."

"Dolya says there is a new file. A separate file on one individual, being kept in a separate place."

The lips puckered again. "How untidy," he said sadly.

"Dolya is friendly with the woman Khobotovna in Archives. Strelbitsky has visited this particular file twice. Personally. She was curious because it is kept in a section reserved for the Third Department."

Voslov nodded, as if all of this was quite in the ordinary course. "And yet," Voslov said, "the meticulous Comrade Gresko failed to remark on this file during your chat of this morning." Here, he was simply taking the boy's temperature. He was reasonably certain of receiving the appropriate response.

"I conclude," Yuri said, "that Gresko is not involved."

"Because?"

"Gresko would not have the spine to join a cabal against you. Discovery would mean the end of his career. If he knew of Strelbitsky's deception, he would report it to me at once, confirming for all time his loyalty to you and the Secretary."

"And?"

"If Gresko had been part of the plot, he would have made the file available to Strelbitsky in a less conspicuous way. Strelbitsky would not have taken the risk of recording two visits to Third Department Archives if he had Gresko's cooperation. Gresko is not involved."

"You are certain?"

The boy looked at the smooth, round face of his master. "No," Yuri said, and cast his eyes toward his lap.

"Good. Nonetheless, you are most probably correct."

The boy smiled shyly, the slightest compliment a cherished moment.

"Why, one wonders," Voslov murmured, "would this separate file be sitting in the Third Department?"

Voslov knew that Dolya must have already breached every known commandment by reading the file. For Yuri had said a file "on one individual." Yet Yuri had thus far hesitated to mention Dolya's outrageous imprudence. Voslov wondered whether Yuri was protecting Dolya. This would please him in one sense, since Voslov had long been apprehensive of Yuri's tendency to view young colleagues as competition. Loyalty to one's comrades was admirable. Sadly, however, loyalty to Voslov himself was even more essential.

Yuri's effort to compose himself was effective, but discernable. Voslov had his answer.

Yuri said, "If I were to ask for permission to let Dolya read this file . . ."

"Denied," Voslov said quietly.

Yuri's head nodded slowly. The limb had been sawed off behind him. There was no alternative but to face the fall.

"He has already read it," Yuri said. And waited for his master's blow.

"Did it say anything of interest?" Voslov inquired mildly. "I don't mean to pry."

Voslov's smile was friendly. The boy's shoulders relaxed. This was the first moment of the slightest wavering of Yuri's loyalty to him in four years of service. Voslov would leave for later the question of whether Yuri must now be reassigned. First the file. Then cribbage with Tatiana. Yuri's fate would hold.

"Dolya photographed the file," Yuri said. "He says it concerns the activities of a previously unknown agent during the last Marco Polo meetings in London. The file rests in the Third Department, since England is in their jurisdiction. Apparently, Strelbitsky had been secretly asked to monitor the appearance of this agent at the forthcoming meeting in Venice, since Italy is the responsibility of the Fifth Department."

Yuri had said that Dolya was waiting for a final piece of information to complete the package.

"One wonders," Voslov mused, "whether this file makes so bold as to disclose the identity of this previously unknown agent."

Yuri shook his head slightly. "It gives only a code

name and a cross-reference. The reference number appears to be in the section reserved for the First Department. I assume, therefore, that this agent must be an American. Or Canadian."

No reaction from Voslov. Yuri began to wonder for the first time whether Voslov might already be aware of this. Perhaps, have participated in it.

"I suppose," Voslov said absently, "that if one were to suggest to Konstantin Dolya that he not pursue his little girlfriends, or boyfriends, in the First Department, toward the end of naming this previously unknown American or Canadian, I would suppose that such a suggestion might already be . . . untimely."

Yuri bowed his head. "Dolya," he said, "expects the answer within a week. He assures us that his contacts are loyal and discreet."

"Oh," Voslov said. "Well, that's a relief."

Yuri's hands were gripping each other. He could not quite keep from staring at them as though they were alien objects.

"We had," Voslov said, "been so pleased with the fullness of SIA cooperation in the Marco Polo matter. I take it that 'previously unknown' indicates that this particular individual's identity had not been shared with us by Mr. Buckley."

Yuri only stared at his fingers.

"Yuri," Voslov said gently, "that was a question."

"Correct. The file says that the man is not one of ours. He may or may not be one of theirs. The file speculates as to whether the Americans even know of his existence. Lepeshkin will analyze the situation further before deciding whether to disclose our awareness of this man to Buckley."

There was a long silence.

"One should also wonder, I suppose, why this file is

in Third Department Archives at all. Why not locked in Chairman Lepeshkin's safe?"

"It's mistitled," Yuri said quietly, "as a file dealing with minor budgetary matters concerning British operatives. Buried with a million others in the Archives, Lepeshkin probably feels it's safer there. No one really trusts the security of his own safe these days."

"Sad times," Voslov said wistfully. "Colleagues mistrusting their fellows."

Another silence.

"Does Konstantin offer speculation as to why this previously unknown gentleman is of any real importance?"

Yuri looked up.

"Only," he said, "that Lepeshkin is hiding this matter from us. If it is important enough for him to risk his position, his career . . ."

Voslov nodded absently. His mind now appeared to be elsewhere.

TWENTY

Claude Mairet hummed softly to himself as he stepped into the brilliant sunlight of the street. If you could call anything in the tangled patchwork of Venice a street. To France's Minister of Energy, the city was one long, twisting alleyway, intersected periodically by the foul sewers Venetians chose to call canals.

It was incomprehensible to him that civilized people could live in this claustrophobic squalor. At every hand, decaying remnants of buildings in the gaudiest of colors. Dingy bridges spanning slimy, fetid waterways, where gondoliers in absurd costumes grimly milked the failing tourist trade. Shops, tavernas and faded Cinzano umbrellas, like toadstools, crammed the tiny squares and pathways. Everywhere, people moving, selling, shouting. It was, Mairet had always thought, as if all of Istanbul or Cairo had been compacted into a few square kilometers, and left to rot in the sun.

Nonetheless, Mairet had to admit that he was enjoying his visit.

There had been a passable meal last night at Cuadri's, even it the wine had gone over and his belly still rumbled from the grease. His table had offered a view across St. Mark's to the Grand Canal, and the sunset had been little short of magnificent. He could say the same for the dark lady his bellhop had provided for the balance of the evening.

Mairet had spent as much time as possible sipping brandy in St. Mark's Square, since it was the only open space available with enough room to keep his skin from crawling. And, he was forced to admit, there was a certain pagan charm, perhaps even grandeur, to the sweep and color of that particular setting. Alone with his cognac in the sunlight, he had dreamed of his student days passed lazily in this square and the other grand places of Europe. Days passed in places where the young and idle gathered to dream and talk of beauty and liberty and love, and dwell on elegant forevers.

Venice, the symbol, could call all of this back to him, however degenerate the reality. And despite the glass trinkets and outrageous prices of the sub-standard leather and lacework, he had found a lovely pin for Monique, after all. Monique, his treasure, whom he missed terribly in the early morning hours, after the bellhop's dark lady had continued on to her appointed rounds.

It might have been the simple fact that he came three times in one evening. Or the excellent carbonara he had just dispatched in full view of the blazing white dome of Santa Maria della Salute. Ignoring, of course, the ghastly red liquid called wine which had washed it down. No, if he were to account for the undeniable pleasure of his mood, he would have to grudgingly credit the city itself. For no one could ever truly make him believe that people worked and lived out the mundane details of life here. It was a place for students, for holidays, for lovers. A fantasy, however faded, that sang of a moment's escape from the life to be lived somewhere else.

It was in these spirits that Mairet stepped lightly across the last bridge, and into the Piazza fronting the Teatro Al Fenice.

Directly to his right was his destination, Hotel Al Fenice. This, of course, would be a gathering in full public view, and nothing of consequence would be discussed. The next true meeting would be tonight at the beach house the Saudis had taken on Lido.

Mairet filled his lungs and stretched the muscles of his back. He looked smilingly about the Square, seeing nothing. As he moved toward the hotel, he stepped behind a young woman posing prettily for her boyfriend's snapshot. The shutter clicked as he passed.

Mairet had entered the hotel by the time the young woman spoke to her boyfriend.

"Can you really get a proper likeness with the sun slanting in from over there? Seems like it would wash everything out."

The man smiled slightly. "Next time," he said softly, "you take the goddam pictures. This used to be my business, you know. I've got twenty-four faces in here. Every one a portrait. Believe me."

She nodded with mock confidence, and formed a circle with her thumb and forefinger. Affectionately, it said, nice job, Mr. Bigshot. Don't blame me if your portraits are washed out.

"So," she said, "when are you going to tell me?"

"Tell you?"

"Your faces. Anyone you know?"

"I know them all," said Harry. Photos, bio, psychological profile. Twenty-six countries. Sitting in the fluorescent glare of Taradan's cubbyhole. Eight hundred twenty-three faces. Nineteen days. Fifteen hours a day. Twenty minutes for each face and file.

"Anyone of interest?" Cassie asked breezily.

"French," he said, "Germans. Italians. But no British. No other Europeans. Saudis. But no other Arabs. Chinese. Japanese. That's it. Six countries. Three professions. Energy. Military. Intelligence. No diplomats."

His voice was oddly flat. Her face registered the difference, and he smiled immediately. "I've got to admit," he said, "these guys are beginning to provoke my curiosity."

TWENTY-ONE

It had taken three drinks to finish the conversation.

Giacomo actually stocked Bombay gin, and each drink was pretty much a double. Harry left the bar a little unsteady, a little happy.

He picked his way slowly through the alleys and across the squares. He was taking the long way to the Rialto Bridge because, simply, he wanted the walk to last. Harry was thrilled to be back in Venice. He wanted to lose himself in the alleyways and never come out. To freeze the moment, live in it.

Harry didn't know if Venice had caused the dream. It wasn't really a dream. It was a memory that came to him in his sleep that night. A moment lost for ten years.

Harry had been working late. He brought a box of chicken home and he and Jenny were sitting in their big bed in Georgetown. They were watching a football game, so it was Monday. Eating chicken out of yellow plastic bowls, a third bowl between them for the bones.

Lissa was on the bed with them. She had just learned to crawl.

On her hands and knees, Lissa rocked back and forth, eyeing her father with total delight. Suddenly, she attacked. Squealing madly, she scrambled across the bed toward Daddy's chicken, over his legs and across his belly and face first into the yellow bowl.

He pulled her out, her face covered with grease and ecstasy. Fat cheeks bursting with the grin of victory.

Jenny looked up from her magazine. Her smile was tolerant and amused. Then her gray eyes caught his. She touched his arm very lightly. The smile became a smile for him.

And there was, in that moment, the absolute reality that the dream of his life had come true forever. He loved. He was loved. He was safe in that love. He would never ask, never want, anything more.

Harry was on Rialto Bridge now, and then over it. He buried himself in the open-air market. He had been here in the loneliness of his student-childhood. He had been here on his honeymoon with his gray-eyed love. He would be here again. He peered at the same squid that would always be there behind the frosty glass, peering back at him. He bought his hundred grams of soft Dutch cheese. He poked a wad of the cheese into his mouth and crossed Rialto Bridge again.

The longer he walked, the drunker he got.

He wobbled ever so slightly on his way to St. Mark's Square. He told himself the same thing he'd always told himself. It didn't matter if you thought your dreams were no good. They were your dreams. They were what your heart really wanted from this life. If you gave up on them, ever, you were dead inside.

Harry passed through the archway, and the vast openness of Piazza San Marco was suddenly before him. For a city boy, for a man who loved places where people gather, this was one of the truly remarkable places of the world. The arcades stretched forever to the golden cupolas and tile of the Basilica. It was mid-afternoon now, and the music had begun. Lovers in twos, loners alone, they sat and sipped coffee or brandy or whatever was their pleasure.

Harry knew what was his pleasure. His pleasure was to step into a vaporetto and go straight to the airport. To fly to San Francisco, to climb up Russian Hill, to pound on the door at Macondray Lane. To take his love in his arms, and smile the smile that would make the difference. Hold her, kiss her, tell her that her home was with him. To claim his wife and his daughter and carry them back here, to this square, for luncheon tomorrow. To be whole again.

What Harry saw as he moved through the Square was a slim girl in a sundress. Her bare shoulders were browning, and the limp hair had been swept back and tied with a black ribbon.

The escape from Paris had been the adventure of her life. Dead of night. Three swift métro changes, all probably unnecessary. The tickets to Stockholm. Switching planes at Copenhagen before dawn. The flight to Milan. The slow train across Lombardy and Venetia. The fat little family who shared their picnic and their laughter, as they rolled through the soft green hills.

She sat now turning the pages of an Italian grammar, pretty and fresh and waiting for Harry. To his eyes, she was the first in what would be a lifelong procession. Nice girls, lovely girls, intelligent girls. Each, at bottom, nothing more to him than a reminder of the woman she was not. Whoever they were, they were for someone else.

He sat down quietly across the table. She looked up with eyes so tender, so personal, that he was suddenly almost reviled. With all his heart, he wanted only to get up from that table and go to Jenny.

"How was your bartender friend?" she asked. "Any help?"

"Well, Giacomo and I had a nice long chat. First we talked about sports. Basketball. Fighters. Then we talked about his kids. Paolo plays soccer. Then his girlfriend. She's a little young, but that keeps it exciting for him."

"All that stuff necessary?"

"It's my training. Interrogation. That was my primary skill."

"To talk about the bartender's girlfriend?"

"Sometimes it's possible to manage things so that what you're interested in gets brought up by the other guy. Then he doesn't know you were interested in the first place."

"And how did you manage that?"

"I was hoping that when our friends finished lunch, someone would amble into the hotel bar. They did. Two Frenchmen, one Chinese. Had a drink, left. I made some nasty remark about frogs in general. Giacomo appreciated my taste. I told him I'd never seen frogs with a Chinaman before. He was off and running."

The waiter appeared. Harry ordered two dishes of ice cream. She was still beaming at him, but his revulsion was gone. He liked her. She was good company and getting better.

"Giacomo says they call themselves the Marco Polo Society. One of the Germans was at the bar last night, talked a lot about it, but there wasn't much to tell. It started as an historical society. Marco Polo linking Europe, the Middle East and the Orient. After a couple of years, some government people had joined up, and the organization started to swing toward cultural exchanges, even improving trade relations. They get together three times a year, get drunk, get laid, have a good time."

"Sounds harmless," she said.

He nodded.

"You don't believe it?" she smiled.

"Giacomo told me the German's name. It's a phony. He told Giacomo he buys magnesium. The man he described was Heinrich Weber. Army. He's their top man in NATO."

"So when he takes a trip with the boys, to get laid, he changes his name. Sounds reasonable."

Harry sighed. He was starting to wonder if somehow he had done little Cassie more harm than good by bringing her along. He had been wondering that ever since he snapped those twenty-four pictures in front of Teatro Al Fenice. It did not, however, enter his mind to lie to her.

"Cassie, these people, these twenty-four guys, they are very, very important fellas. They are not here for a Rotary lunch, not even Kiwanis, okay? Everyone's in drag. The military aren't wearing uniforms. The Saudis are wearing Saville Row suits. These guys haven't been seen in public without their ghotras since they left college."

She locked her fingers together and rested her chin on them.

"Energy, military, intelligence," she said, repeating Harry's words at Al Fenice. "What do your people say?"

"My people?"

"Your people. The CIA, or whomever you report to."

Harry thought for a moment. "I haven't told anyone about this yet."

"In three days?" She was slightly astounded. "Why not?"

Harry sat back and looked at the tower. It was nearly four, and soon the hammers would strike the great bell. White clouds were floating just beyond the Campanile, and he watched them for a while.

"They probably already know," Harry said. "They're the best intelligence service on this earth. Obviously, they know."

Cassie traced her fingertip along the corners of her book. "Don't you think you should tell them anyway? I mean, if it's this important, wouldn't you want to be sure they know?"

He looked at her. "They know," he said. "They have to know. It would be a waste."

"Waste of what? Where's the harm in just reporting it?"

Harry smiled gently. "How shall I tell them I ran across this little Marco Polo Society? See, guys, I picked up this girl in Paris. We decided to take a little holiday in Venice. Well, we're having our pasta in this little square, when the power elite of six different countries parades by in drag . . ."

"Coincidences happen," she said, with a playful grin.

"In some other solar system. Maybe. Some of the bureaucrats I work for will suddenly develop their paranoid tendencies into an advanced art form."

"They don't know you're a spy?"

She was definitely asking better questions than Harry was giving answers. He sighed again. "I'm a spy who sort of went straight. I was out for nine years. They brought me back in. I don't know why. Not yet."

She nodded as if it made sense. "Thoughtless of them not to have mentioned," she offered.

"They told me I'm to negotiate oil treaties. That it's not an intelligence function. I'm not working for the Agency, I'm a diplomat."

"So, of course, you figure they're lying to you. And you're calling *them* paranoid?"

Suddenly, his smile was gone. His eyes were serious. His voice made her feel very close to him.

"There is," Harry said, "a reason for everything in this life. For everything. I left the Agency under very unusual circumstances. They would never have asked me back without a reason. The reason is not that I'm the best man available to negotiate an oil treaty. Until I find the reason, I won't trust them."

"And then?"

"Then I still won't trust them," he smiled, "but I'll know why."

She laughed. "How come," she said softly, "I like you so much?"

Harry wondered the same thing. "I'm a boring guy," he said, "in an un-boring circumstance. It's an appealing contrast."

She nodded, with obvious delight. "Well," she said, "I hope you tell them about Marco Polo anyway. It just might be a major international crisis, you know."

"Might be," he grinned.

"Maybe they'll name it after you," she said. "You know, like Haley's Comet. Then you'll be in all the textbooks. Lime's Crisis."

"I'll be famous," he nodded. "But I won't forget my old friends."

She bit her lip.

"Will you forget me?" she said.

"Never," he said. "Count on that."

"Was," she said, "I mean, is . . . your wife very beautiful?"

Yes. Yes, very beautiful.

"She's attractive," he said.

"How could I . . . make myself more attractive?" she said, and looked down at her fingers.

He thought of all the right things to say, but he couldn't make the words come.

"Cut your hair," was what he said.

She looked up sharply.

"Cut it very short," he said, "like a boy."

"You like boys?" she asked with a grin.

"Your features are delicate," he said. "Very feminine. Short hair would accentuate that. I think you'd look . . . be . . . irresistible."

TWENTY-TWO

Harry pressed his fingers to his temples. The pressure eased the dull throbbing for only an instant.

The steward approached for a second try. Cold poached salmon, perhaps. Without opening his eyes, Harry smiled gently and shook his head. A little sleep was all he needed.

Harry tried to breathe more deeply. Shake loose the muscles of his neck and shoulders. It seemed he had boarded in Frankfurt, switched at Geneva, a hundred hours ago. The damn flight was never going to end, and Harry would grow old and die in his plush first-class seat. The steward, growing old with him, reduced to pleading with Harry to sample the antique poached salmon.

It may or may not have been Marco Polo. But there was no doubt that Paris and Bonn could scarcely have been more disastrous.

Energy Minister Mairet had been a priggish little technocrat. Dull as a post, yet stupefyingly arrogant. As a true Francophile, Harry found himself pushed to the limit. This banal little twit, in his tortoise-shell glasses for godsake, had been authorized, no, ordered, to tell Harry off. This seemed to have given the distasteful fellow the thrill of his life. Sardonic wit was not the man's long suit, but apparently no one had ever let him in on that secret.

The German Minister had been a whole lot worse. Harry decided that he would rather be married to Claude Mairet than take one more lunch with Herr Jósef Hoch. Obese, vulgar and most disturbing, rather intelligent. There was a glint in his porcine little eye that made the jackboot obsolete.

Harry didn't know why Hubert Longview had dispatched a Jew to the two most anti-Semitic capitals on the Continent, but he had the definite impression that he had just lived through a diplomatic pogrom. This, of course, made his present destination seem a bit comical, and even Harry had to force a smile through his migraine.

One more demonstration of graceful hospitality from a staunch American ally, and Harry was going to have no choice but to whisper the words "Marco Polo" into the General's leathery ear. Just mention in an off-hand way that he had stumbled across an apparently secret alliance between Europe, China and the Saudis. That could be a rather costly whisper. For if the General concluded that this was a dangerous morsel of information to be rattling around in the brain of someone like Harry . . . well, then the General would naturally consider Harry to be a dangerous man, a sometimes terminal disease. Or worse, perhaps, cause for six-green. Code six-green, maximum surveillance for the rest of one's natural life. Harry smiled again as he envisioned himself ninety years old, trying to take a leak in the face of whirring robot cameras, catching his stream from three revealing angles.

He thought, for the briefest moment, of Cassie. Lime's Crisis. In all the textbooks.

The steward returned. Dark and sincere.

"Something for your headache, sir?"

Heroin, please. Hemlock chaser. "Nothing, thanks," Harry said. "You're very kind. I'm really all right."

The flight droned on. Harry pretended to read. As he turned each page, his mind saw only the faces, bios and psychological profiles of the men who would soon be his hosts. Soon, that is, as measured by siderial time, as if the million-hour flight was ever going to end.

Then, as if in a single moment, the jet dipped. Below him, the Red Sea. Beyond, glittering in the incredible sunlight, the port of Jiddah.

Of all cities Harry had approached by air, only Athens had come close to this vision of a city dressed entirely in sparkling, sun-reflecting white. Skyscrapers, thoroughfares, there was nothing to hint at the backward desert land this once had been, before Allah's own oil had transformed Saudi Arabia into the savior and the master of the civilized world.

Master and hostage, Harry thought, and the dull humming turned to a roar as the Saudia jet swooped down across the waters of the Manqabah. On the ground, the steward reappeared with Harry's small leather case. The other passengers would deplane through the rear, he said. Could Harry please wait a few moments, and the steward would escort him personally.

Harry waited thirty minutes, alone with the steward, whose anxiety increased geometrically with each passing second. About five minutes in, the air went off and the heat began to bleed through the steel and into the cabin. The steward stammered his apologies. Harry smiled through the sweat gathering on his face, and assured the man that he scarcely noticed.

"This is insufferable," the steward announced near the end, and charged off to do something about the situation. Harry saw him on the tarmac, talking with three men in white ghotras, the headcloth of the summer months. Despite the heat, they wore mishlahs, loose gowns of a soft brown color. Each held an automatic weapon.

The steward raced back up the steps to Harry. Firing squad ready for the infidel Jew?

"Any problem?" Harry asked mildly.

The steward had been greatly chastised by his visit with the armed men. "A few more moments," he said.

Harry smiled and nodded, as if that were a wonderful explanation indeed. No blindfold, please. Just ship what's left to Arlington National.

Finally, from a far corner of the terminal, a small motorcade approached. Each vehicle, Harry was relieved to note, a black Mercedes. He fully expected to see Herr Jósef Hoch waddle out, leg of pork in one hand, luger in the other.

Instead, as the five limos glided to a halt on the steaming tarmac, only Arabs got out. Most of them with weapons. Some without. In the shadows of their ghotras, no face was recognizable at this distance.

The steward led Harry down the steps. Harry had thought nothing could be hotter than the inside of the jetliner. He was very wrong. As the first blast hit him, Harry figured maybe a hundred fifty. Actually, it was a mere 117°. He was later advised that this was only 47° Celsius, which sounded a lot cooler.

On the tarmac, a tall, elegant man stepped forward. He extended his hand. The man introduced himself as Asad. He apologized that the Minister had been unavoidably detained in Riyadh. The Minister had very much wanted to greet him personally.

The man was Asad al-Qahtan. He was First Deputy Minister of Petroleum and Mineral Resources. He was educated at Columbia and M.I.T. He was forty-three years old. He was not a member of the royal family, but had been personally selected by the Minister, Prince Majid, for his blend of technical background and diplomatic aptitude. He was a rising star. He had six children. The fourth, a son, was severely retarded and institutionalized in Switzerland. He liked French wines, burgundies particularly. He liked girls, blondes particularly. He was affable, he was flexible, he was reasonable. He held the Minister's absolute confidence.

"Thank you," Harry said, "for coming personally to meet me. General Longview has told me many wonderful things about you."

The man smiled. His lean face was amused, and very friendly.

"Including, I expect," Asad said, "what I eat for breakfast, and what I do to amuse myself in late hours on the Continent."

"I expect," Harry grinned.

"I have never had the honor to meet the General, but I assume that he probably knows almost as much about me as I do about him. He is an interesting man, Mr. Lime."

"Fascinating man," Harry concurred. "Just out of idle curiosity, what *does* the General eat for breakfast?"

Asad looked Harry straight in the eye. "Four strips bacon, very crisp. Two eggs, scrambled. No toast. Black coffee."

Harry grinned. "You made that up."

Asad grinned back. "I thought the bacon was a nice touch," he said. "Demonstrates our tolerance for the infidel."

Harry decided he was probably going to like this man.

Asad took his arm, guiding him toward the limo. "But then," Asad confided, "I think the most fascinating men are the ones I know the least about. The ones on whom there is simply no available information. Don't you agree?"

Harry shook his head. "Usually less to those guys than meets the eye," he said.

They slipped into the rear of the limo. The doors closed softly and the silence was broken only by the blessed air conditioning.

"The Minister," Asad said, "will be detained for a few days. He has asked me to escort you in some travels about our nation."

"He has asked you," Harry said simply, "to size me up."

The man looked at Harry for a moment. "Will that be convenient?" he said.

"Size away."

Asad kept looking at Harry. He knocked on the glass partition and the limo began to roll forward.

"Let me put you completely at ease," Asad said, his eyes playful and warm. "None of my best friends are Jews."

Harry shrugged. "I never met a wog I didn't like," he said.

Asad's smile was pure delight. "This," he laughed, "you call diplomacy?"

"This," Harry said, "you call establishing rapport."

TWENTY-THREE

Over the next five days, Harry Lime and Asad al-Qahtan continued to establish rapport.

Asad spent little time in Jiddah. "Embassies, banks," he said with a sigh, "who needs it?" There was an afternoon's walk through the Old Quarter, alive with markets and rich smells. The men with the weapons had been left behind. Asad and Harry strolled the dirt alleys alone, Asad stopping to buy fruit. They ate oranges and figs as they walked.

Asad casually interspersed tidbits of the history of the city, Bride of the Red Sea. As he talked, he would repeatedly fix Harry's eyes, or place a firm hand on Harry's elbow. There was a directness and a strength to the man. His grandfather was a Bedu from the Najd. His father, barely literate in early childhood, had persevered to become a civil servant in the Ministry of Labor and Social Affairs. The government had tested young Asad, had quickly seen that his intellect merited a substantial investment, and had lavished upon him as fine an education as money could provide. After half a lifetime in the decadent West, Asad al-Qahtan had returned to repay that investment.

The limo purred across new highway, heading south. "This is central Hijaz," he said. "Our western prov-

ince. We are going to Asir, in the Southwest. You will
see there mountains and green valleys. Very lush.
Propaganda. Only 1 percent of our land is cultivated.
We talk agriculture, but don't listen. Allah feeds us
with oil. We must make do."

The villages of the Hijaz slipped by. Low, white-
washed buildings, each with its elaborate screens in
every combination and variety, guarding those within
from view.

"I'm going to tell you some things, Harry, that you
probably already know. Indulge me with your patience. I want you to hear about them from me."

With that, Asad al-Qahtan began the story of how
his nation came to be. Not from the pre-Cambrian
days, when Allah first wrested the crust of the earth
into the configuration that would make this all possible. Not from the seventh century, when the warrior-
prophet Muhammad gave Islam the breath of its
beginning. Asad's story began in the late eighteenth
century, in a Najdi village called ad-Diriyah.

In that village lived a scholar, Muhammad ibn
Abdulwahhab, who spoke out against the corruption
of his religion. Idolatry must be scourged from the
face of Islam, so that nothing could stand between
God and man. Not unlike Moses and Luther before
him, his words struck fire in many hearts. Among
them, the village leader, Muhammad ibn Saud. By
1806, the Al Sauds had conquered Mecca and Me-
dina. By 1818, the Ottoman Empire had crushed them
forever.

Forever ended in 1932. A huge and extraordinary
man named Abdul Aziz ibn Saud united the dispersed
tribes of his homeland, and created a homeland for
them all, the Kingdom of Saudi Arabia. Arabia had
become forever linked to the House of Saud.

When Abdul Aziz died in 1953, there were thirty-four sons and an uncounted number of daughters. His eldest son, Saud ibn Abdulaziz, became King. When the profligate Saud was eventually ruled unfit by the ulama, the religious leadership, he was succeeded not by his own son, but by his younger brother, Faisal. An unusual pattern of succession had been established. Each of the royal brothers, all sons of the great Abdul Aziz, would have his chance before the next generation could take its turn. Faisal was succeeded by Khalid. Khalid, by his younger brother, Fahd. And as Harry's black Mercedes sped on to the South, King Fahd, now a frail seventy-seven, still ruled the world's richest land. The Crown Prince was brother Sultan, one year younger. The next eight brothers in line were already over sixty. The vitality of the succession had become a growing concern.

Asad and Harry lingered in Asir, wandering in and near Rijal, a stone village set along both sides of a narrow valley. They rose before dawn, and headed up into the hills for a private stroll. Late in the morning, Asad disappeared for an hour. Harry assumed he was seeking long-distance guidance from his Prince.

At last Asad told Harry that they were to visit Ghawar, the world's largest oil field.

They flew from Abha to the Persian Gulf. Asad directed the pilot to swing across a large corner of the Rub al-Khali, the Empty Quarter. They saw an ocean, the size of Texas, its waves only of sand, the abandoned place of Allah's earth. From time long before man, no living creature had broken its perfect, wind-swept silence. Until now. Until the rigs and teams and pipelines.

They landed in Dhahran, nerve-center of the petroleum industry and home of the Aramco community, with its American-style golf course and suburban shopping malls. Asad hustled Harry out of there as quickly as possible.

From Dhahran, they drove to Ghawar. Throughout his day there, the statistics, his meetings with officials and workmen, Harry could not clear his mind of the sheer immensity of the field. One single continuous oil field, one hundred thirty miles long. No king, no conqueror, no god in any time or fable, could have conceived of a prize so priceless. Yet here it sat, with its sister fields, Safaniyah, Zuluf, Marjan, Khurays, Barri and the others. Here it sat in a land so unable to protect itself that, without the shield of foreigners and infidels, the prize would surely fall in a matter of days to attack by the State of Israel, let alone the Soviet Union.

And so, as Harry rode and walked Ghawar, his mind returned to Venice. Twenty-four faces on a single roll of film, four of them Chinese.

On the fifth day, Asad took Harry at last to Riyadh. They arrived in late afternoon, driving the length of Matar Street from the airport to the heart of the city.

"Forgive the lack of opportunity to freshen up," Asad said, "the Minister has asked to see you directly."

Harry was taken to al-Maather Palace, to a large hall lined with paintings and tapestries, and filled with Arabs from all walks of life.

At one end of the hall, a man was seated in an overstuffed chair. Next to him, another man on his knees, whispering, explaining, pleading. Both men wore ghotra and robes. The man kneeling wore garments that were coarse. The stubble on his face shone with sweat. His eyes were shining as he poured his soul into the ear of his Prince.

The seated man was immaculate. The sleeve of his mishlah was pulled slightly back, and Harry could see a broad Rolex. The man's face was impassive, serene, yet there was no doubt that he was truly listening to the supplicant. As the man finished, the Prince gave instruction to one of the men standing beside him. With a word, the kneeling man's prayer had been answered.

"This," Asad said softly, "is a majlis. An audience. Many times each week, members of the royal family hold majlis. Any man may come and make a request for help or for justice. He addresses his Prince by his first name, for under the Qur'an, all men are equal before God. We have no parliament here, no representatives of the people. Here, the relationship between a man and his government is direct. Man to man."

As Asad spoke, another supplicant took the place of the first, kneeling at his Prince's ear. As before, the Prince leaned forward, eyes calm, attentive. Standing directly above the humble petitioner was a fearsome-looking guard. Automatic weapon at his side, golden khanjar, dagger, at his waist. Harry knew that King Faisal, savior of his nation from the ruinous excesses of Saud, had been assassinated at just such an occasion. The risk of the majlis to the Prince's person could never truly be controlled. For it was this intimacy, this moment to reach and touch the arm of his ruler, that meant everything to the man on his knees. They were men together, under God and the Qur'an.

There were twenty-six more petitions before the majlis ended. Harry stood, without moving, and watched a man's face.

Prince Majid ibn Fawwaz. A collateral branch to be sure, but royal family all the same. Minister of Petroleum and Mineral Resources. And whether King Fahd would die to be succeeded by Abdullah, Sultan or any of the others, Majid ibn Fawwaz would remain at the right hand of the King, so clearly had he proven his worth to his people in these past twelve years, so clearly was he needed to guide and husband his nation's treasure in these days.

The majlis ended. In accordance with the custom begun by the great Abdul Aziz himself, all within the palace, of whatever station in life, knew they were invited to remain as guests for supper.

But this night, Majid would not be joining them at table. As the great hall cleared, Majid looked the length of the room to the lone figures of Harry and Asad. He rose and walked to them.

He took Harry's hand directly, without introduction.

"Mr. Lime. Thank you for coming. And thank you for your patience these past days."

He was a large, soft-looking man. His dark face round and perfectly smooth, but for the small traditional beard. The eyes gave no hint of superior intellect. Rather, they were kindly. There was nothing fearsome about this man who wielded a weapon as potent as any nuclear arsenal.

"Asad," he said, looking only at Harry, "I would be grateful if you could take my place at evening meal tonight. If Mr. Lime will indulge my impatience, I should like to speak with him directly."

TWENTY-FOUR

The room was very small. The doorway to the balcony was open, and Harry could hear the sounds of the garden below. His host had seated him comfortably, had poured him a small cup of cardamom-flavored coffee from an exquisite service. The coffee was bitter, and Harry sipped slowly.

"I trust," Majid said, without the slightest small talk, "that your meetings in Europe have been successful."

If Venice meant anything at all, he already had his answer. "I'm sorry to tell you," Harry said, "that my conversations in Paris and Bonn were not productive."

Majid looked at him, directly but without challenge. Once again, it was a look that Harry could only describe as kindly.

"I am," Majid said at last, "truly saddened to hear that. I know that our dear friend, your General, might question the sincerity of my reaction. He will suspect that we are delighted by your difficulties in Europe. He is wrong."

"Why," Harry asked, "would he suspect such a thing?"

"Because your government is attempting to establish an anti-OPEC cartel among oil-consuming nations. For this, you need the cooperation of Western Europe and Japan. Your General, I am afraid, thinks in terms of traditional alliances. Thus, he thinks that we would fear and oppose such a cartel."

Harry sipped his coffee. The man clearly had correct information. Whatever credibility Harry could hope to establish with this man would not be furthered by useless lies and denial. Direct confirmation of the truth, however, would be an absolute violation of instructions. So Harry kept sipping. Very slowly.

"Those at OPEC," Majid said, "who are guided by reason, do not fear the effect of such a cartel on our prices. So long as production is in our hands, so long as our commodity remains useful, we will set prices as we choose. And I must quickly tell you of our awareness that prices are absurdly high. Dollars arrive so much faster than they can be invested. Inflation alone makes the entire situation rather ridiculous. No, my friend, we would not fear your consumers' cartel. What we fear is the status quo."

"You would," Harry said slowly, "welcome such a cartel?"

The Arab shrugged slightly. "We would not fear it. We would welcome it only if it would help the situation. If your great nation and its allies could truly band together to reduce their demand for oil, this would lower prices and give us what we truly desire. More of our resources could be left in the ground for our grandchildren's future."

"We all," Harry said, "worry for our grandchildren's future."

"Why, then," Majid said sadly, "will your great country, our strongest ally and friend, do everything on earth but the one thing that would truly remedy the situation? Discipline itself to consume less petroleum."

"Are we," Harry said softly, "such a selfish and wasteful people?"

The Arab shook his head. "A generous people," he said. "Strong, proud. But, on this one question, perhaps, not well-advised by its leaders. The discipline would be fierce, I know. Please know that I understand that. But yours is a people familiar with sacrifice and struggle. And what must be done . . . must be done."

Harry nodded. "The sacrifice," Harry said, "and the struggle were long ago. People are human."

The Arab sighed. "The French," he said, "and German people are also human. Perhaps this is why your effort was doomed from the first. I am truly sorry, my friend. Sorry for us all. You must persevere, however. You must find another way."

The cup was refilled. Harry kept sipping. The silence lengthened.

"You have come," Majid said at last, "to ask us for a favor."

"I have come," Harry said, "to listen and to learn."

"You have come," Majid said gently, "to ask that we increase our production. You have come as a friend, a good friend, to ask a friend's aid in a time of great need."

Harry smiled. "This is my majlis," Harry said. "My time to petition."

The smile was returned. "I am not your Prince," Majid said. "Only your friend. Please know how deeply we have valued that friendship. For decades now, your might and your resolve have been our only security against the godless Soviets. Your weapons, your men. Your promise. These have been the gifts of a true friend."

"The assurance of your security," Harry said, "has been my country's most vital self-interest."

The Arab smiled and nodded. "And how glorious," he said, "when the self-interest of friends coincides. How sad when it does not."

Harry did not take the cue. He sipped as slowly as he could, holding the Arab's eyes. It was going to take a gallon of this wretched coffee to get him through the conversation.

"Technology," Majid said. "Another precious gift. We have built the beginnings of an industrial nation on the sliding surface of the sands. We could never have begun without technology from the West. Now that we have begun, we need that help more than ever."

Harry nodded slowly. "When self-interests do not coincide. You were speaking of the supply and demand of petroleum?"

Now it was the Arab's turn to wait. "Primarily," Majid said finally. "Have you ever visited the State of Israel?"

"Yes," Harry said. "It is very beautiful. As is your nation. And mine."

Majid nodded. His eyes now seemed very wise. "It is beautiful," he said. "Our Palestinian brothers remember the beauty of their homes. They cannot rest until the day they are home once more."

"Nor," Harry said, "can their brothers in Islam rest until that day."

Majid put the tips of his fingers together and looked at them for a moment. "Such a simple issue," he said, "from one perspective. Yet, how complex. For as much as a Palestinian homeland means to my people, it means so much to others as well. Our brothers in Iraq, Yemen, Africa. My government, as a monarchy and spokesman of moderation, cannot find easy answers to those who urge revolution and the sword. If there is anything more frightening to my family than the specter of the Soviets, it would be the instability of our own region, our own brothers."

"The strong wind," Harry said, "cannot help but move the sand. The sand cannot help but cover what was there before the wind."

Majid smiled. He nodded his agreement.

"Shelter from that wind," he said, "would take still another form of discipline from your people. To look anew at Palestine and do what must be done."

"And this," Harry said, "is a favor you have long asked from us, as our true friend, a most important favor we have been unable to grant. Instead, we have asked you for the gift of understanding. To truly understand our position in this matter, despite the peril that exists for your people and your family, and to remain our true friend through it all. We have asked a great deal."

Majid took a deep breath. His robes seemed to billow about him for a moment. Harry knew what would come. It would not come with the arrogance of Claude Mairet, or the jackboot of Jósef Hoch. It would come as quietly, as inevitably, as the wind blows the sand.

"Always," Majid said, "your people have given more than they have asked. That is the greatness of your people. When you have refused us, as in the question of Palestine, it has been with the truest sadness. There is no sadness to surpass the refusal of a friend."

Harry nodded. The only question left was how bad it was going to be.

"Nothing in this," Majid said, "is of Palestine. That is not the issue of this moment. We spoke of it only because I know of your faith, and I felt we should share our hearts on this. What I have to tell you is a matter purely of economics, the economics of our own survival. Do you accept this?"

"Yes," Harry said.

"In our current fiscal year, we have kept production at 8.1 million barrels per day. I know that you have come this long journey to ask that we substantially increase this for the coming year. Yet, what I must tell you is that our decision has already been made. Next year, our production will be decreased to 6.4 million barrels per day. Even this will put the most severe strain upon the responsibilities which we bear to conserve the resources of our nation."

The Arab searched Harry's eyes for a moment. "We ask," Majid said, "in your words, that you remain our true friend, through the disappointment this news must bring to you."

Particularly since there is no earthly alternative. "Of that," Harry said quietly, "you must have no fear. In your words, what must be done must be done."

TWENTY-FIVE

Harry could scarcely keep his eyes in focus. He had flown through the night and the day and the night again. He dimly remembered that it had been dark in Washington when Taradan had collected him at the airport.

Harry had sat in the Victorian library, in the center of the earth, waiting for Longview to arrive. Taradan had sat with him, but had said very little. When the General had arrived, Taradan had quickly left.

The General had questioned him for two hours. Mairet, Hoch, Asad and, finally, Majid ibn Fawwaz. Every word, every inflection, every nuance of facial expression had been reported, repeated, analyzed and then rehashed anew.

The interview was drawing to a close. Longview himself was tired now. It must have been quite late. Harry felt pummeled and terribly stale. But there would be no other moment.

Longview was saying good night, urging him, for chrissake, to get a little sleep. They would have supper tomorrow. Harry was bending to the carpet by his chair, gathering his notes and papers together.

"I'd like Dave to pull a file for me," Harry said

off-handedly, without looking up. "Anything you've got on something called the Marco Polo Society."

There was no sound but the rustling of Harry's papers. He half expected that when he looked up, Longview would be pointing a pistol at him, smile, and quietly blow him to pieces.

When he did look up, Longview was staring at him with no expression at all.

Attack. Old John Knowles. When you're scared enough to pee in your drawers, attack.

"I'd like the file tomorrow morning, Hubert. With my coffee and eggs. And, Hubert, the next time I catch you holding out on me, I'm out of this. And I'm out for good."

Harry had taken his shot. His face was as cold and as strong as he could manage, but his mouth was very dry.

"What," the General said quite calmly, "do you know about Marco Polo?"

"Not a goddam thing, Hubert, and that's a disgrace. You sent me off naked, and those assholes ate me for breakfast."

"What," the General repeated, in precisely the same tone, "do you know about Marco Polo?"

Harry's mouth was full of ashes now. His heart was really pounding.

"The Saudis," Harry said, "are cooking something with the Germans, French, Italians. They've got Japanese and Chinese in there too. They all met in Venice. My bloody government doesn't see fit to let me in on the jokes, so I stumble through Paris, Bonn and Riyadh with an unloaded gun. I'm in this thing to help, Hubert. Not to play fall-guy for you and Buck. If you can't take me into your confidence, let's end it right here."

Longview sat and stared. "You're tired," Longview

said at last. "Dave'll take you to the hotel. We'll talk about it tomorrow."

If I'm alive tomorrow.

"Hubert, take your formula Agency response and shove it straight up your ass. Better, shove it up Buck's ass. I'm on the team or I'm off the team, and you don't need twenty-four hours to make up your mind. You make up your mind right now. I mean this fuckin' minute."

Before Buck can talk you out of it. Before Buck can kill me.

"There's very little to tell," Longview said blandly.

"Fine. Tell it now. Pretend you trust me, Hubert. Make it convincing."

Longview stared at him a little longer. "How," he said, "did you come to hear about all this?"

"That's a separate conversation," Harry replied. "It starts five minutes from now. If I like what goes on in-between."

Longview ran his hand along the back of his head to his neck. He twisted his head from side to side, as if shaking the muscles free.

"The Dutch are in it too," he said at last. "And the Belgians. They didn't go to Venice, but they were all in London in March. They met last year in Djakarta, but we have nothing on that."

Nothing in this world could have squeezed a sound out of Harry.

"We've been in contact with the KGB," the General said. "That's how scared we were. The Saudis fart and we jump. Jump, hell, we stained our goddam shorts. I mean, we had twenty of our men and God knows how many Russians crawling all over London, trying to wire those guys. Came up with one tape. Five hours. The voices are coming through eight inches of wood, and it sounds like you pointed a mike at the moon."

Longview looked at Harry's eyes. The General smiled. "You gonna tell me what you know, Harry?"

Harry said nothing.

"I just want your word, Harry. You want a drink? You drink Bombay gin, don't you? Rocks and a twist."

He sat staring at Harry. He looked very calm.

"Hubert, you tell me the truth and I'm going to tell you the truth. Nothing else makes any sense. And I'll take that drink, thanks."

The General stood very slowly and ambled to the bar across the room. He kept his back squarely to Harry and mixed the drinks.

"I used to drink gin," he said, "before I got old. Now I drink scotch. It's an old fart's drink. My daddy drank Irish whisky, but I never could stomach the stuff. The smell of it."

He brought Harry his drink. He moved slowly, but his hand was firm and steady. He eased himself back into the deep leather chair.

"Harry, I'm going to tell you whatever you want to know. You're going to read the transcript of that tape. Let you hear the damn thing, if you want to. If Buck doesn't like it, he can fly a kite."

Longview lifted his glass in a silent toast. He took a long swallow. Harry did the same.

"Lot of talk on that tape," Longview said. "Not much meat. The Saudis are cutting back production. OPEC is going to follow suit. But they're slightly *increasing* their supply to Europe and Japan. They're cutting way back on us. They're cutting Russia off, which is going to really put some pressure on getting the juice squeezed out of Siberia. Anyway, that's basically what's on the tape. The rest we've had to piece together."

The General studied the ice cubes bobbing in his scotch. "How those pieces fit depends on who you ask."

"I'm asking you," Harry said.

The General nodded. "We know that Marco Polo is a secret alliance. We don't know yet why it's been formed or why it's secret. I think, Buck thinks, we've become an unstable market for the Saudis. We give them technology and security from the Russians. But we're too demanding. We need too much oil, way too much. The Germans and the Japanese can sure supply the technology."

Longview shook his head. His lips formed a tight, rueful grin. And Harry saw John Knowles in that little smile.

"Europeans don't have our hangup about Israel, Harry. And the Saudis have to appease the radicals to stabilize the area. As they slowly cut off our water, we'll be down there on our knees, looking over at Israel and saying, 'Sorry, chum.' The Israelis will hand over the West Bank or face something a whole lot worse."

"And who protects the Saudis from the Russians?"

"Well, here's where you get to that difference of opinion. As I read the Saudis, they figure it would take a lot before we'd make good on any threat to pull our protection away. If we hand the Russians the Persian Gulf, we've had it. So that's a piece of brinksmanship they figure they can push pretty far."

The General put his hand across his eyes and squeezed his temples. Did Knowles used to do that, just that way? Harry had forgotten.

"As I see it," Longview said, "the Saudis' only real worry is pushing us so far our economy, our society, goes under altogether. Or gets so damn desperate we send in the Marines and call their bluff about blowing their own oil fields. 'Course, if we send in the Ma-rines, do the Russians just sit back? I don't think the Saudis want us desperate enough to even start think-ing that way. They'll give us enough oil, just enough, to keep that from happening."

There was a long silence. The General had finished his drink. His hands were slowly turning the empty glass.

"So, as I see it," he said, "we're in for some real pain, maybe even a depression. But not Armaggedon."

"There is," Harry asked, "a contrary opinion?"

The General nodded.

"Chairman Lepeshkin of the KGB seems to think that Marco Polo is more than a purely economic alli-ance. Show him a Chinaman and he sees the devil. You ever heard of the Condominium Theory?"

Harry had.

"The Condominium Theory," the General said, "is the fear that we and the Soviets are finally forced to band together to rule the world. Everyone else would be our slaves. The Chinese, the Germans, the French, they're pretty susceptible to that fantasy, at least their military. Their diplomats know that such a partner-ship would be impossible. But then, who listens to diplomats?"

The General was searching his eyes.

"Lepeshkin thinks there's more to Marco Polo than hoarding oil and screwing Israel. He thinks it's a plot to make the Marco Polo Alliance the dominant super-power on this planet."

"The Chinese . . ." Harry said.

"And the Germans. The Chinese already have enough nuclear weapons and medium-range delivery to have Russia hysterical. Whether they have enough range to reach us, we just don't know. As for our European friends, Lepeshkin says we're fools if we don't think that the Germans and French could suddenly pull out of NATO with enough nuclear hardware and technology to handle their end. Between the Chinese and the Europeans, Marco Polo could be an effective nuclear third force, at least enough to hold the rest of us at bay. Then, with OPEC's domination of the money markets and control of petroleum reserves, Lepeshkin figures the Alliance would have the world by the balls."

Harry thought for a long moment. "Bullshit."

The General nodded slowly. "I'm ninety-nine percent sure you're right," Longview said. "First, it makes no sense strategically. Whatever they've got, it couldn't be enough to stand up to us *or* the Russians. And, God knows, if they ever really forced us to throw in with the Russians, we'd blow them all the fuck off the earth."

For the briefest moment, the General looked as if that weren't exactly the worst idea that had ever passed his mind.

"And politically," Longview said, "it makes even less sense. Why the hell would Marco Polo want to challenge us with nukes and get our macho bubbling over? They can get everything they want with the slow squeeze. Turn the screw one notch at a time. These are a smart bunch of bastards, Harry. Why would they suddenly turn stupid?"

"You've made that point to Lepeshkin?"

"Buck has. Buck doesn't believe the Alliance is any kind of military threat. Nikolai's answer is some gibberish about world domination. Lepeshkin's army, you know, he came from GRU. He was on the Intelligence Directorate for the General Staff for thirteen years, and it just simply fried his brain. Germans, Chinese, even Japanese. In his mind, they're obsessed with lust for ruling the world. It's pathetic, isn't it?"

And that slight smile hung again. And the General's dispute with Nikolai Lepeshkin seemed something less than ninety-nine percent.

"Yes," Harry said, as if the question had wanted an answer. "It's pathetic."

The General nodded his accord. Shrugged his broad shoulders. "Cherny, of course, isn't buying what Lepeshkin's trying to sell. Cherny is the brightest man to lead Russia in thirty years. Maybe ever. He's got Nikolai on a very tight leash. He'll replace him when the time is right. I think Nikolai knows that."

Now it was Harry's turn to think for a moment.

"That be good for the good guys?" he asked.

Longview shook his head slowly.

"Lepeshkin is a guy Buck can outsmart at every turn. Has for years. Be a shame to see Cherny replace him. We've paid some attention to making Nikolai look good from time to time. Little things here and there. But the guy's his own worst enemy."

Harry gathered up his papers again, and held them on his lap.

"Marco Polo," Harry said. "Next class reunion?"

The General looked at Harry, and just kept looking. "Vienna," he said finally. "Christmas in Vienna. Professional curiosity?"

Harry smiled.

"You ask Buck," Harry said. "I'm a civil servant. I do what I'm told. But I need access to relevant information. I need your word that I'll get everything you learn about Marco Polo."

There was a long silence.

"Given," Longview said. "For the present. If that changes, I'll let you know. I want you on the team, Harry. You worked a little magic with our Mexican friends. The President feels maybe you can do it again. The President likes you, Harry."

Harry told the General how he came to hear of Marco Polo. He told him the truth. The General seemed relieved and greatly amused. The General shared a spicy little story about Jósef Hoch. He insisted that they have another drink. Harry obliged. The General's tiredness had gone. Disregarding the hour, Longview lapsed into stories about his days as a line officer in the Vietnam War. Harry drank and listened and laughed in most of the right places.

When the General finally called Taradan into the library, it was an hour before dawn. Longview spoke to Taradan privately for a moment, then said Taradan would drive Harry back to the hotel.

Throughout the drive, Harry was too tired to be truly frightened. If Taradan did not wheel him off to some lonely spot, if Taradan did not kill him somewhere between the Pentagon and the Mayflower, Harry thought he might indeed be past the worst.

Taradan took him straight to the hotel.

Harry lay awake through the dawn and the sounds of early morning. Finally, he slipped into unconsciousness so deep and dreamless that when he awoke it was dark again. Harry was still alive, and beginning to believe he might remain that way for a while.

TWENTY-SIX

Andrei Ilyich Voslov walked alone along the Garden Ring, his hands thrust deep into his coat pockets. Behind him, the birches of the Lenin Hills were still green, but the chill of dusk surely meant that autumn had begun.

He walked, as always, with his small shoulders hunched forward, as if bending into a cold and hostile wind. His thick coat, warm for the season, was at least a size large for him. He seemed lost in its great wool folds.

Crossing the river, he continued along the northern edge of Gorky Park. Rush-hour traffic surged by unnoticed as he plodded onward. He should have worn a hat, he thought. His ears would freeze over, or at least he'd have a proper headache. From his childhood, through his years in England, through all of his manhood, Voslov was the oddest of anomalies, a Russian who had never come to terms with the cold. All right, in the dead of winter when you know what you're facing, when you're properly dressed and your mind is set to deal with it. But God save him from the end of summer, with only a light suit under his coat and his hat back in Kutuzovsky Prospekt.

He cursed himself for not having Yuri simply drive

him. Still set in the old ways, the old precautions. A
dirty, jostling ride on the train, and now this interminable stroll along the Garden Ring, while his face
tensed against the chill and all body heat fled. Idiotic.
Old. That was it, of course. If a man had to get old,
did he have to do so at the North Pole?

Just before Dimitrov Street, he disappeared into an
alleyway. If anyone had been watching, which no one
was, they might have been amazed at the ease with
which the round little man had simply vanished.

Two blocks away, Voslov surfaced, still muttering
to himself. At an unmarked doorway, he fumbled with
his key for a moment, and then let himself in. The
stairway was dark, although night had not yet settled
on the city. He stubbed his toe on the first step,
certainly scuffing the black polish from his newly
shined shoe, and giving himself something fresh to
mutter about all the way up the stairs.

There was a lone bulb in the hallway, and he shuf-
fled along slowly until he reached number eleven.
Another key, and Voslov entered the small, well-lit
parlor.

Konstantin Dolya rose from the table to greet him.
A thick shock of dark hair hung above merry eyes.
The youngster was a rogue and a charmer, and his
greeting was its hearty best. Voslov noted, without
surprise, that Dolya seemed nervous beneath it all.

Dolya helped the older man with his coat. Voslov
rubbed his plump fingers together as if he had just
trekked in through a blizzard. The room was mercifully warm.

Voslov seated himself in a straight-backed wooden
chair across the table. He smiled pleasantly, but not
enough to take the edge from the young man's appre-
hension. He said nothing.

Dolya passed a manila folder across the table.

Voslov opened the folder to find copies of two files. They were barely legible. Dolya had filmed the papers, poorly, and had developed and enlarged the product himself.

The first file was from the Third Department Archives, which held KGB records of United Kingdom operations. Voslov read the file very slowly, his face utterly devoid of expression. When he had finished, he read the material again, even more slowly. To Dolya, it seemed as if the little man were committing each word forever to memory.

The file described an American agent, identified only by the code name Harbinger. The material was considerably more specific than Yuri had suggested. Apparently, Dolya had only told Yuri a fraction of what he already knew.

Harbinger had visited London March 11–18 of that year, coinciding with the dates of the Marco Polo meetings in that city. He had stayed at the Hyde Park Hotel in Knightsbridge. He had dined, shopped and strolled alone, for the most part. On two occasions, he had obtained the services of a rather expensive escort for the evening. The call girl's name was not included in the file. Voslov found this odd.

On the morning of March 14, and again on the evening of March 16, Harbinger attended meetings of the Marco Polo Society. These were chronicled as the only known instances of participation by any national of a nonmember country. He attended the first meeting for one hour, the second for six.

Although intelligence operations surrounding the London meetings had been conducted in broad collaboration with the American SIA, it was a KGB team which had been responsible for visual surveillance of the meeting site on the two occasions in question.

Harbinger was among that portion of their product which the KGB had withheld from the Americans.

The file was uncertain as to whether the Americans knew of Harbinger's existence. If the Americans had planted Harbinger, why would they have permitted him to attend meetings under surveillance by the KGB team? Unless, of course, there was some devious purpose with precisely that intent. If the Americans had not planted Harbinger, but had discovered his presence through a secret duplicative surveillance of their own (which the Soviets had suspected, searched for, but not detected), they would most likely not have shared their knowledge with the KGB, particularly upon learning that the Russians had withheld disclosure themselves. It was entirely possible, therefore, that Ross Buckley of the American SIA was pondering whether the man was actually in the employ of the KGB, which, considering Harbinger's background, would be a fearsome thing to ponder. The utility and disutility of each permutation for a broad range of KGB objectives was carefully analyzed. A "senior official," the file stated, would decide at the appropriate time whether this data would be shared with SIA.

A meticulous search had been conducted to determine whether Harbinger had attended the only other known Marco Polo gathering, in Djakarta the previous October. Nothing was found. This was not conclusive, however, since Harbinger might have attended the conference under an undiscovered alias.

Harbinger, apparently, was a man of some mystery. He had recently been engaged in low-profile, but extremely sensitive, diplomatic activities for the American Government. Curiously, nothing had been discovered of his past thus far, but KGB operatives were furiously at work in Rome, Bonn, Paris, Tokyo and

Washington, including well-placed personnel with intelligence services of certain of these nations. It was only a matter of time until more complete data would be available on this man and his utility to the Marco Polo Alliance.

There was no cross-reference to another file. Apparently, Dolya had simply taken the initiative to scour the First Department Archives, which contained KGB files on Americans, for any file using the word "harbinger" in its title. Thus, the second file which now lay before Voslov. Its title was "Radical Press of the American Southwest: Harbingers of Discontent."

The file had apparently contained dozens of pages of reports and photographic reprints from rural American newspapers. Toward the back, a tantalizingly brief dossier on an American agent, code-named Harbinger.

Voslov rubbed his eyes. He sighed, and offered Dolya a weak smile.

"Would it be possible," he said, "to have some tea?"

Dolya stood, almost reluctantly, as if he could not bear to take his eyes from the sight of Voslov's silent reading.

As he departed for the kitchen, Voslov's eyes returned to the second file.

Harbinger was a man named Harry Lime. He was known to have been an SIA agent some ten years past, as a very young man. He had been a personal assistant to John Knowles, and was headed for a most promising career. He resigned his post suddenly, without warning, and had disappeared into private life. Somehow, he had managed to excise all record of his Agency career, both files and computer data. This demonstration of the Agency's inept security capability led to a violent but secret upheaval, which ended in Knowles' resignation. So complete was both Lime's destruction of his records and the official shroud which dropped over the incident, that the KGB was not certain to this day whether their appreciation of the affair was wholly accurate, partially so or perhaps entirely apocryphal.

Harry Lime was a mixture. One part footnote to the history of the American intelligence community, and two parts pure myth.

Until London.

The balance of the dossier was three items. The first, a photocopy of Harry Lime's registration card from the Hyde Park Hotel. Name: Harry Lime. Citizenship: USA. Profession: Attorney. Residence: 2047 Connecticut Avenue, Washington, D.C.

Dolya returned with the tea. He set it very carefully before Voslov. Napkin, lemon, spoon.

Voslov looked up with a smile that now seemed very tired. "The address . . ." he said mildly.

"Fictitious, of course," Dolya responded. "By this time, Lepeshkin probably has everything this man did for the past ten years. I expect it will all wind up in this file. Beautifully complete and thoroughly useless."

Voslov nodded absently. As if to say he supposed that was quite correct.

The next item in the file was a photograph.

Four people were seated in a booth at a restaurant. Voslov thought at first that the restaurant might be Mirabelle, though he had not been in London for many years. It was nonetheless his first association, and so he filed it away.

At one side of the booth sat a large, handsome man with powerful shoulders and steel-gray mane. He was Heinrich Weber. German. Perhaps his nation's foremost soldier, certainly its most important link to NATO. Weber was smiling slightly, looking down at his hands, which were folded comfortably before him.

At Weber's left was a small Oriental gentleman, older, balding, dressed incredibly in a neat Western business suit. Incredibly, because this was Xing Dzulin, hero of the People's Republic of China. To see this man in Western clothing was as much a shock to Voslov as spotting a member of the Presidium wearing a dress. Xing was beaming widely, raffishly, at the woman to his left. His hands were below the table, and he was leaning forward slightly.

The woman was a stunning, if somewhat aging, blonde. She was tossing her head to one side, as if to free her hair. She was dressed expensively, tastefully. She looked like every high-priced hooker in London.

The third man was Harbinger. His face was slightly in shadow, but there was still a reasonably clear view. Dark hair and large dark eyes. He seemed attractive, confident, calm. Surprisingly young, or perhaps simply baby-faced. His fingertips rested lightly together. His eyes seemed to look across the table to Weber.

The final item in the file was a brief summary of the conversation at the dinner party in the photograph. The name of the reporting KGB agent was not included, nor was there mention of whether the conversation had been recorded.

It was reported that the supper was lengthy and cordial. There were three references to a meeting which the men had attended together that morning. There was a single reference to another meeting two days hence. The references were discreet, and added nothing to existing information. No other matters of relevance to the report were discussed.

Voslov carefully gathered the papers together and placed them into the manila folder. He pulled them into his lap. Dolya would never see them again, unless, of course, he had copies of his own.

"I should like the negatives of your photography,

Konstantin. Any remaining copies to be burned. Tonight."

Dolya nodded.

"This is excellent work, Konstantin. You fulfill my hopes for you. I am very pleased."

Dolya actually blushed. His delight was complete.

Voslov stood, and Dolya sprang to help with his coat.

At the door, Voslov turned.

"The final element of perfect work," he said, "is knowing when to stop. For you, that moment is now."

TWENTY-SEVEN

Sunday morning and Voslov was strolling once again, through the Kremlin itself this time, through the green of Taynitsky Garden. The morning air was mild, but Voslov now wore his hat, soft brown fur, and certainly the only hat on the street in all of Moscow this balmy autumn morning.

No matter. Andrei Voslov possessed the thorough genius of passing unnoticed in any setting. He was congenitally inconspicuous.

He passed behind the Assumption Cathedral with its five brooding domes, and out of the Kremlin at Spassky Gate.

The clouds were pure white billows, altogether wondrous, but Voslov's eyes were only on the stone before him. Shoulders hunched forward, hands deep in the pockets of his wool coat, he walked the length of Red Square and turned toward Marx Prospekt. Each plodding step in its turn, eyes cast absently down, until he reached Dzerzhinsky Square. There, at number two, he entered the headquarters of the KGB, the Committee for State Security.

Smiling pleasantly, a light wave of his hand passing for identification at each checkpoint, Voslov made his way at last to the Archives. Signing in at the small desk, he complimented the young woman on the way she had done her hair. She seemed very pleased. Although she had never seen Voslov before, she most certainly knew the name.

"First Department, this morning," he said.

She reached for the clearance form necessary to admit him to the area reserved for First Department files.

"No," he said softly, "no files this morning. I'm only visiting the reference area."

She smiled and pressed the button releasing the gate to the section reserved for general reference only. No clearance was needed for this area.

Voslov moved through the corriders and aisles of what seemed to be a gigantic library, up the steel steps to the third level. He paused to glance through a card catalogue for a moment, jotting down two numbers on a slip of paper from his inside coat pocket. There was not another soul within sight or hearing on this early Sunday morning.

At last he came to a dimly lit section which seemed unvisited for centuries. The shelf was marked: Attorneys, American. There were seven khaki-colored volumes bearing the title *Martindale-Hubbell Law Directory*.

Voslov looked for the book that would include Washington, D.C. It was quite heavy and, unfortunately, on the bottom shelf. He wheezed a bit as he straightened his legs again. Sharing its weight between his belly and the shelf, he scanned the alphabetical listing. Finding nothing of interest, he carefully replaced the book exactly as he had found it, perfectly flush with its neighbors.

The process was repeated with the volume for New York. Again for Illinois.

Next, the volume for California. Beverly Hills, California. Lime, Harry. Bernstein, Fischer, Maxwell and

Stone. Pages turning. A plump finger tracing down the list.

Harry Lime, born Los Angeles, California, March 26, 1955; admitted to bar, 1981, District of Columbia; 1988, California. Preparatory education, Stanford University (A.B., magna cum laude, 1976), Yale University (M.A., 1977); Legal education, Harvard University (LL.B., cum laude, 1980). Member: Beverly Hills Bar Association; the State Bar of California; Los Angeles Copyright Society.

And Voslov, who never permitted himself such flights of indulgence, stood and stared at the page long after he had committed its contents to memory. Stood and wondered, perhaps for the first time in just that way, of this man's meaning.

Though Dolya would never know it, though circumstances might require that he be transferred or even sacked, no matter. Konstantin Dolya was a Hero of the State. He had achieved a sublime moment at the age of twenty-seven, a moment of true and consequential service.

The first confirmation of Voslov's instincts would be quite simple.

Two aisles over, four shelves up, a row of volumes almost certainly untouched from the moment they had been placed on those shelves. There was a small table at the end of the aisle, with a reading lamp. Although there was less than one chance in a thousand that any human soul could happen by, Voslov reflexively bridled at the notion of removing the volume so far from its resting place. Still, the added light would be useful.

He took four other books at random. If he heard any footsteps, he would bury his treasure among them. Seated at last, he found the wretched bulb had burned out after all. Sighing to himself, Voslov opened the Harvard Law School Yearbook of 1980. And there, on page 47, were the dark eyes and shy smile of Harry Lime.

TWENTY-EIGHT

A man sat alone in a darkened room.

Motionless, thoroughly at peace, he sat in silence. When the knock came, it was so soft as to barely be audible.

"Come," he said. And the second man entered.

As the door opened, the first man pulled the chain on the Tiffany lamp above his chair. A soft golden light filtered through the room.

The second man found his way to a chair. He sat waiting. The summons, at this hour and in this way, was unprecedented in their relationship.

There was a long silence before the first man spoke.

"Harry Lime," he said, "has discovered the Marco Polo Alliance."

"How?"

"We don't know."

"What was his explanation?"

"Coincidence."

The second man smiled. Living in a world in which coincidence did not exist, he was amused that Lime could have supposed such an explanation credible.

"How much does he know?" the second man asked.

"He claimed to know nothing. He was then told of

the London tape. Given that transcript. He was told of the Christmas meeting in Vienna."

The second man digested this for a moment.

"I assume," he said, "that no formal interrogation procedures are contemplated?"

"Of course not."

The second man massaged his knees with strong fingers. Dozens of images were bursting and disappearing in his mind.

"It will," the first man said, "affect nothing. Except, perhaps, certain elements of timing. In fact, I suspect this will all prove immensely useful."

The second man nodded slowly. His face assumed a rather chilling grin.

"Yes," he said. "It might at that."

TWENTY-NINE

It was evening as Harry's jetliner touched down at Charles De Gaulle. The wait for the baggage had been absurd, even by De Gaulle standards.

Harry rode the escalator ramps through the maze of glass tubing. This always made him feel that he was somewhere east of Mars. The closest thing in life to a Folon lithograph. Silent rows of people moved through glass tubes above, below, slowly passing at every angle and direction.

At the cabstand, he unfolded the scrap of paper he had been sent.

"Rue Vavin," he said, "cinquante-neuf. Dernière du Luxembourg."

As the drive to town began, Harry thought of nothing until the lights of Paris came up before him. Then he thought of the city, and of how he had always promised himself that this was the place he would die.

Harry knew that he would die very soon. There wasn't much logic to it. Harry himself could not explain the certainty that now gripped him. Perhaps only Andy Maclennon could understand.

Harry was not resigned to it, he was not at peace with it. There were moments, sometimes more than moments, where it simply scared the living crap out of him. He would not go gentle into that good night. He would go suddenly, without warning. He would go in utter confusion as to who and why. He would go, as all of us, because he had no choice.

The cab left him at the row of gray apartments, a student quarter, each building with its scollery about the windows. The iron balconies on the upper floors were too small for anything more than a flower box.

He pressed the button and a moment passed. Then the answering buzzer, and the door was released.

The lift was tiny and disreputable. He carried his bags up the two flights, slowly in the poor lighting. The stairwell seemed clean enough. The corridors had been recently painted. Despite the age of the building, these were not inexpensive flats. Location alone told him that.

On the door to number 31, a small piece of paper had been folded and taped just above the latch. He opened it to find a key.

The note said, "Come on in. P.S., this is your key, keep it clean."

Harry smiled and unlocked the door.

He entered into a dimy lit parlor. The furnishings were old and comfortable-looking. His first thought was that it looked friendly. It looked like a home.

There was a bright light coming from the hallway at the far end of the room.

"Harry?" her voice came from beyond the light.

"Plumber," he said back at the voice. "I'm here to check out your tubes."

She laughed.

"Make yourself comfortable," the voice came back. "I'm just finishing up."

Harry heard what sounded like the scratching of a phonograph needle. The speakers must have been quite near him. From the sound of the needle, the volume was turned way up.

In a moment, standing in his coat in the doorway, Harry's eyes were slowly filling with tears. For the sound of the needle had been followed by the sharp, incredibly rapid soaring of a zither, the zither of Anton Karas. The rest of the world, if they knew the music at all, knew it as *The Third Man Theme*. Its true name, of course, was *The Harry Lime Theme*. Where in the world she had gone to find it, Harry could not imagine. Brussels, he learned later.

Cassie appeared in the light of the doorway across the room. Her hair had been cut very short and parted neatly to one side. At her tiny ears were thin hoops of gold. Whatever lashes or shadow or liner could do for a woman's eyes had been done. They seemed enormous and brilliant blue, glowing at him across the parlor.

"Welcome home," she said, almost shyly. And stretched out her arms.

It was one of the few moments in Harry's life when the reason simply didn't matter. It could have been that she looked so goddam beautiful standing there. It could have been that only a moment earlier he knew his life was ending. It could have been simply that someone had wanted to do, had done, something wonderful just for him. Harry only knew that there had never been a happier moment in his life, and he couldn't run to her fast enough, crush her tightly enough. Tell her, show her, he loved her.

THIRTY

The visit was unannounced and unexpected.

Before Chairman Lepeshkin could order his secretary to report that he was indisposed, Voslov had come straight through the door.

There he stood, struggling out of his coat and muttering quietly to himself. He wore a large fur hat, absurd for the season, and looked helplessly about for a rack to hang it on.

"Thank you, Nikolai," he said absently to the wall, "for sparing the time to see me. I assure you I won't . . ."

His eyes searched the corners of the room. The hat and coat seemed lead weights in his hands.

"Where, after all," Voslov said, "do you hang *your* coat?"

Lepeshkin smiled in spite of himself. "It is warm, Andrei," the huge man said kindly. "I don't wear a coat. There is no need."

Voslov looked at him as though he had just uttered a sad put profound truth.

"Yes," Voslov said, "warm." And dropped hat and coat together into the nearest overstuffed armchair.

"Do you mind terribly," he said, "if I sit down?"

"An unexpected honor. I think Sonya has made tea."

Once again, there was a beat of silence before the little man responded.

"Lemon," he said. "Thank you. And a spoon."

He looked at Lepeshkin so strangely. His eyes were unusually direct, almost questioning, but in a regretful way. There was nothing of threat or challenge there. Still, the visit would have its reason. Lepeshkin relaxed, but not completely.

"I remember now," Lepeshkin boomed. "Andrei and his war against the cold. Thin blood."

Voslov looked at him for a long moment. Suddenly, the small tired eyes glazed over, grew strangely cold. Somewhere in the back of his brain, Lepeshkin felt a twinge, as a swimmer feels the shark nudging his arm, just before the arm disappears.

"Chilling breeze on the Square," Voslov said. "Harbinger of winter. More or less."

And in spite of himself, regretting as the very words left his lips, Lepeshkin blurted: "What? I didn't quite catch that."

Voslov looked at him for another moment. A slight smile began to play at his lips.

"Winter, Nikolai. I said, 'Winter. More or less.' Your family is well? Alexandra, the grandchildren?"

"Well," Lepeshkin said. "All are well. Thank you. And Tatiana?"

"Never better. You seem flushed, Nikolai. Is something wrong?"

"Nothing. I was preoccupied with a small emergency. Perhaps this is not the best of times for a chat."

Voslov's face was soft and harmless once more.

"I just came from the most pleasant chat with one of your department heads, Nikolai. Pavel Strelbitsky."

The twinge in Lepeshkin's brain was now a pounding in his ears.

"We chatted," Voslov offered, "about a wide range of matters. We talked about loyalty, Nikolai. And judgment, that sense of responsibility that we see too lttle of in these days. Don't you agree?"

Lepeshkin's intestines were now slowly constricting.

"Indeed," Lepeshkin said. "Pavel is a good man. A good worker. He is very loyal."

Voslov smiled quite suddenly.

"Loyal," Voslov said. "Yes."

Strelbitsky now dead and buried, Voslov was content to sit and watch. Lepeshkin was immobilized by terror.

"Nikolai," Voslov said gently, "do you have something to tell me? Some report perhaps still in process of completion? Something you were holding only because you wanted to present it to the Committee in its finished form?"

Certainly there was no alternative.

"Well," Lepeshkin said slowly, choking down the rage and panic, "there are always a number of such matters in process. One in particular has now reached a stage where I had intended to brief the Committee at its next meeting."

Voslov seemed pleased. "How timely," he mused.

Lepeshkin's mind actually leapt to the possibility of killing the little man on the spot. Lunging, and taking the soft, pasty throat in his hands. So quick, so sure, there would be no sound.

"If you would care, Andrei, to have the data before the meeting, I can have Ovechin bring the files around for you. In the morning, if you like."

A slight wave of the pudgy, hated little fingers.

"Oh, no need for files, Nikolai. That can wait for the Committee. I would be grateful for just the briefest explanation from yourself. Now, if it is convenient."

Lepeshkin looked at the small golden clock on the sideboard.

"Actually . . ." he began.

"So grateful," Voslov interrupted.

Lepeshkin nodded thoughtfully. "Of course, Andrei. As you wish."

Lepeshkin leaned back and brought a battered cigarette pack from his inside pocket. Forcing a smile, he kept his eyes on the pack. His oversized fingers fumbled with the task of extracting a single cigarette. His rage, he knew, was irrational. There was nothing catastrophic in this. At the worst, this could only push his timetable up by perhaps a month.

"The matter," Lepeshkin began, "concerns the Marco Polo Alliance. It had come to our attention that an American attended two of their meetings in London. He consorted with various delegates to those meetings in public and private places. We know that this same individual was seen in Venice during the most recent convention, but apparently he did not attend any of the official meetings there."

Lepeshkin now produced a book of matches, and carefully lit his cigarette. He drew heavily, and willed his muscles to relax.

"The man," he went on, "is a retired SIA agent. He had contrived somehow to obtain a position of considerable responsibility in these last months, negotiating highly sensitive matters as a personal assistant to Hubert Longview."

Lepeshkin took a puff and smiled as he watched the smoke drift upward.

"I can tell you," he said, "that Ross Buckley had a minor stroke when informed of the situation."

Voslov's face was a picture of attention and respect.

"You thought it best," Voslov said quietly, "to share this information with the Americans."

Lepeshkin nodded firmly. "At first," he said, "I was of two minds. There were so many possibilities to consider. But as we began to have the man followed, we discovered that he was under American surveillance, as well. We thought this indicated that Buckley was already aware of the man's involvement with the Alliance. When contacted, Buckley denied any such knowledge. He had only been observing the man as a routine procedural precaution, since there had been some question of the man's reliability. Apparently, relating to his past SIA service. Buckley was shocked by the man's contact with the Alliance. And very grateful, I might add, for the information. He made a point of acknowledging that he owes us one."

Voslov nodded, his eyes a bit blank, as if he were having difficulty digesting all this.

"You had," he said, "no difficulty convincing Buckley that you had the right man?"

Lepeshkin shood his head. "Not really. We had a photograph of the man in London, dining with senior German and Chinese military personnel. This was in March, of course, and long before Buckley's own surveillance of the man had begun. Buckley said that he simply could not believe his eyes. I understand that he had the photograph tested extensively to establish that it was not a composite or some such."

Voslov nodded, quite content with the response.

"And who," he asked, "is tracking our American friend at this point?"

Lepeshkin pushed his large fingertips together. He smiled broadly. "It is a collaborative effort. Which is to say, neither of us will let this man out of sight for five seconds."

Voslov smiled supportively. "And what," he asked, "is your appreciation of this man's role in the Alliance's affairs?"

Lepeshkin raised his shaggy brows. "To this moment, we don't really know. At first, I had a lingering concern that Buckley was deceiving me, that we had actually uncovered some clandestine participation by the American Government in the Alliance itself. I now discount this entirely. If this man were working for Buckley, he would never have attended meetings which Buckley knew we were monitoring. I conclude that this man is collaborating with the Alliance, against the interests of his own nation."

"Buckley agrees?"

"He cannot quite accept it, even now. He contends that the man may simply be reverting to the lone-wolf methods he used in his earlier SIA career, infiltrating the Alliance on his own initiative, without reporting to his superiors."

Voslov shook his head ever so slightly. His disbelief at Buckley's self-delusion was evident. "Obviously," Voslov said, "your conclusions are correct. What form of collaboration do you suggest is involved?"

Compulsively, Lepeshkin stubbed out his half-finished smoke. He fought the urge to light another, as this might make him appear to be anxious. "I suppose," Lepeshkin said, "that he could be advising Longview in a manner beneficial to the Alliance. If so, his effectiveness in that direction has ended. The only other possibility is that he is providing classified information to the Alliance. Of course, Buckley can now use the situation to feed the man whatever he wants the Alliance to hear."

Voslov's eyes made it evident that he understood fully. The initial strangeness of his manner was completely gone. They were two colleagues now, working together.

"Buckley, then, intends to keep the man in place?"

"For the present. He feels it might provide something interesting. Neither of us, however, are placing a great deal of hope in this."

"Because?"

"The Alliance will never trust this man with any knowledge that would be terribly important. In their eyes, he is already a double. Therefore, he could easily be a triple. This man is an aspect we must observe, but he should not distract us from the more direct efforts we have already begun."

Voslov nodded thoughtfully. Again, in complete agreement. "And how goes the work in Paris?"

Lepeshkin smiled and leaned forward slightly. Here was the truly exciting news. His voice lowered slightly to underscore the drama.

"France has proved to be a dead end. The scene has shifted, however, to Rome. We have a man named Correlli in AGIP, a bureaucrat, brilliant, a Christian Democrat. He has now been told by his superiors about the Alliance, though only in broad terms thus far. He will be part of the energy team preparing for the Vienna meetings. Apparently, he has passed every security check with flying colors. He anticipates a full briefing within a matter of weeks. This is the breakthrough we have been waiting for. I'm certain of it."

Voslov's eyelids drooped slightly, always the sign of sudden intense interest.

"And this man, Correlli. He has your full confidence?"

Lepeshkin stared at the little man. It had begun. Each domino would fall into the next without effort.

"Absolutely. I know the man personally. Strelbitsky placed him six years ago."

Voslov smiled, ever so slightly. "The Americans . . ."

"They know nothing of Correlli, of course. When his product begins to flow, we will decide how to make the best use of Mr. Buckley."

The smile lingered on the cherubic face. Voslov was unquestionably very pleased.

"Andrei," Lepeshkin said hesitantly, "I really must apologize for not having come to you about the American before this."

Another slight wave of the fingers.

"Nonsense, Nikolai. This is splendid news, splendid work. With your permission, I would share this with the Secretary at supper this evening."

It had begun.

THIRTY-ONE

The morning air was crisp and very cold. It was November now, and the sky was a bitter gray.

Reika moved slowly through the open-air market-place of Rue Lebon. Reika always moved slowly.

He stood at the cabbage stand, fingering the leaves of a particularly healthy specimen. Around him flowed the foot traffic of the early morning. There were house-wives with their net baskets, children chattering and gently shoving one another on their walk to school. Here and there, a businessman hurried by in a warm coat of gray or brown. A hundred citizens of Paris strolled past the tall man with blank eyes as he bought his cabbage, as thousands of citizens of other cities had strolled past him before. And as always, if there had ever been anyone to ask the question, none of them could quite remember who the man had been or exactly what he looked like. If Andrei Voslov was a man made inconspicuous by nature, Reika was a man invisible by profession.

Slowly, carefully, Reika counted out the change for the vendor. Without a word, he tucked the parcel beneath his arm, and headed off for his own day's work.

Reika took the métro to his morning's destination.

He had purchased a copy of *Le Monde* at the station. Although he did not read French, he slowly turned the pages of the paper as the train clattered its way below the Champs Elysées. His eyes studied each page. His face and hands were quiet. And if anyone had for any reason chosen to look into those eyes, he could not tell you later what was their color. Gray, you might be told, or hazel. Green, perhaps, with yellow or brown fleks. The hair? A middle shade of brown. With some gray. His age? Depending on the day, depending on the light, you might be told anything from forty to sixty.

It did not matter. No one looked.

At Châtelet, Reika changed trains, moving with the flow of commuters toward Direction Porte D'Orléans. He stood this time, long, slender fingers holding the strap. Hands of an artist. Pianist, perhaps. Eyes blankly staring at the dark beyond the window.

Reika took the train to St. Placide. The sky had brightened somewhat. It would be a passable morning to sit in the park. He walked up the Rue de Fleurus to the Luxembourg Gardens. It was after eight o'clock.

Reika knew where the lovers would be. In fact, during these past weeks, Reika had acquainted himself reasonably well with their habits and their hideaways. Reika could track with the best. But he was not a tracker.

He strolled to a grassy knoll above and seventy meters behind where the couple usually sat in the mornings. She taught on Wednesday and Friday afternoons, and always came to this spot to read on those mornings. Her lover was not always in town these past weeks, but today he would be. They would come together. They would spread a soft tartan blanket under that particular tree. He would carry a basket with bread and yellow cheese and wine, sometimes a pâté or a cold sausage. They would read and talk. They would cuddle from time to time. Before noon, they would eat. Then he would walk her to the Lycée.

Seventy meters away, Reika would watch.

The couple had not arrived as yet. As he sat, his parcel of cabbage at his side, Reika read from a well-thumbed paperback. He read more in these past few years, and drank less. Very slowly, Reika was growing older, and his minor adjustments to this fact had been carefully thought through. He slept one hour longer now. He had his eyes examined twice each year, always by a different ophthalmologist. The result was always the same. Reika's vision was astonishingly acute.

Reika was quite precise in his diet. In each city, he would take a small flat so that he could cook for himself. His weight never varied. His pulse was that of a finely tuned athlete. His care of his tools, bodily and mechanical, had always been meticulous. In his private unknown world, Reika was a professional without peer. His assignments had always been the most sensitive, the most signficant. Hence, his appearance in Paris this gray November.

A young woman approached, wheeling her bundled child in a bright blue stroller. She stopped on the path directly in front of Reika, and knelt to adjust the straps holding the child. The baby, of indistinguishable gender, cried suddenly, loudly, at the intrusion upon his/her reverie. The mother was quite startled by the volume of the noise. Once begun, the child warmed to its task. The wailing increased.

The mother, pretty and young, looked helplessly up at Reika. Her eyes apologizing for the din.

Without a word, Reika leaned forward. He placed his fingertips on the back of the child's hand. The child looked up into Reika's eyes and the noise suddenly ceased. For an instant, the quiet seemed almost unearthly. The child did not smile, did not give any indication of its thoughts as it stared into the eyes of the stranger.

After a long moment, the mother broke the spell. Thanking Reika in a grateful burst of French, which he did not understand, she wheeled the child away. For a few steps, the child turned in its stroller to look back at the man, until its mother's body blocked the view.

Reika, of course, had never killed a child. Forty-three men. Four women. One at a time. But never a child.

After a while, Reika saw the couple picking their way along the grass far below his knoll. Hand in hand, Harry and Cassie brought their picnic basket to their favorite tree. They spread their tartan blanket. She cuddled into him, and they settled down to read.

Below and far off to the right, Reika saw the trackers. The couple Harry had named Charlie Team. They knew now, of course, that Harry was aware of their presence. But they had been kept in place because Harry would be more comfortable without a visible change in surveillance procedures.

In a sense, Reika and the trackers were co-workers. He knew everything there was to know about each of them. Yet, if they passed on the street, or sat side by side in a bar, the trackers would most certainly not know Reika.

Fewer than a dozen men on earth knew his face or his name. He could be placed by one man only, and he was required always to deliver perfection. For Reika was a collector. And with understandable pride, he was the very best.

THIRTY-TWO

The moment Voslov walked into the room, he knew.

Tatiana lay under the soft folds of their good down coverlet. She was wearing a dressing gown of pure silk, carefully taken from the chest where she had stored so many memories. Her face was more beautiful than he could remember.

Resting lightly between her fingers was the letter.

Voslov sat gently by her side. as if careful not to wake her. He took the cold fingers into his own, and held them tightly as he read.

Our love is not over, it said. This is the first, the most important, thing for you to know. We have said good-bye. That was at breakfast this morning. You kissed me. You smiled. It was perfect.

We have said good-bye. And our love is not over. Our good-bye was perfect, as our love will always be. Forgive me for wanting that. Forgive me for fearing the other good-bye. My pain bringing you pain, your sadness bringing mine. Leaving you with the lie that there could be sadness between us. Have we lived our love so that wicked little cells, growing in darkness, could cheat us at the end? No. We cheat them. We say good-bye with a kiss and a smile. And our love goes on forever.

Our love has been my life. It has made my whole life wonderous. You have made me a queen, my love. I can never repay that. What you must know is that in my last hours I have lived our life again, in tears of joy that so exquisite a life could have been mine.

Now you must do something for me. You must live long and well. You must live as though you are saving each moment to share with me, in my arms, when we are together again. And if you find another love before your life is over, treasure those moments most of all, and know that nothing could make me happier.

Our love is not over. We are apart *and* we are together always.

It was a fiercely cold morning when Tatiana Serafinovna's body was gently placed into the earth.

Vladimir Cherny, General Secretary of the Party, stood at his friend's side, a firm, strong hand on his arm. He looked down at the little man in wonder. Not at the tears. For Cherny knew that no matter how many tears had fallen, how certain one may be that no tears could remain, there were always more. Cherny's astonishment was rather of something quite mundane. The little man wore only a light summer coat. And as the balding head bent in its grief, there was no hat to save it from the cold.

THIRTY-THREE

Cherny had understood that his friend would need to be alone for a while, to get away somewhere, to be with his thoughts. Despite the considerable red tape which would inevitably surround any trip abroad by a member of the Politburo, Cherny saw to it that visas were quietly and secretly arranged. His friend could go where he wished, do as he pleased, return when he chose.

So it was without public notice that Voslov boarded the Aeroflot jetliner for Helsinki. In the pocket of his coat was a commercial ticket for Madrid. Next to the ticket rested a worn leather case. Photographs. Passport and visas.

There was a second passport. British. Henry Watersby. Born, Blackpool, January 25, 1933. Occupation, salesperson. Residence, 62 Great Titchfield Street, London. Widower. The passport bore a skillful forgery of a departure stamp from Heathrow Airport, some seven days before. Below, in a deep maroon ink, a stamp of the same day welcoming Mr. Watersby to Finland.

At the airport in Helsinki, Voslov had a large breakfast. His connecting Swissair flight to Madrid departed long before his coffee arrived.

Voslov made his way to the ticket counter for British Airways. His English was flawless, his accent refined through six years at Cambridge. He presented the Watersby passport, and purchased a first-class one-way ticket through to Heathrow, paid for in cash with British currency.

Through the long flight, Voslov's thoughts were filled with Tatiana. Not the graveside. Not their wedding trip, nor the night they first met. It was a moment in a boat on a lake. There was sun on her hair and the world was very still. That was all. But his mind was locked to it, obsessed by it. Not a word, not a sound. Tatiana's eyes. Her lovely throat. And the silence of the sunlight.

Heathrow came, and customs and luggage and taxicabs. And then he was in Chelsea, in Sloane Square.

Henry Watersby took a small room at the Royal Court Hotel. He drew himself a very hot bath and, although it was well into the evening, he hiked himself down to the large cherrywood bar off the lobby. There he resolutely downed one large cognac after another, until he could scarcely find the lift. He slept for twelve hours.

Voslov awoke to a morning of rare sunshine. He bathed and shaved again. By this time, it was past noon. He dressed in the English-made suit he had brought with him, expensive but five years out of style. He set off for Beauchamp Street and a grand luncheon. Prosciutto and veal and most of a liter of drinkable wine. Thus fortified, he strolled on to Knightsbridge.

The multi-colored brick of the Hyde Park Hotel loomed before him, pennants flapping briskly. The lobby was quiet and large.

It was mid-afternoon and the bar was nearly empty. One red jacketed barman patrolling his post, hands clasped behind him. With no little difficulty, Voslov lifted his rump onto one of the stools. The barman approached with a polite smile and raised brows.

"Hello," Voslov said, somewhat nervously.

"And good afternoon to you, sir." There was a taste of Ireland long ago in his voice. "What would be your pleasure?"

Voslov's hands were clasped on the bar before him. "Brandy, I suppose." His smile was friendly, but shy.

"Anything in par-tic-u-lar, sir?"

Voslov shook his head. "I don't know," and he giggled slightly. "I don't really drink brandy."

The barman nodded most knowingly. "I see, sir. Well, we'll just fix you up with the best, then. Nothing better'n the best."

The barman returned with a large snifter. Voslov smiled gratefully, and placed a ten-pound note on the bar.

"That's for you," Voslov said meekly.

The man's brows raised again. "And thank you very much for that, sir."

He looked down at the small, round creature perched on the stool. "Would there be," he asked directly, "anything else I might do for you today, sir?"

The little man now seemed truly embarrassed. "Actually," he said, "I suppose there might be. I understand that occasionally a fellow could find . . . suitable feminine . . . companionship . . . if . . ."

The barman chuckled. "Well, I wouldn't know anything for sure about that, sir."

"Oh," the little man said. Deeply disappointed.

" 'Course, I hear rumors, same as anyone. Some of the young ladies who stop by for something sweet and wet . . . well, some of them, I imagine, would enjoy meeting a gentleman such as yourself. They usually pop by a bit later in the day, sir."

Voslov bit his lip. He seemed uncertain as to what he should do next. Then, slowly, he pulled a worn leather case from his inside pocket. He took out a photograph and placed it on the bar. He covered the photo with another ten-pound note.

The barman gently pushed the note aside, and looked down at the picture. It was a reproduction of Dolya's photo from the Harbinger file, cropped to show only the woman. The barman's eyes flickered at once. It was clear to Voslov that he recognized her.

"That would be Lesley, sir. Yes, it would. A very lovely lady. Professional lady, sir, as I expect you know."

Voslov gulped a little and lowered his eyes. He nodded, to confirm his awareness of Lesley's professional status.

"Haven't seen Lesley about for maybe five, six months now. Sorry to tell you that, sir. You seem to have your heart set."

The little man was crestfallen. He took one more ten-pound note from his wallet, and folded it around a card.

"If anything occurs to you," he said, "I'm at the Royal Court in Sloane Square."

Voslov did not get off the stool. He just kept looking up at the man.

Finally, the bartender said, "Well, you know, there is this fellow. Jerry. Why don't you come back around, say, eight o'clock. Might have a nice surprise for you."

Voslov returned to the bar at eight o'clock. He sat at a table in the rear, and sipped brandy for more than an hour. When Jerry arrived, the barman ushered him to Voslov's table with a hearty smile.

Jerry was wearing a suit made of raw silk. It was very bright blue, and nicely set off his paisley ascot of electric orange. Jerry had a great deal of something oily rubbed into his hair. His scent was heavy and sweet.

"My man Martin," he said in theatrical tones, "tells me that you have a photograph for me."

Slowly, shyly, as if the man planned to snatch the precious object from him, Voslov produced the picture of Lesley.

"Yes, yes, yes," Jerry said admiringly. "I think we can come up with something to your full satisfaction."

Voslov looked hurt.

"It's not something," he said. "It's someone, someone very particular."

He snatched the photo off the table. Jerry smiled and held up his hands.

"No offense intended," he said. "Little Lesley hasn't been around of late. Left London, as a matter of fact. I know we could find something, someone, you'd fancy. Look just the same, couldn't tell the difference."

Voslov looked down at the table. "No one," he said so softly, "no one else ever understood. Do you ... know what I mean?"

Jerry drummed his fingers on the table. The nails gleamed from their afternoon manicure. A ring with a large purple stone. Drumming. His smile fixed in place. Apparently, Jerry was thinking it over.

Voslov pulled out his billfold. He laid a fifty-pound note on the table, just to see if it helped Jerry's thought process. The drumming stopped.

"Used to live with her mum, you know. In Bayswater. Paddington, maybe. I'd have to check through my files. Be a hell of a job."

Voslov laid a hundred-pound note atop the fifty.

The next afternoon, Voslov found himself at a flat in Leinster Gardens, just off Cleveland Square. Dull mustard with white trim. The steps to the door were very clean.

A tiny woman answered the door. She was scrawny to the point of being emaciated. Her gingham housedress hung from her bones. It, too, was very clean. Her hair was gray and pulled tightly into a large bun at the back of her head. Her nose was slightly hooked, like the beak of a parrot, and her hands held each other as she stood in the doorway.

"Good afternoon," Voslov said softly. "I do hope that you can forgive this intrusion."

The woman stared up at him. There was no recognition, and obviously Jerry had not prepared her for the visit. This was just as well.

"I'm not selling anything," he said, and smiled very gently. "I've come to have a word with you about Lesley. Would you be kind enough to let me sit down? I've walked such a way."

She looked a little defensive, perhaps even frightened, at the mention of her daughter's name. Something in his warmth, though, had found its mark. This man was, apparently, a gentleman. She was too much a lady to leave him standing in the cold.

She took him to a faded parlor, which looked and smelled just as one would suspect at first sight of her. Voslov carefully moved the lace pillow to one side, so as not to crush it with his bulk. She smiled, timidly grateful for the gesture.

"Would you have some tea?" she said. These were her first words, and her voice squeaked as if it had not been used in years.

"How lovely. With a bit of lemon, please."

She disappeared without a word. They had not so much as exchanged names. There he sat, in the stale fragrance of her parlor, waiting for his tea. The tea, as it happened, was peppermint and revoltingly sweet.

"My name is Henry Watersby," he said. She perched on the edge of her seat, bony elbows on bony knees.

She looked at him as if he were the executioner, but such a nice man.

"I am trying to find your daughter. I need to have a brief word with her, on a matter important to my heart."

She looked at him with all the pain her eyes could bear. The pain of a good woman whose only child is a whore. She cleared her throat.

"She's out of it, you know."

He raised his brows politely.

"Out of it," she repeated firmly. "She's married now. To a good man. Very wealthy, he is. He loves her, you know."

Voslov's eyes lowered with respect.

"I'm sure he does," Voslov said. "I'm sure of it. As she well deserves."

He left the silence there between them.

"So, you can see," she said, "why we can't have no one from her old life coming to her. For no reason. You see, he doesn't know."

Voslov understood completely. "Of course he doesn't," Voslov smiled benignly. "And why should he? Past is dead and buried now, thank our Lord."

The silence again.

"So, you see," she nearly pleaded, "how I couldn't send no one to her. She's off in a new world now."

Voslov nodded with sympathy, but his eyes were sad. Slowly, they drifted into the distance.

"Men," he said, and sighed deeply. He searched her eyes. "Isn't it always the way?" he said. "It always comes back to a man."

She wanted to understand. Her eyes were questioning.

"When a woman has been ruined," he said. "When a good woman's life is disgraced."

She was leaning forward now.

"My own daughter," he said softly, "my own Emily. We lived in Surrey. After her dear mother went to her reward. Until a certain gentleman came into our lives."

And it was clear from his voice that the term "gentleman" did not truly apply.

"He was American," Voslov said. "He was her first love. They were to be married last Christmas. Do you understand?"

She did not.

"Now," he said so softly, "there is a baby. Little Michael. But there is no father for Michael. And no husband for my little girl."

Her eyes were glistening. If she had been less timid, she would have reached out to take his hand.

"The police ... laughed. The sergeant actually laughed at me. Can you believe such a thing?"

She shook her head. A small tear made its errant way down her cheek.

"All these months," he said, "I have given up my trade. Given my life to finding this ... this man. Forgive the indelicacy of what I must tell you. The only lead I have been able to uncover is that, this March, your daughter was this man's ... escort. On at least two occasions. I do not know what she will be able to tell me of him. But in her conversations with this man, there must be some clue that will help me. Without her help, I am utterly ... lost."

She was shaking her head, slowly. "I am more sorry for you than you could know," she said. "But I promised her I would never ..."

Voslov held up his hand. "Never," he said gently, "break a promise to someone you love. That is how the world got to be in such a state, isn't it? Just give her my card, tell her my story. I am staying at the

Royal Court in Chelsea. Tell her I can only beg for her kindness."

He fumbled in his pocket to find the card. He laid it gently on the side table.

"Tell her one thing more," he said gently, looking down only at the card. "Tell her to trust my discretion. Tell her that her husband, her . . ."

The silence hung for only a second.

"George," the woman said.

"Tell her that her George will certainly never hear of her past from my lips. Be particularly sure to tell her that. I know that will ease her mind."

THIRTY-FOUR

It was Sunday. Reika had taken the day off.

He stood in the Jeu de Paume, before the rich colors of Gauguin. He looked at the copper skin of the Tahitian women who had modeled for the master, and at the calm, dark secrets of their eyes.

He stood before Monet's paintings of the Cathedral of Rouen. Five paintings of the same facade, each in the light of a different time of day. No one knew how many times Monet had painted that cathedral. More than twenty paintings in 1874 alone, each to explore the same subject in the mood of a different light.

This was a labor Reika could particularly respect. To truly know one's subject, it must be studied in every possible light. Each element seen, analyzed, repeated, until the understanding was fully rounded and complete.

Careful, dedicated work was Reika's only standard of worth. His only god.

Reika's only personal relationships were with his subjects. A curious relationship, to be sure, since the subject never met, or even saw, his executioner. But Reika's interest was as intense, as real, as any scientist who ever peered through a microscope. Reika's work was the ending of a human life, and Reika insisted

upon an understanding of that life before he took
it.

Reika's understanding came only from personal
observation. He watched at distances ranging from
hundreds of meters to a matter of inches. He watched
in every light, in every mood. In an astonishing array
of private moments, each small moment its own small
revelation.

He disdained briefings and psychological profiles,
for he was certain that his superiors had no true
knowledge of his subject. It was for them to choose. It
was for Reika to understand.

As he left the Jeu de Paume, the day was cold and
incredibly clear. He walked up Avenue Gabriel with
the sunlight on his face.

In his mind, Reika pieced together what he had
seen of Harry Lime. It was not the sort of description
one would convey in words. He was putting Harry
Lime together in his thoughts, as a composer would
construct an orchestral work. Yet the composition was
in pictures. Images of Harry turning, smiling, lost in
thought. Sleeping on the grass, nuzzling Cassie's hair.
Sniffing at his wine or stumbling at a curb. Harry
tired. Harry anxious. Harry very much alone.

Reika had his man now. He waited only for word of
the proper date. It would be very soon.

Atypically, Reika dined out that evening. It was
something of a celebration. For Reika had concluded
that Harry Lime was a worthy subject. It was not
always so. What Reika noted as worthy in such a
circumstance would have been difficult for him to
articulate. Intelligence, yes. He always looked first
for visible manifestations of intellect. Awareness of
life, of others. A man who observed, always, reflexively.
These, too, were significant. But above all, there
was a certain matter of tone. A bittersweet color of

a man who knew loneliness. Whether he knew it in pain, as Harry, or in the comfort of solitude, was not important. To be a man, one must have that sense of himself apart. Only alone could a man face the idea, the reality, of his death.

And so, Reika sat in the corner of the darkened bistro, and finished his whitefish and wine. He strolled in the evening chill down to the river. The grand buildings along the Seine were lighted, and their reflections danced on the blackness of the water.

And as Reika walked down at the river's edge, he did not look up at the stone barrier running along the Quai far above his path. He did not see the face. The face that had tracked him, at a distance of greatest respect, for most of the day. The face of Harry Lime.

THIRTY-FIVE

Cassie was reading in bed. Harry had been pretending to do the same. At last he reached over and took the book from her hands.

"Playtime already?" she said, with a small and slightly dirty smile.

"Time for a talk," he said.

"Any talk in particular?"

"Anything you want to know about anything. This is the time to ask."

He was smiling, all right, the sweet gentle smile that always came so easily. But the dark eyes were strange and sad.

"Do you love me?" came the first question. Because suddenly, without reason, without warning, there had been the stabbing fear that his eyes were saying he would leave her.

"Very much." His voice was soft, but very firm.

"The way you love Jenny?"

It had just come out. No thought. Just straight from her heart to her mouth.

"Jenny and I shared thirteen years. We shared Lissa. There's a lot of stuff in thirteen years."

Her eyes looked down. "Lot of stuff," she said very softly, "in thirteen weeks."

"Lot of wonderful stuff," he agreed.

She thought for a moment. There was no reason to ask it, since she knew the answer. He would have to lie, and she didn't really want to make him lie. There was no reason to ask it. And she had to.

"When Jenny calls you," she said, looking straight at his eyes, "will you go?"

"She never, never will, Cassie. Believe that."

"That's some dumb kind of answer."

"I wouldn't know the answer," he said, "until it happened. If it happened today, if it happened right this minute, I'd go. I'd never forget you. But I'd go."

Her eyes began to fill. She knew it would happen. She hated herself for doing this. At least he hadn't lied.

"And," he said, "if it happens later, she might just be out of luck."

She threw her arms around his neck. At least he'd said it. She loved him for saying it.

"Later," she whispered. "Later is my favorite time. You let me know when later gets here. Okay?"

He couldn't believe all this was happening, that he had done all this to this woman, who only loved him. Of course, there would be no later. The tall man would see to that.

"When later comes," he said, his dark eyes very wet, "you'll be the first to know. Okay? Far as I'm concerned, the sooner it gets here, the better."

She smiled now, sniffing back her tears. She put her head on his bare chest.

"Questions all through?" he asked.

He could not see her face. But very directly, the small voice came back at him.

"Why," she said, "did you leave the Agency? You said 'unusual circumstances.' In Venice. Remember?"

She sat up and looked at him.

'I used to work," he said, 'for a man named John Knowles. He was Director. I was his personal assistant. We were very close."

"You loved him?"

"And something like hated him. He was an extraordinary man. Fierce, cunning. But he could feel. He read. He wrote poetry, Japanese haiku."

"He was grooming you to replace him?'

"No. He had groomed another man to be Director. A man named Buckley. He's Director today. No, John was grooming me for something else. Son, maybe. Or maybe even friend."

"And you hated him?"

Harry's eyes were far away now.

"Knowles was a genius and a disaster. He believed that America should rule the earth. Communists, radicals, revolutionists were vermin, lice. If he could, John would have controlled each government on this planet by the simple expedient of killing off the bad guys. He did it in Pakistan. He did it in Iraq."

Harry said nothing for a while, and Cassie just waited.

"I had to learn each of the operations. He insisted. I was primarily a questioner, an interrogator. That is not to be confused with deep questioner. Those are the fellas who deal in torture. I never saw them work, but Knowles would tell me stories. He put me in cryptography for a while. I liked that. From time to time, I would track for him. Like our friends on Charlie Team."

He was quiet again.

"I was tracking for John in Vienna. Some German guy named Dreiser. He was NATO and John thought he was working for the KGB. God knows what terrible secrets John thought this guy was whispering to the opposition. Anyway, I thought John was in Wash ington all this time. One evening, I come back to my little flat, and there he is. You just graduated, he tells me. Tracker with a stinger. And he shows me a gun. Little tiny silver thing. Pretty, almost looked like a toy."

Cassie cleared her throat. She didn't know why it suddenly seemed so dry. He looked at her.

"Time to prove," she said, "that you were a man, huh?"

"Time to prove I was *his* man."

Cassie just shook her head. "How ... were you supposed to do it?"

"John told me that Dreiser would be meeting his contact at the Prater on Sunday afternoon. It's an amusement park. It's very simple, he said. You'll come up behind him in a large crowd. Very tight, very noisy crowd. You'll put the gun just below his left shoulder blade, pointing up and in. You squeeze one shot immediately. You blow his fucking heart out. Your arm falls to your side, you drop the gun, you keep walking. Don't worry about his rib cage, the bullet will explode inside him. There will be very little sound. By the time he drops, you'll be well past him. Just react with the rest of the crowd when he falls. Ease your way to the periphery of the crowd. Then just walk away."

"What if someone sees you do it?"

"Too fast. Tiny gun in your hand, in your pocket. You brush past him from his left rear. Your hand moves only a few inches. It's all one quick motion. Like a pickpocket, only easier."

Cassie shuddered a little. "You told him you wouldn't do it?"

"That's right."

"What did he say?"

"He just stared at me at first. I didn't have the

slightest idea what was going through his mind. He looked like he detested me, and was reaching out to me, all at the same time. Then he put the gun on the floor between us. You'll do it for one reason only. If you don't, you'll never see me again. Then he walked out."

"What happened?"

"I went to the Prater on Sunday. I knew John would have me tracked. I tracked Dreiser for an hour. There's a big ferris wheel, always a good long queue. The traffic flow gets compacted trying to move past that line. As he headed toward that point, I measured the speed of his progress, moved in about ten yards to the rear. I caught him just as he was passing the ferris wheel. It was a tremendous mob. I came up from behind, took my hand out of my pocket and put it under his left shoulder blade just as I brushed by him."

"Oh my God."

"I said, 'Bang, bang, you're dead.' Very softly."

"You didn't shoot him?"

"I've never touched that gun. Last I saw, it was lying on the floor of that flat. Right where John had left it."

"Oh my God."

He smiled the boyish smile again. "You're repeating yourself," he said.

"What about Knowles?"

"I never saw him again."

"Just like that?"

"I walked out of the Prater, into a cab, went to the airport, flew to Miami. Changed planes four times on the way. I figured John was going to kill me. He should have. In fact, it was the biggest mistake of his life."

"You're dangerous when you're mad, huh?"

He smiled. "It's a long story," he said.

"I'll stick around."

"I called Ross Buckley. We met somewhere in Maryland. I told him I had left the Agency. He already knew why."

He looked at her, at the way her eyes narrowed slightly. She was thinking. Couldn't help herself.

"Did Mr. Buckley try to talk you out of quitting?"

"At first. He liked me."

She offered a sly grin. "How nice for you. If he liked you so damn much, why didn't you become *his* right hand when he took over?"

He stared into her eyes. He really liked her. No doubt about it.

"He and I worked this plan. We were going to precipitate John's immediate retirement. I disappeared. Buck saw to it that a lot of highly classified material disappeared with me. It was all replaced three days later, except that every reference to me had been excised. Files, computers, everything. As if I'd never existed."

"Sounds hard to do."

"Buck was very talented. Also motivated. John resigned in disgrace and Buck took over as Director. The whole thing took six days from beginning to end. There were a few Congressmen who wanted to try me for treason. Buck persuaded them that I was a well-meaning idealist, who had sacrificed his own career to bring down John's decadent reign. More to the point, everyone involved wanted the SIA to remain low profile. Any action against me would bring the same kind of publicity that had emasculated the CIA."

She was shaking her head in utter disbelief. "How could you let that . . . that man Buckley . . . *use* you? How could you think he was any better than the guy you got rid of?"

Such cynicism in one so young. He loved her, all right.

"We need an intelligence service," he said. "All the crap aside. Like we need an army. Like we need nuclear weapons. It's tragic that we need them. It's monstrous. But we do."

"I don't happen to agree with you," she said softly. "But you didn't answer my question."

"Vienna taught me something. I was repelled because John had wanted *me* to pull the trigger. He knew that someday I'd realize that loading the gun from his inner office was the same thing as sticking it into that guy's ribs. He could never really count on me until he made me face up to that. So he did."

"And you 'failed' him?"

"I learned. I didn't belong. We need policemen, we need soldiers. If you can't kill, you're not one of them. As to the difference between John and Buck, I thought the difference was pretty clear. John was a madman. For him, violence was a policy. Buck is a technician, an administrator. Violence is the tool of last resort. Buck didn't use me any more than I used him. The Agency had to go on, it had to go on without me, and it had to go on without John Knowles."

She was looking at him. Differently, now. "Just one more question," she said. "Why are we having this little talk? Why are your eyes so strange? You look like something awful has happened. You know that? Like somebody died."

He sank back against the pillows.

"I saw someone today," he said. "A tall man. I was on the Champs Elysées and his face just passed in front of me. Very close. And it was like someone jammed a gun barrel straight down my throat."

She didn't look frightened. She didn't look anything. She just reached for his hand and held it.

"I didn't recognize the face at all. Just my stomach did, just that part that wants to go on living. I doubled back. I tracked him. All day. I'm still not completely sure I'm right. He's a lot older than the picture. Maybe ten years."

"Who in God's name . . . ?"

"If I'm right, he's a collector. His name is Reika."

"What does that mean?"

"A collector is a master assassin, an artist. He works for the Agency. Practically no one knows who they are or what they look like. I saw this man's picture once. It's a very old picture, and I haven't seen it in a long time. I could be wrong."

She licked her lips. "Even if you're right. He could be here for somebody else. Or on holiday."

Harry nodded. "The hell of it," he said softly, "is that it would be impolite to ask him."

She looked as if she understood it all. So quickly, so completely.

"Lime's Crisis?" she said.

Harry smiled. "In all the textbooks. Remember how I said it might be kind of dumb to tell my people that I knew about Marco Polo?"

She nodded and smiled very warmly. "So I guess you were kind of dumb, huh?"

"Gonna look bad in the textbooks, I'm afraid."

She reached out and smoothed his hair away from his forehead.

"Hey," she said, "just so long as they spell your name right."

He folded his arms around her. "These guys are legendary," he said. "They never miss."

Her eyes were brimming full again. But her little jaw was set. Very stubborn.

"Until now," she said. "You're Harry goddam Lime.

You're not just anybody. Nobody's gonna beat you. Nobody's gonna beat us."

He squeezed her so tightly. Then held her arm's length. "We've got to talk about you," he said. "I don't think he'd kill you. Under John, they never did that. But then, John was a chivalrous sort. Buck, I'm not so sure. If this is big enough to rate a collector, Buck may want to ask you some questions. So you have to listen to me now. Very carefully . . ."

She drew his face to her until their noses touched. "Hey," she whispered, "forget all that stuff. We're sticking together. Okay? I'd be scared to death without you. Anyway, we're responsible for each other."

It would be an insane risk to take her.

"See what happens," she said, "when you get a girl in trouble?"

She was very frightened now. He could feel her heart beating as he held her.

"I have to run," he said. "Really run. You don't know what that means. It's the most terrible thing there is. I've got one step's grace. Reika doesn't know I've recognized him. Once I'm gone, he'll track me till he finds me."

She was crying now, sobbing freely, her slender fingers clutching at his shoulders. He was leaving her. She would never see him again.

He held her to him. He put his lips against her ear. "I'm not leaving you behind," he said. "Not for anything."

The sobbing choked off instantly. She pulled back to look at him, her eyes wide and unbelieving.

"I like," he said so softly, "the way you take good care of me."

THIRTY-SIX

Maude Frisón shifted her weight to the left leg again. She wondered, for the thousandth time, why the Consul always insisted that she stand. Americans. Every civil wedding performed by a magistrate, for every decent French couple, witnesses sat like gentlemen and ladies.

She was dreadfully late for lunch as it was. Half of Lyon was already fed and back to work. She had let herself think about the lunch, the leftover goose and the tarts. She had thought this would see her through her boredom, as the Consul droned on to the poor couple of the responsibilities of wedlock. My God, the man could take ten minutes just to clear his throat.

Why on earth she had to stand through these ceremonies was wholly beyond understanding. Consul thought he was some sort of priest, she suspected. These things always seemed set for noon and then lingered with delays and paperwork, until a person's stomach burbled loudly at the indignity.

Maude shifted her weight one last time and kept her grim stare of respect firmly in place. Finally, the old fellow was drawing to a close.

"And do you, Samuel, take this woman as your

lawfully wedded wife? To cherish and love and protect her until death do you part?"

The man looked down at his bride and smiled with a tenderness that Maude didn't often see in men these days. Of course, Maude had been fooled by a smile at the altar before. Twice, to be exact.

"I do," the man said.

The Consul beamed, the old fool.

"Then, Mr. and Mrs. Samuel Allen, by the authority vested in me by the Government of the United States of America, I now pronounce you husband and wife. By all means, Sam, kiss the little lady before I do it for you."

And Harry took Cassie in his arms and gave her a deep, lingering kiss. True to his word, the Consul was next in line. Then it was Harry's turn to kiss the Consul's wife and Maude herself.

After Maude toddled off to her lunch, the others retired to the Consul's study for large glasses of sherry.

"I can't tell you," Harry said, "how grateful we will always be. I'm sure these things usually take weeks of red tape and so forth."

"Well," the Consul said with a broad wink at his tiny wife, "one learns a thing or two through the years about red tape and how to cut it. A thing or two."

Harry beamed his undying appreciation.

"Where are the lovebirds off to next?" the old man wondered.

"Italy," Harry said. "Cassie's never been to Florence."

"Ah," the Consul nodded approvingly, "Firenze, eh? The Accademia, the Uffizi, the Pitti Palace. What could be more splendid?"

Cassie looked demurely at Harry. "It's the honeymoon," she said, "that I've dreamed of since I was a little girl."

The Consul and his wife responded with smiles of pure delight.

Cassie looked up at the old man. "How long will it take for our new passport to get here?"

He waved his hand. "Don't worry about that, darling. You just travel on your old ones. They'll send the new one home to Colorado for you. Shiny and new for your next trip."

Cassie bit her lip. She seemed suddenly very distressed.

"What's the matter, honey?" Harry asked.

"You said we'd have *one* passport. Husband and wife. I don't want all those people, at the hotels and everything, thinking we're . . . you know, thinking we're not married or anything."

Harry chuckled. He shared a glance with the Consul. Women, God love them.

"We'll have our marriage certificate, honey. What's the difference?"

She was very embarrassed. She stared at her lap.

"Samuel. You know no one's going to see that. It's not the same. You know how those men will look at me. Those Italian men. At the hotel. Samuel, you *promised* me. You did."

Harry bit his lip. He was on the spot for sure.

"I know I did, honey. I just didn't really stop to think it all through."

Cassie's eyes were beginning to glisten. The old man was already out of his seat. He was holding his handkerchief to her, and she took it with a shy nod.

The old man tapped his belt buckle and leaned back on his heels.

"Two days over, two days back," he said to the ceiling. Then he clapped his hands like a sultan about to issue a proclamation.

"Five days," he said. "You children drive around in

Burgundy till next Tuesday, and you'll have your passport, little darlin'. Just the way Sam promised."

She turned her face up to the old man. A very small tear tracing down each cheek. "Do . . . you really mean that?"

The Consul beamed down at her. "It *will* be something of a world's record," he intoned without a trace of false modesty, "but after thirty-five years, I've got a few chits I can call back at home base. This is *your* government, little lady, and if you can't call on your government for a little help when you're in a fix far from home, well, what's the whole damn State Department in business for?"

THIRTY-SEVEN

There is a little street in Soho called Sutton Row, he had said. She knew that, of course, quite well. It runs into Charing Cross, he'd said, just below St. Giles Circus. She'd known that as well. A small pub. The Thorn and Blossom. Seven o'clock. Please be very much alone.

She had taken the tube to Tottenham Court Road. She was early. Much too early. She was glad she'd taken her fur against the cold, even if it did certify the wealth of her new station in life. He obviously knew that already. One had to stand up to a blackmailer. One had to draw her fur around her shoulders and stare imperiously down at the weasel. To have credibility, there must be dignity. And one always has a bit more dignity when wrapped in quality fur.

Twenty minutes early. She couldn't just walk into the pub and wait for the man. Gathering the fur around her, she set off on a chilly stroll down Charing Cross Road toward Cambridge Circus. Walk ten minutes out, turn 'round, walk back just a bit slower.

Every step of the way, her stomach rolled and tossed. In her bag was an envelope. Five hundred pounds in small bills. She knew it would never be enough. It had to be. Not because she couldn't get more, she could get whatever was required. But she couldn't get away from Leeds again. Not so easily. George had been astonishingly suspicious. She had telephoned the sweet sonofabitch five times today already.

By the time she entered the pub, she had worked herself into a proper state. She didn't know whether to claw at the man's eyes or burst into tears and beg him to take her money.

The pub's lighting was mercifully nonexistent. The place was full and incredibly noisy. Her tormentor had chosen well.

She stood for a moment, squinting into the smoke and darkness. Off in a corner, an elegantly dressed man caught her eye. He motioned to her with the slightest movement of his head. She pushed her way through the crowded tables.

The man did not rise as she approached. Neither did he smile. He was far older than she had expected, and far better dressed. As she seated herself across from him, her belly turned cold. The man sat appraising her blandly, almost as if deciding whether to buy her. His face was soft and pasty, but the eyes were too intelligent. She was no match for this man.

"Good evening, Lesley," he said.

"Good evening," she heard herself say. Miserably, she heard the clear, whining panic in her voice. She knew her face must be a wreck.

The man just sat. Looking. What on God's earth was he looking for?

"I don't want to hurt you," he said suddenly. His voice seemed amazingly gentle. "I don't want to hurt you or George. I don't want your money. In fact, after these few moments together, you will never see me or hear of me again, if you tell me the truth. If you tell me the truth."

She would tell him anything.

'Do you believe me?" he said gently

She did. Terrified and trusting at once. She nodded her head like a child.

His hand came up from under the table. She flinched slightly, as if expecting a whipping. In his hand was the photograph.

"Tell me," Voslov said evenly, "about the man seated to your left."

Lesley squinted, but she really did not have to. She recognized the scene instantly.

"His name," she said, "is Harry Lime."

The man just looked at her. "Tell me," he said at last, "everything."

She shook her head.

"I . . . dated the man twice. In April."

"In March," he corrected.

His voice was fatherly, and not devoid of compassion. Something in it, however, was suggesting straightforwardly that she take particular pains to be accurate. She would sure as hell try. Whatever this little man wanted that Johnnie for, let him find him, go away and let them rot in hell together.

"Sure," she said, as if she had just remembered, "it was March. He's an American solicitor. He was a nice enough sort, good-looking, kept in good shape. He was real quiet, you know. I'd try to get him to talk about his work or his family. You know, try to lighten up the evening a little. He wouldn't get mad or anything. He'd just look at me and say, 'You don't have to do that. You don't have to talk.' A little creepy. But just a little. Mostly, I mean, he seemed nice enough."

The little man just kept looking at her. "You're doing very well," Voslov said. "It's important that you only tell me the truth. Don't make something up, just because there isn't much to say. All I want is all you know."

She nodded. Gratefully. "Well," she said, "I think that's really all. Unless you want to know how he was in bed. He was all right. Took a bit to get him started, but he was all right."

Voslov smiled patiently. "Anything particularly memorable about him?"

She thought for a moment. "His eyes. He had big, dark eyes. Bedroom eyes."

"How old a man would you say is Mr. Lime?"

She thought for a second. "I would have thought maybe early thirties. I said that to him. He just smiled and said he was older. Clean-living, he said."

The little man was smiling comfortably now. Everything was going to be fine. He pointed to the picture in front of her. "Mirabelle?" he said.

"Yes," she said. He was right.

"Good supper?"

She gave him a slight shrug. "We didn't eat there," she said.

"Oh," said the little man. His eyelids drooped slightly. He seemed to be losing interest.

"Very peculiar," she said. "He took me in there just to look for these friends of his, he said. The ones in the picture. But it turned out he didn't really know them at all."

"Really?" And the eyelids seemed to droop a little further. He really was a cute little old man, after all. She wondered how she could have thought him menacing.

"It was very funny. He spots them right away, and drags me over to their booth. He sort of shoves me in, you know, next to the Chinaman. The other chap, the big one, was a German. Harry tells him how he's always admired him and how they met once in Stockholm or somewhere. Well, it's obvious the German doesn't know Harry from Adam, but Harry insists on the honor of buying a drink. Just one drink, he says, and we'll be off. Well, the German didn't like it one bit."

The little man nodded.

"Well," he said, "you know the Jerries."

"Yes, well, I could see that Harry wanted to buy him this drink. So I flirt a little bit with the Chinaman. You know, touch his arm, smile at him. Toss the hair about. You know what I mean."

Voslov smiled with good nature. "Yes," he said, "I expect I do."

"The Chinaman wanted us to stay, but the German wouldn't hear of it. He was very polite, but Harry could see we weren't welcome. So we left."

"Yes," the man said absently, "I expect that's all you could do."

"We were only at the table for two or three minutes. God only knows who took that picture. Or why."

"God only knows," the little man agreed.

THIRTY-EIGHT

It was a very simple room, nothing more, really, than a metal box. The walls and ceiling were steel, painted green, the steel floor was covered with thick carpeting.

It was a small room. It held a round wooden table and eight chairs. The chairs were leather. They swiveled and rested on casters, which moved with difficulty on the deep pile of the carpet.

It was a room with a name. The Quiet Room.

Three men sat in the room. Hubert Longview seemed rather tired. Perhaps it was just uncertainty, perhaps impatience. He would let Woolly take the ball. Woolly would be only too eager.

Next to Longview sat a small, wiry man in full uniform. His thinning hair cropped closer than Longview's, if such a thing were possible. Four stars proudly on each shoulder. The man's hands were clasped firmly in front of him, and his eyes were fixed dead ahead. This was Gen. Otis A. "Woolly" Sharpening, Chairman of the Joint Chiefs of Staff. Woolly Sharpening knew why he was here. He prayed to God that the President was man enough for what lay ahead.

The third man was short and very square. His head seemed too large for its body, with lantern jaw and small bright eyes. He was the calmest of the three. In his stubby hand rested the bowl of a large cherrywood pipe, which he puffed with maddening slowness. The thing would always appear just on the verge of going out, but with a soft, soundless puff at the last instant, Ross Buckley would manage to keep it alive.

They had been sitting, in virtual silence, for more than an hour. Sharpening was tight enough to snap. Each moment had now become excruciating. And there was no help for it. He could only sit and wind himself tighter.

At last, without ceremony, without sound, the door opened. The three men came to their feet.

Through the door stepped William Parkens. Golden, immaculate. The President's aide let his eyes meet those of each man in turn, and for each there was a small, personal smile of greeting. Throats were cleared. Nothing was said.

Through the door came Robert Manders Cole. With the appearance of the President, the meeting had begun.

Papers now spread themselves across the table. Throats were cleared once more. Ross Buckley slowly refilled the bowl of his pipe, the curious smile of light amusement always at his lips.

Parkens turned to Longview. "Hubert . . ." he said softly, to begin in the proceedings.

Longview gestured toward Sharpening. "I think we should let Woolly start us off. He seems to have a complete appreciation of the circumstances."

Parkens looked to Sharpening. "Slowly, General," he said, "from square one."

"Right," the General's voice came a bit too loudly. He turned his eyes to meet Cole's. Squared his shoulders around to make it clear he was addressing Cole directly.

"Mr. President. Six days ago, General Longview

advised me of a piece of intelligence which had just been communicated to SIA by the Soviets. It concerned the so-called Marco Polo Alliance, and was obviously of the greatest sensitivity and urgency."

Sharpening adjusted his scrawny butt in the swivel chair with an indignant manner, but his eyes stayed on Cole.

"I strongly urged General Longview to inform you of this intelligence immediately. He said that Buck had convinced him to wait until our boys could independently verify the information. That has now been accomplished."

Cole was leaning back comfortably, his face impassive. Too comfortable for Sharpening's taste. This man was, after all, an intellectual and a politician. There would be nothing he could say to this man to truly make him see. Hubert and Buck, that was another matter. In the end, it would rest in their hands.

"There is a man," Sharpening said, "named Harry Lime. As you know, sir, he has been attached to Hubert. Apparently, SIA has been aware for some time that Lime has been in clandestine contact with representatives of the so-called Marco Polo Alliance. He attended their conventions in London and Venice. Both SIA and KGB have uncovered other contacts as well."

Sharpening had been told that the President had no prior knowledge of this. If that were true, the man had one hell of a poker face. Not a flicker, not a muscle changed position.

"Buck had prevailed upon Hubert to leave him in place. For one thing, Buck could not really believe that the man would do anything detrimental to national interest. Buck and this man go way back, apparently. And if he *were* operating as a double, we could make use of this by feeding him information of our choice. I must say that leaving the man in place was a standard and seemingly appropriate procedure, and I don't believe Buck should be faulted in this. Would have done the same thing myself."

"What," Cole asked simply, "has Harry done?"

"There have been, Mr. President, over the years, a great many studies conducted concerning possible military and para-military operations in various theaters. There are hundreds of these contingency studies, some more detailed than others. Those of us in the military and intelligence communities are aware that, in a time of crisis, the Commander-in-Chief is entitled to turn to us and say, 'What are my options, boys?' If we don't have some options ready, we've let you down."

"General," the President said very softly, and the resulting silence was powerful indeed. "Please now come to your point."

Sharpening looked as if he had been slapped, hard.

Cole's voice became supportive. "That sounded rude," Cole said. "I'm sorry. We haven't spent much time together, General. You don't know me very well. I like my information straight. If I feel someone is preparing me for what I'm about to hear, then I get the sensation that I'm being set up. Ever feel that way yourself?"

Sharpening cleared his throat. "Yes, sir, I have."

Cole smiled. His voice became still warmer. "I was never in the service, Woolly. I suspect that bothers you. I'm not going to let it bother me. You're a brilliant and dedicated man. I have all the respect in the world for who you are and what you've contributed. You're never going to let this country down. And, Woolly, neither am I."

Sharpening looked down at his hands. Cleared his throat again. "Sir, if my manner seemed improper in any way . . ."

"You were speaking," Cole said gently, "of contingency operations."

"Many years ago," Sharpening said, "a study was begun of the feasibility of launching a military operation in the Persian Gulf, for the purpose of seizing the oil fields there. Over the years, the study was refined several times. Three years ago, these studies resulted in the formulation of a contingency operation now known as Sandstorm. The plan is detailed, well thought out. It's there if we need it, that's all. Of course, we have every reason to believe that the Soviets have detailed operations of their own for the same objective."

Cole said nothing. His face was respectful, attentive. Sharpening felt more at ease.

"Harry Lime," he said, "has apparently uncovered Sandstorm, and has disclosed the plan in detail to the Saudis and other members of the Alliance."

"How," William Parkens asked quietly, "did Mr. Lime come by this information?"

"We don't know," Sharpening said. "Apparently, Mr. Lime has a history of being surprisingly good at that sort of thing."

Parkens thought on this for a moment.

Longview noticed that Parkens had easily assumed the President's place in the dialogue. This was common practice. Cole often preferred to observe you while you were speaking to Billy. It was a habit that always unnerved Longview slightly, as perhaps it was intended to. There were times, of course, when Longview admired detachment, even indirection, in an executive. Somehow, though, Longview still held the old-fashioned notion that a President was more than an executive. He was a man who stared you in the eye and said his piece. Cole could do this when prompted by style or circumstance, but directness did not come from the man's soul.

"Surely," Parkens said at last, "the Alliance could not have been entirely taken aback that such a contingency had been planned for?"

Sharpening took a short breath. "Sandstorm," he said, "was not conveyed by Lime as a remote contingency plan. He told them it would be operational within six months."

Longview had to smile to himself. Billy was such a goddam magician that everyone in the room, even Longview himself, was watching Parkens' face for reaction. As if Parkens were in command. Cole was off in the shadows a thousand miles away, watching through field glasses. He would remain the unobserved observer now for as long as it suited him.

"Why," Parkens said, "would our Harry tell such a . . . provocative . . . untruth?"

"Just a theory," Buckley spoke up, "just speculation now. Harry is a boy of some ideals, Billy, a boy who loves his country. My guess is that when he learned about the project, he figured, sweet Jesus, these crazy hawks are gonna blow up the world. I think he told the Alliance it was operational so that they would take all immediate steps to protect themselves. Thereby preventing Sandstorm from ever being tried. Thereby averting nuclear holocaust. Harry is just one of those guys who feels like saving the world every once in a while. Cycle of the moon or some such."

Parkens looked directly at Buckley. Without noticeable change of expression, the deadly cold had settled in.

"There wouldn't," Parkens said, "be even just the slightest possibility that Lime was right, after all? About Sandstorm being operational within six months?"

The slight smile never left Buckley's lips. "Not to worry," he said. "Before SIA elects to blow up the world, we always notify the Commander-in-Chief. It's in the manual."

Parkens just looked cold enough to snow. There was a long silence. "Might I suggest," the President's aide said very quietly, "that Mr. Lime be recalled for some polite inquiries?"

"He's gone," Longview said. "He disappeared ten days ago."

Parkens' eyes never wavered from Buckley.

"We've misplaced Harry for a bit," Buckley said. "He'll turn up."

Longview forced his eyes across the table to the President of the United States. Cole was watching Buckley. Eyes moving slightly over the man's face.

"Consequences?" they heard Parkens say.

Sharpening cleared his throat again. "Our intelligence," Sharpening said, again too loudly, "is still in a preliminary stage. The Soviets are ahead of us here, but they seem to be sharing information very freely. Apparently, Lime's story has been accepted by the Alliance. Previously, there had been opposition by some of their members to the use of joint military action. Mr. Lime has succeeded in unifying them."

Sharpening stopped. He looked at Parkens expectantly, as if waiting for a corroborating expression of indignation or dismay. Getting none, he had no choice but to plunge ahead anyway.

"The Alliance has activated its contingency plan for protection of Saudi and Kuwaiti oil fields. Our familiarity with the plan is fragmentary, but growing. The plan includes the introduction of nuclear weapons into the area itself. Chinese weapons, with Chinese controls and personnel. The Germans are itching to get in on the action before the Saudis become completely dependent on the Chinese. The French don't want to be left behind by the Germans."

"What, exactly," Parkens said, "is the point of placing the weapons in Arabia?"

"Where," Longview interjected, "is the most impregnable place in the world to put a nuclear missile silo? Right in the middle of the Ghawar oil field."

A small but clearly audible puff of air escaped from William Parkens.

"Every site," Longview added, "will be a major field. They call it Checkmate. If there is a nuclear exchange . . . win or lose, we lose."

The room was still. Parkens tapped the tips of his fingers together. He was lost in thought.

"Of course," Sharpening added, "they still have the warheads they can launch from China, Germany and France. But missiles in Arabian oil fields give them a crucial added dimension. At least this portion of their nuclear capability will be immune to preemptive first strike."

Longview's voice was low and soothing. He sounded almost apologetic.

"Once this stuff is in place," Longview said, "the risks of a confrontation in the area could become prohibitive. If we go over the edge, we're risking stone-cold cutoff of maybe thirty percent of our petroleum for whatever years it would take to get everything back on line. We'd go under, Billy. It can't happen."

"There's no time to waste," Sharpening threw in a beat too quickly, "because we don't know how much time we've got."

Parkens turned to him in very slow motion. "How much time we've got . . . to do what?" Parkens asked.

Sharpening's hands were squeezing each other for dear life. He was selling now, no question about it.

"Gentlemen, in three months, maybe less, the Persian

Gulf is going to be locked up tight. Forever. Then they're going to slowly squeeze us to death. If we freeze up now, we're going to watch this country go from a depression to chaos to revolution. There is no choice, gentlemen. We're going in."

"Into the Gulf?" Parkens asked incredulously.

"In the next thirty days," came the answer. "All we need is the word from you, Mr. President."

Sharpening had turned now to Cole. The General's eyes were not challenging or defiant. They were begging. They were pleading for the one word that would end it all, the decades of frustration and impotence, the humiliation of watching the nation he loved groveling at the feet of the Saudis. One word. Now. And it would be over. The boys would go in and beat the living crap out of those smug little bastards. We would mop the goddam floor with the sonsofbitches. We would have the oil. We would have our balls back. We would have a country again, goddammit. One word. Say it.

Cole was looking at Sharpening with a level gaze.

"What," they heard Parkens say, "will the Russians be doing, General, while we just send in the Marines?"

"The Russians," Longview said, with a softness bordering on intimacy, "want to go in with us."

"What the hell," Parkens nearly whispered, "is that supposed to mean?"

Longview had never seen Parkens appear to be unnerved before. He didn't think he had it in him.

It was Ross Buckley's turn to take command of the room. "The Soviets," Buckley said, "are past hysteria. China taking over the Persian Gulf? Germans pointing nukes down their throat? Listen, give the Soviets their choice of enemies and they'll take us every time. We're the fuzzy-minded bunglers. The chinks and the krauts are just a little different story. Mr. President, you think Woolly here is a bit excitable about the situation? You try to talk to the Russians about Operation Checkmate. You have to scrape them off the ceiling first."

And now Cole was ready at last to speak for himself. "Go in ... *with* the Russians?" as if he were translating from the original Aramaic.

"Comrade Lepeshkin," Buckley said quietly, "has spoken with me personally. In English, if you can believe that. In the interest of the stability and peace of the world, he said, our great nations must enter this arena immediately, and administer its resources jointly. For the good of humankind. That was his personal recommendation. He said he will have Cherny's authority within the next few days."

Cole's eyes were steady. He was digesting, analyzing. "Even if you were to discount retaliation from the Alliance," Cole said, "and who knows what they may already be capable of throwing at us. And even if you discount the chance that the Saudis could and would blow up their own fields if we invaded. Looking past all of that, how in the world could you ever trust the Soviets in such a partnership? We would be 'jointly' administering the Persian Gulf in *their* backyard. We're half a world away. We would be at an impossible disadvantage."

"No worse," Sharpening said, "than we are today. It's our nuclear deterrent that's kept the Reds from owning the Gulf for the last forty years. That wouldn't change. Remember, Berlin is still free, geography notwithstanding."

"Stakes here," Parkens said evenly, "are somewhat higher."

"Of course," Cole added, "we've neglected the moral component of this question, General."

Sharpening's eyes made it clear that this particular component had eluded him.

"I mean," Cole said straightforwardly, "it *is* the Saudis' country, after all. It's their oil. There is something, is there not, to the thought that they should be able to choose their own friends, sell their own oil to whom they wish, and defend their homeland against foreign invasion."

Sharpening looked absolutely stupefied.

"Point-of-view," Cole said softly. "We each look to our role models, Woolly. I suppose General Patton, if he were here, might say 'Mr. President, I am talking about saving America.' Now, if Thomas Jefferson were here to respond, General, he might get us into a little discussion of what America is all about in the first place."

"Mr. President," Sharpening said, holding his astonishment in very loose reins, "what exactly are you saying?"

"I'm saying, General, that I find your suggestion somewhat distasteful."

"If you want the truth," Buckley cut in, "it gets a whole lot more distasteful. See, the Russians know that by cutting us in on the Gulf, they'd be giving up more than they're getting. Hell, they always figured they were two or three local revolutions away from controlling the whole damn area without us. Now they need our cooperation, but they still want a little something extra from us in exchange for sharing the Gulf."

"Something extra . . ." Cole repeated tonelessly.

Buckley's smile had become sardonic. "They want to launch a preemptive strike on China and Germany. I can talk them out of Germany. Lepeshkin threw them in so he'd have something to give up. China's the key. We don't have to do anything, you understand. Just sit back and let them nuke the People's Republic back to ... well, hopefully, not the Stone Age ... maybe just to the Industrial Revolution. Lepeshkin says military targets only, of course. You can take that for what it's worth."

Buckley's smile had disappeared. His face was grim and his eyes were locked on Cole.

"That's the grisly trade-off, Mr. President. The Soviets get China off the map, we split up the Middle East. We set up a joint economic and military dictatorship of this planet, and get back to a nice, civilized, two-way Cold War, the way God intended. For the good of humankind, he said to me."

The President's face was chiseled in granite.

"Is that," Parkens' voice was heard, "all of it?"

"Except," Buckley said, "for the very worst. Mr. President, I don't have any choice but to tell you that, if we tell the Soviets to go fish, well, they're gonna do their fishing in the Gulf. Without us."

Cole blinked. His shoulders sagged a little. For he knew in an instant that Buckley and Longview had to be right.

"Bobby," Longview said to Cole, "you've got to put yourself in their mind for a moment. Chinese controlling the Gulf. A two-front nuclear threat from China and Europe, fueled and backed by OPEC. Increasingly isolated as the Alliance takes over the third world. It's unacceptable, Bobby. They're gonna go in, with or without us."

Cole's eyes were off somewhere in middle distance. "Hubert," he said, "what kind of time frame ...?"

"You mean," Longview said, "how long do we have to accept their offer before they decide they can't wait any longer? We'll never know until it's too late."

"No one knows," Sharpening added, "how long it would take the Alliance to set up the various elements

of Checkmate. Or how far along they are already. But
if we're going to be immobilized by indecision, in the
name of caution . . ."

Cole turned his eyes at last to Buckley. Sharpening
shut up.

"Mr. President," Buckley said, "the Soviets will act
decisively. They are scared to death. This is their
moment of truth. We have to conclude here that we
are talking not about a couple of months. It's a matter
of days."

THIRTY-NINE

Mr. and Mrs. Samuel Allen crossed the Swiss border at Basel. The immigration guard smiled as he glanced at the date in their joint passport.

"So," he said with a very German grin, "The newlyweds now take the honeymoon?"

The bride smiled. His command of the idiom was most impressive.

"Switzerland," he added, "is so perfect for such a holiday."

"Actually," the bride said, "we're going through to Italy. Samuel is taking me to Greece. To the islands."

Actually, that was not quite the case.

The happy couple left their gleaming express train at the city of Brig. It took Harry less than two hours and three thousand francs to buy everything he would need. They shared a beer and a large sausage at the station, while waiting for the tiny blue train that would take them on to Visp.

At Visp, they switched to a tram which clattered still deeper into the Alps, to the village of Stalden. It was dusk now, and Cassie was very tired. Gently, Harry insisted on catching the last bus up the mountain. There was no point in leaving names and faces with one more hotel clerk than necessary.

In darkness, the bus picked its way slowly through the steep curves. For Cassie, the ride seemed interminable, and she dozed on Harry's shoulder.

When the bus finally reached the village of Saas Fee, the air was cold and incredibly clear. Their feet sank into the snow as they gave their luggage over to the porter. The strangely long canvas bag remained strapped across Harry's back as they walked behind the porter to Hotel Wallerserhof.

They shared a large supper, and slept deeply in each other's arms.

The morning sky was crisp and pale as they set off through the village. Although Saas Fee relied heavily on its tourists, there was little skiing to attract the hordes which flocked to nearby Zermatt and St. Moritz. The village depended instead on the charm of its native architecture and the natural beauty of its setting, which were considerable.

As they reached the meadows just beyond the village, they found small boys in black cloaks leading their cattle up into the mountain. Cassie spoke to one of them in German. It seemed that there were patches higher up where grass was to be found.

And then they were alone, walking carefully through the crusted snow and over icy rock. Up into the mountain, their breath frosting in the cold. The long canvas bag was heavy across Harry's back, but he knew it would be lighter coming home.

She walked behind him and said nothing. She knew he was memorizing their trail. He stopped twice, giving her a chance to catch her breath, but they said very little as they sat in the snow. Always his eyes were moving over every tree and boulder, always checking his wristwatch against the position of the sun.

At last they left the path, came around a sharp curve and onto a clearing. Astonishingly, the village, which Cassie had not seen for more than an hour, lay in full view far below them. Hotels, shops, the meadows they had crossed on the way to the mountain.

Below and to the right, they could look down the slope of the mountain itself. Small chunks of the path they had taken were visible at several points.

Harry set the canvas bag onto the ground. He unzipped the bag and lifted out the shovel.

"Waste of time," he muttered to himself as he looked around.

He walked further off the road and stood the shovel on end behind a small tree. He returned to Cassie, brushing the snow and cold from his hands.

"I should live so long," he said with a small smile, "to ever use that thing."

She smiled back. Cassie had already taken both pairs of binoculars from the bag. They crouched at the edge, looking down at the village.

"How often do we come up here?" she asked.

"Every day," he said. "The same way, the same time. We do everything the same each day. At the same time."

She was watching the tiny clearing at the far end of the village, where the bus would stop.

"When does the first bus arrive?" she said softly.

"Thirty-five minutes."

She said nothing. Crouched in the snow, watching through the heavy glasses, she looked so frail and small.

"There are four buses each day," he said. "Five on weekends. We watch them all."

"You're sure he's coming?"

"I'm not sure. But I'm right. He's coming. Not today or tomorrow. Take him maybe a week."

He did not say that it would be easy for Reika because they had changed passports only once. If he had been alone, Samuel Allen would have become Walter Clarke. Then Terrence Wilkes, then Philip Cooke. And he would have moved differently, lived differently.

He did not say any of this. But he thought about it all the time. How stupidly he had increased the risk to both of them by bringing her along. And how glad he was that she was here.

"Why are you so sure he'll come on the bus?" she asked.

"I'm not sure."

"You're just right," she said with a smile. "Tell me how you know."

"It's the only public transportation up here. Otherwise, he would have to rent a car, which hardly anyone does. He's trained to do the normal thing. He picks the least conspicuous alternative at every turn. Besides, he's not worried about being spotted. He doesn't dream I know what he looks like."

"Then why does he think you ran?"

"Lime's Crisis. Whatever he was sent to kill me for. I could have a hundred reasons for running. But he doesn't think I know his face."

"Why not?"

"Maybe two or three people in the world know his face. The picture I saw was one of a kind, and he probably doesn't even know it exists. He's killed dozens of people over twenty years, and no one's ever known his face before."

"You sound pretty sure."

"I'm pretty sure."

"That's good enough for me," she said softly.

She put the glasses down and looked at Harry's face. "You don't seem nervous," she said. "Not the least bit."

"I'm scared to death," he said simply.

"Don't look it."

"Haven't you noticed? I stopped whistling in the shower."

She smiled up at him. "So be scared," she said. "You're allowed. We're allowed."

"I keep thinking about John Knowles," he said. "All the things he told me. He said that when you have to kill a man, that's business as usual. But when it's reversed, when someone is out to kill you, you have to take that very, very personally. You have to let your anger and your terror come right to the surface of your mind. You have to hate him."

He was staring over the edge at nothing in particular.

"Hate and panic are going to be there anyway. If you don't keep them right in front of your eyes, you'll trip over them."

Then he was quiet for a long time, his eyes still staring down off the mountain.

"You just keep thinking," he said at last, "of all the things this man will take away. All the people. Little . . . times you've had . . ."

He was quiet. He was saying the rest behind his eyes.

She watched his face. For two weeks now, she had been fighting what she already knew. This man was tender and loving with her. He was a soft man. Gentle and confused in the familiar way of the over-bright. He did have some dark knowledge from the world of these other men, the men who would kill them. But he was no match for them, not in that world. He was far beyond his depth. And so, she and Harry would die.

It must have been inevitable for weeks. From the moment the man Reika was chosen. Her own death had begun then. Nothing she would dream or do would stop it. Not today or tomorrow, Harry had said. Take him maybe a week.

Cassie turned the heavy glasses toward the clearing below. Her heart pounding now, she waited for the bus.

FORTY

Vladimir Cherny ran his slender fingers the full length of his nose. Until they reached his eyes. He closed his lids and massaged the eyeballs gently with his fingertips. As if they would help him see more clearly.

The General Secretary of the Communist Party sat in the darkened study. His mind raced to digest and analyze and sort.

With a small motion of his hand, he called his private secretary to his side.

"Lepeshkin," Cherny said. "And Voslov. Please ask the others to reassemble at ten o'clock tomorrow."

In a matter of moments, the two men were seated before him. Cherny's mind was clear. He was fully in focus. Yet, he was lost. Lepeshkin was unusually calm. He spread his massive palms upward, almost in a gesture of resignation.

"It is a decision," Lepeshkin said, "which comes to us already made. It is for us to seize the moment. To turn this pivotal instant of history to our will. This is the moment we were born for."

Cherny's eyes searched Lepeshkin's. The huge man smiled supportively. He had never dreamed Cherny could look so shaken.

"If we hesitate," Lepeshkin said softly, "the Americans will go into the Gulf without us. Their panic is absolute. All they can see is inevitable strangulation as the Alliance closes the flow of mother's milk. I know we are not accustomed to decisive action from the Americans. But they will be decisive here. They have no choice."

Cherny's fingers interlocked with one another. He shook his head, not in disagreement, clearly, but in disbelief.

"One swift stroke," Lepeshkin nearly whispered, "and the Chinese nuclear threat is obliterated. The Alliance disintegrates in that moment. We occupy the Gulf with the Americans. We share its wealth in stable coexistence, until our natural geographic advantage can be most effectively asserted."

"Other advantages come to mind," Voslov said.

Voslov's voice seemed to float toward Cherny, as if from a considerable distance.

"For decades, the influences of China and OPEC have been most detrimental to our role of leadership in Africa, Latin America and, of course, Asia itself. That could change rather dramatically under Nikolai's scenario."

Lepeshkin looked at the little man and smiled his assent.

"Then, too," Voslov seemed now almost to be murmuring to himself, "if our intelligence is accurate, the choices may well be all but made for us here. There is certainly that smell of destiny that Nikolai has alluded to."

"The time," Lepeshkin said softly, "is so very short. We may be dealing with a matter of only a few days."

There was silence for a moment.

"Nikolai," Voslov's tone now seemed quite weary, "what is your personal estimate of the damage we would sustain from Chinese retaliation to our strike?

Military, industrial? Moscow, other population centers?"

Lepeshkin shifted his bulk. The KGB Chairman's tone remained even and objective.

"As General Orzhurmov stated, that would be impossible to predict with any accuracy. But if we ever intend to eliminate this problem, the risk and the damage will never again be as low as it is today. China's retaliatory capacity would continue to increase, even if left to their own devices. With European technology and OPEC capital, this could be significantly accelerated. Then, too, if the future were to bring the Chinese a protective treaty with the Americans, as we have long suspected, or should I say 'feared' . . ."

The silence settled over the three men.

"Nikolai," came Voslov's drowsy voice at last, "these are fearful things you have proposed. And yet, one returns constantly to the idea that our time for reflection is swiftly being overtaken by events. The premises that will shape, perhaps impel, our decisions, are the product of your own intelligence efforts. Largely, the product of your man, Correlli, I believe, in Rome."

Lepeshkin's blood was suddenly rising. He fought to keep his hands still.

"What, Andrei, exactly is your point?"

"So much," Voslov said, "weighs on the reliability of this one man. I would think that Signor Correlli should be brought to Moscow. With the stakes you have proposed, I would like the opportunity of interrogating this man. Personally."

"That would be most inadvisable," Lepeshkin said. A beat too quickly.

"Why?" Secretary Cherny asked simply.

"This man is the most valuable agent we have in the field today. Any irregularity, anything that could bring him under suspicion, and his future usefulness to us would be ended."

"Surely," Voslov said, "you have no further need of this man. He has done his job heroically. What 'future usefulness' could you be speaking of?"

Lepeshkin could offer only the first thought which tumbled into his mind.

"In two weeks, the Alliance begins its scheduled meetings in Vienna. Correlli has been chosen to attend. I would say it is imperative that we do nothing to endanger the flow of that product."

Voslov's drooping lids opened slightly. He nodded as if he suddenly understood.

"The Vienna product," he said, "could be that important?"

"It could be most significant," Lepeshkin answered solemnly. "Of course, we cannot know until we have it."

Voslov nodded. He was obviously in complete agreement.

"Then by all means," Voslov mused, "we must wait for it."

He turned to his old and good friend. "We must tell the Americans," he said, "that we cannot respond to their proposal until after Vienna. We shall examine Signor Correlli and his Vienna product. And we shall give Mr. Buckley our answer by, let us say, the fifth of January. Americans respect dates and specificity."

Voslov turned back to Lepeshkin and locked eyes.

"The Americans will wait that long, Nikolai. They need us. They will wait."

Cherny's throat cleared in the distance.

"Andrei is right, Nikolai. Tell Buckley we are favorably disposed. But we will not decide until the fifth."

FORTY-ONE

Reika's feet moved lazily through the snow. It was not the stride of a man with a purpose, only a man, lost in thought, enjoying an aimless stroll.

His hands were thrust deep into his pockets. His smile was loosely in place. His eyes seemed to casually drink in the beauty of the mountain as he walked.

Reika had arrived on the last bus the previous evening. He had registered at the Hotel Dom. He had checked his bags and taken a tourist's walk through the village. Stopping in each hotel, he visited lobbies, bars and dining rooms. His fourth stop had been Hotel Wallerserhof. The dining room was nearly filled. In a far corner, Harry and Cassie were just beginning their salad.

Reika returned to the Wallerserhof in the morning. He read his paper in an overstuffed chair to one side of the fireplace as the couple shared their breakfast. He did not seem to notice as they passed through the lobby.

He had watched them from a great distance as they passed through the meadow and headed up into the mountain. Since Harry wore a backpack, Reika knew that they would be on the mountain for some time. He waited an hour before crossing the meadows.

The couple left a distinctive trail in the snow. They were alone. They were not using the main path.

This, then, would be the proper time for Reika to finish with this matter. It was just as well, since he had less than a week to complete the other assignment in Vienna.

Reika had been on the mountain for well over an hour. The tracks were fresher now. It was evident that their pace had slowed considerably, and that Reika was gaining ground on them. He had just passed the second place where they had obviously stopped to rest. Reika had not seen another soul since he started up the mountain. The silencer would not even be necessary, although it was already in place.

As he walked, his thoughts turned to the assignment in Vienna. A less interesting subject, to be sure, but far more of a challenge. Rarely was Reika called upon to kill another of his kind. Of course, the man was not nearly in Reika's class, but a killer and a professional, nonetheless.

The assignment in Vienna would require some thought, and no little delicacy. The man was indeed a professional, and therefore a paranoid. He would suspect that he was hunted, even though there would be no reason or indication. He would have the tools and the training to protect himself. There would be no complexity of mind or spirit in this man. There would be only the simplicity and directness of a creature bred to act.

Reika stopped.

His smile stayed in place, and instinctively he reached for a cigarette. As if to explain to the unseen eyes that were not there why he had stopped for a moment in the snow.

Reika had not really heard a sound. It was more the fleeting sensation of a subtle change of air pressure.

Just the barest wisp of a feeling that something had changed, if ever so slightly.

And so, Reika had stopped. Vienna had gone from his mind now. Smile easily in place, cigarette coming to his lips, his eyes moved naturally about the mountainside. He wondered in which pocket he would find a match.

It was Reika's last thought.

There was a sound, but there was no way for Reika to truly hear it. It arrived more slowly than the object that blew away three quarters of his skull.

Bone and skin and tiny bits of brain tissue scattered and fell to the snow. The rest of Reika stood in place for what seemed an incredible length of time. Then crumpled. Limp and liquid, as if there were no bones beneath the flesh.

And somewhere up the hill, the hands and cheek of Harry Lime were frozen to the rifle stock. He was still looking through the telescopic sight, but the image now danced and swam before him.

The sound of the shot seemed to take forever to die away. Harry thought that all of Switzerland must have heard it. Must be running to its source.

From deep within him, there was a lurch. There was only an instant of wondering whether he could fight it. Then everything in his stomach rushed up through his esophagus, past his lips, and spilled over his arms and hands. Over the rifle and the rock on which it rested, staining the snow.

Cassie was running to him now, from her hiding place farther up the trail. At the sound of her steps, Harry's hands released the rifle. He staggered to his feet.

She fell into his arms, crying and holding him. When he looked into her face, he saw such inexpressible joy and relief. To her eyes, it was suddenly over. Over and finished forever. They had won.

Andy Maclennon had saved their lives this once. Now they were alone. There would come the moment when she realized it was not over, could never be over. The men who sent Reika still lived. He could never kill them all.

He looked into her brimming eyes and summoned a smile for her. For this moment, let it be over.

He pushed his smile into something tender and playful.

"Piece of cake," he said softly. His breakfast was still freezing into crusted slush over his arms and hands.

"My hero," she said, sniffling and giggling and trying to wipe the crud from his hands with her own sleeve.

Harry dismantled the rifle into its three separate pieces and returned them to his backpack. The pack would be left, for the moment, buried under rock and snow.

They picked their way down the path toward the body. If others arrived, Harry and Cassie were shocked tourists who had heard something almost like a rifle shot. But there was no one.

Reika's body lay in the pile Harry had last seen through the telescopic sight. He would have thought the freezing weather would have stopped the blood. But blood was everywhere.

Cassie busied herself kicking and piling new snow over the area.

Harry stripped off his gloves and quickly went through Reika's pockets. If he were to have only a moment alone with the corpse, this was the first priority.

There was a passport wallet. There was a slim

leather notebook. A hotel key. Harry pocketed these, and left the rest in place.

Cassie had finished grooming the area. Amazingly, it seemed utterly unmarked.

Harry had pulled Reika's coat over what was left of his head, to reduce the loss of blood as they moved the body. He dug his hands under Reika's armpits. Cassie took the legs, which were, of course, much lighter.

Harry knew that there would be little explanation for why even two frightened and confused tourists would be dragging this body uphill. Harry figured the trip would take ten minutes, and he would just have to pray to somebody's God that no one showed up for ten minutes.

It took twenty-five.

They cleared away the loose branches. They placed Reika in the shallow grave Harry had dug during his first few trips up the mountain. They put the shovel in last, after the hole was nearly filled, and finished covering the grave with their hands.

They strolled back down the trail, searching for spots that needed grooming. They found none. The only clothing with any bloodstains appeared to be Harry's parka. He folded this under his arm and they headed back toward the village.

Harry sat in a steaming bathtub, room service brandy at his side. Harry was reading.

Reika's passport. Christopher Martin, Albany, New York. Corroborating identification. Notebook meticulously prepared as part of Reika's cover. Appointments and notes of a merchant who imported children's toys and clothing. All incomprehensible, unusable.

With one exception.

At the bottom of the next-to-last page was scrawled, "H. Lime." And next to it, another name that Harry

knew only too well. And below the two names was
written: "Imperial Hotel—Vienna—Dec. 21–27."

At the dinner hour, Harry strolled to the Hotel
Dom. He let himself into Reika's room, bolted the
door behind him and slowly took the place apart.
There was nothing.

Harry took all of Reika's things and packed them.
He took the bags downstairs and left them in the
lobby, among the luggage of a Japanese tour bus that
would be departing in the morning.

The next afternoon, as Harry's train headed east
through the Alps, a chambermaid brought a large envelope to the front desk of the Hotel Dom. In it was
the key, several large bills and a note from Mr. Martin
apologizing for his hasty departure. Any change from
the large bills should be distributed among the staff
as a tip for their gracious service.

The desk clerk gave a little money to the cashier,
put the rest in his pocket, and Mr. Martin's visit had
never happened.

FORTY-TWO

Yuri Mikhailovich stood in the blackened room. There was no sound.

Voslov's aide stood motionless, listening for breathing. Then Yuri realized, with a sudden fear, that he was waiting too long. The man might have awakened when Yuri slipped through the door, might already be reaching for a weapon.

Yuri snapped his flashlight on. Its beam caught the body, then the face. The man stirred, rolled slightly to one side, closed eyes tensing against the light.

The eyes came open, blinked. Large and dark and remarkably calm, as if the visit was not wholly unexpected.

"Mr. Lime?" Yuri said evenly. He held the light directly at the eyes.

"Yes," came the answer.

"Would you please sit up? Hands raised above your head."

Yuri's voice was bland, as if making only a polite and reasonable request.

There was the slightest stirring beneath the covers. But there was no time for Yuri to notice, no time to connect that movement to the unnatural calmness in the man's eyes, no time to think that he *had* been awake these few moments.

The sound and the flash of the shot, then the second shot, burst from beneath the covers.

Before he could even realize that he had not been hit, Yuri had reflexively fired four times at the figure in the bed.

The first shot disappeared into the bedding. The second reached the throat, and a graceful spout of blood arched an amazing distance. The third found a pillow. The fourth tore away a left cheek and ear.

There was a twitch of a shoulder in the light's beam. Then stillness and blood.

Standing, sweating, his pulse pounding, Yuri knew miserably that he had failed. He stared at the dead body for a long and forbidden moment. Voslov would tell him that it did not matter. That he no longer needed this man. But Yuri would never again be certain that he was trusted. He did not know how he would live with that.

FORTY-THREE

The suite was exquisite and ornate. The armoire, the tables, the Chinese rugs, each piece rare and perfectly chosen.

Wide double windows opened onto the darkness. In three hours, there would be dawn. The black beyond the windows would become the massive shape of the Staatsoper, the Vienna State Opera. In six hours, thousands would be filling the Kärntnerstrasse below, lifting their boots through the snow of Vienna's most celebrated shopping street. There were, after all, only three days until Christmas.

Voslov sat beneath the light of his single lamp, his hands folded patiently across his belly. An elegant grandfather clock was ticking softly.

Voslov sat and waited for the sleeping figure to begin to stir against the drugs.

And to Yuri, as he sat attentively in the darkness near the doorway, he had never seen his master quite so alert. Quite so intent. For Yuri, the hours had passed with deadening slowness. But for Voslov, they had been an opportunity to reflect, to sort out the entire affair and order the events, the triumphs, in his mind.

At last, the figure in the bed began to move.

"Ring the other room," Voslov said quietly to Yuri. "Ask them please to wake the girl and ring us back. Remind them to apologize for disturbing her sleep."

Voslov kept his eyes on the man slowly returning to consciousness. To Yuri, the gaze seemed almost fatherly. There was the inescapable sensation that Voslov knew this man in some other time or life.

At last the eyes opened, large and dark and uncomprehending.

"It's all right, Harry," Voslov said so softly. "It's over now. You are with friends. Improbable friends. Still, friends."

The voice was British upper class. Harry did not remember that he had seen the face among the hundreds of photographs and dossiers Longview had provided. There was no trace of accent. The man could be English.

"How do you feel?" Voslov asked.

"Angry."

Voslov chuckled slightly. "I mean, do you feel sick or dizzy?"

Harry just looked at him. His eyes now had picked up Yuri in the far corner, a dark figure, large and strong.

"Forgive us," Voslov said, "for using force. One Harry Lime has already died in a distressing accident. We were more careful with you."

Strangely, this was Harry's first indication that the round little man might be a friend after all.

There was a sharp double buzzing sound. Harry jumped. The sounds repeated. It was the phone next to Harry's bed.

"I think it's for you," Voslov said.

Harry reached for the receiver. Voslov watched Harry's face as he listened. Tense at first. Then a grudging smile. Then a larger one.

"Just so long," Harry said at last, "as they don't stick us with the tab for these rooms. From what I can see of this one, we'd be in big trouble."

Harry listened again. Kept smiling. "Look," he said, "sleep through breakfast. You can buy me an expensive lunch. Okay?"

Listening again. "Me too," he said tenderly. "Very much."

Harry replaced the receiver. He looked up at Voslov in near-wonderment.

"Is the lady all right?" Voslov asked. "I was sorry to wake her, but I knew you would want to talk."

Harry smiled broadly. "She's not sleeping," he said. "She's playing cards with your people. She says their English is lousy, but their German is fine. She taught them a card game called 'tonk.' She's beating the pants off them, and having the time of her life. She says she's won almost a hundred bucks, and she's not quitting till she has enough to buy our freedom."

"This is the Hotel Bristol," Voslov said. "She is four rooms up the hall. You are not prisoners. You can leave any time you wish."

Harry smiled a little sadly.

"She didn't mean buy our freedom from *your* government. She meant from ours."

Voslov returned the smile.

"You are Russian," Harry said. Voslov nodded, his eyes traveling up to Yuri.

Yuri offered a strong hand and helped Harry from the bed. He took Harry to a soft reading chair next to Voslov.

Yuri produced two brandy snifters and poured from a bottle of Rémy which had been waiting in the lamplight. Then Yuri stepped back into the darkness.

"My name is Andrei," Voslov said. "May I call you Harry?"

Harry's eyes drifted off into another thought. He was quiet for a moment.

"You know," he said, "there's only one man in the world who I'm sure is my friend. His name is Andy."

"Now there are two," Voslov said.

Harry nodded. Against all training, there was something in the little man that made Harry feel this was true.

"We have both been victims," Voslov said, "of a great misunderstanding, Harry. You have been most instrumental in getting the matter sorted out."

"Happy to have been of service," Harry said.

Voslov smiled again. Yuri could not remember ever seeing him smile so often and so easily.

"We are all in your debt, Harry. You have saved us from considerable inconvenience."

"Inconvenience?"

Voslov waved a pudgy hand. "World War III. Could have been a dreadful nuisance."

Voslov nodded to Yuri, who walked to Harry's side. He handed Harry a photograph.

Harry looked at the photo. Four figures seated in a restaurant. Three men and a woman.

"Do you know the man at the right hand side of that picture?" Voslov asked.

Harry nodded.

"He is dead," Voslov said.

"That's a pity," Harry said, in a voice gone cold and far away. "I was hoping to speak with him."

Voslov nodded in agreement. "It was an accident. Yuri was sent to collect him, but things took an unfortunate turn. It's not important. In a few days, we should have that information from our end. We're working on it now."

Harry was still staring at the picture.

"His name was Davis Taradan," Harry said quietly. "He worked for Hubert Longview."

Voslov let him think for a while. "I said that we were both victims, Harry. But I had a rather critical advantage. I have friends in high places. You seem burdened with quite the opposite circumstance."

Harry studied the little man. "Until now," Harry said with some conviction.

There was enough trust, Voslov decided, to begin. "Do you remember the Cold War, Harry?"

"The end of it, I guess."

Voslov looked down at the hands folded in his lap. "We were enemies," he mused, "your country and mine. That has been undisputed history. Enemies. But in a certain way, no ally ever brought another greater bliss."

Harry did not understand.

"Each of us," Voslov went on, "ruled half the world. Content. Secure. Our enmity made it so. Two nuclear umbrellas, and everybody had to scramble under one or the other. Economic primacy and nuclear monopoly. That is what we used to share, Harry. And to the minds of some, those were very golden days."

Harry's mind was now working forward to Marco Polo. "Now," Harry said, "the Arabs have all the money, the Germans and Japanese have the technology, and nearly everybody has the bomb."

"Most particularly," Voslov said, "the Chinese. It's an untidy world now, Harry. Some people in your country and some people in mine decided to turn the clock back about forty years."

"The Condominium Conspiracy," Harry said, almost to himself. "America and Russia combine to rule the earth. Could have worked very nicely forty years ago."

Voslov was nodding.

"Now," Voslov said, "the Arabs have the money and the oil. The Chinese and Germans and French have the bomb. Now the world seems very different. What has General Longview told you about the Marco Polo Alliance?"

Harry blinked. John Knowles was stuck in his throat. The little man was, of course, a Red.

"I know it exists," Harry said. "Tell me what it is."

"We have some men in custody now," Voslov said easily, "from our own intelligence community. From KGB. Men very high. We are finally learning, through diligent interrogation, what that Alliance truly is. And what it is not."

Diligent interrogation. John Knowles' stories about the deep questioners flooded over Harry. Men very high. Was Nikolai Lepeshkin himself on the rack? Did this soft little man have a rack waiting for Harry? For Cassie?

"The Alliance," Voslov said quietly, "is an economic community. Very dangerous to our interests and yours, to be sure. Very real and, in the long run, perhaps very deadly. That is what it is. More important, however, is what it is not. We shall come to that in a few moments."

The feeling that this man was telling the truth returned to Harry. Not from the words, as Knowles used to say, but from the music. Harry could not shake that feeling. But he was not through fighting it either.

Voslov sighed. His fingers came to his lips. "Adolf Hitler died when I was twelve years old. He didn't invent the Big Lie, Harry. But he used it well. If the lie is big enough, consistent enough, if it comes from someone very high . . ."

His look was almost playful.

"Intelligence services," he said, "are in a unique position. They control, no, they create, what we call our knowledge of our enemies. We may mistrust their accuracy from time to time, but we cannot permit ourselves to mistrust their basic intent. If we thought they might actually conspire to deceive us, well, we couldn't function at all. We would be afraid to put a foot in any direction. Do you see what I mean?"

Harry did.

"My responsibilities," Voslov said, "include some modest degree of oversight with respect to KGB. Several months ago, I became aware that two secret files were being kept concerning the activities of an American agent code named Harbinger. This agent, Harbinger, was identified as Harry Lime."

"Agent?" Harry asked mildly.

"This agent," Voslov continued, "had attended meetings of the Marco Polo Alliance in London this past March. Lime was identified as the man in that photo."

Voslov watched Harry's eyes, and waited patiently for Harry to assimilate the information.

"It was eventually decided," Voslov said, "to show the photograph to your government. Ross Buckley was appalled. He could not believe that Harry Lime was, in fact, capable of treason. At one time, apparently, you were his friend."

"Has that changed?" Harry asked.

"I knew, of course, that Mr. Buckley had been less than forthright with us."

"Did you?"

"The man in the photo was not Harry Lime. Whether or not KGB knew this, Buckley obviously did."

There was a brief silence, during which Harry did not smile.

"How," he said, "did *you* know?"

Voslov pursed his lips. "Standard reference work," he said. "Harvard Law School Yearbook, 1980. Always at my bedside."

"Not my best likeness," Harry added.

Voslov nodded absently. He seemed to be gathering his thoughts. Harry took this simply as the accustomed manner of an interrogator. The appearance of premeditation was always to be avoided.

"The interesting question," Voslov mused, "was whether Comrade Lepeshkin was actually in on Mr. Buckley's little joke."

Voslov chose this moment to sample the Rémy. He swirled the liquid gently. He spoke down into it.

"My wife passed away," Voslov said.

He looked up at Harry's face. For a moment, it seemed to Voslov that Harry's eyes were damp. In the next moment, he was sure of it. He did not understand why a stranger would reflexively share his grief. Nonetheless, it was there, and Voslov felt the jolt of a sudden bond.

"I lost my wife," Harry said, "two years ago. She left. She didn't die. But I thought I would."

Loss and anger at once, Voslov thought. That was probably worst of all. Loving, and wanting to stop loving.

"My wife died," Voslov said again, voice now softening noticeably at the word, "and so I took myself away to England and did some fieldwork. I used to be a fieldman long ago, Harry. Were you ever?"

He was just a soft little man. Old, and soon older. And his Jennylime had died. Had lived her life with him and loved him and died.

"Long ago," Harry said.

For so young a man, Voslov wondered, could anything really be long ago?

"My fieldwork confirmed my suspicions," Voslov

aid. "The Harry Lime files were a lie. KGB was preparing the lie for the Presidium, and SIA was telling the same lie in Washington."

Patiently, Voslov told each step of the story. The fear that Marco Polo was a nuclear alliance. The treachery of Harry Lime warning the Alliance of a mythical Gulf invasion. The Alliance response of Checkmate, moving nuclear weapons to Arabian oil fields. The appeal for America and Russia to join forces before it was too late. Time slipped, as Voslov laid each brick carefully in its place.

"Lepeshkin told us the Americans are terrified. They are convinced that they must invade now or die slowly. They will go into the Gulf without us if we refuse to cooperate. SIA fed the same story, in reverse, of course, to your President."

Harry stared at the little man.

"But you've stopped it?" he said, hearing the edge of disbelief in his own voice.

"Yes," Voslov said simply, "we have stopped it."

"How?"

"I sat with Secretary Cherny. We talked. It was a long night. He believed me, I think, from the first. At the end, he could believe nothing else."

Harry's eyes seemed far away once more.

"Just that," Harry said at last. "One man believing another."

"Twice," Voslov said quietly. "The Secretary telephoned President Cole on their direct line. It was the only time they have ever spoken. Vladimir's English is only adequate, and I offered to interpret. But he insisted that your President hear his voice alone. The call lasted nearly an hour. Of course, I could hear only Vladimir's end."

Here, Voslov's eyes drifted out into the blackness beyond the window.

"He spoke," Voslov said, "so simply and so directly
Each detail, each deception, in its turn. Quietly, with
such conviction. It was, Harry, a very unusual mo
ment. One Head of State was speaking to another, hi
enemy. He was telling the truth, so completely, so
powerfully, that there was no question it would be
believed. The burden they shared made them closer
than brothers, Harry. For that single moment, made
them one fear, one responsibility, one vision."

Harry understood. As he understood the momen
that made Voslov one with him.

"The Secretary told your President that we were
detaining Lepeshkin and others for intensive interro
gation. He was confident that this would uncover all
conspirators of both sides. He counseled the Presi
dent to discuss this with no one until then."

Harry's mind was locked into a picture. Robert
Manders Cole, face frozen, alone in a room with a
telephone in his hand. Alone with a stranger's voice.

"How," Harry said at last, "did you find me?"

The little man refilled their glasses.

"Lepeshkin said his chief informer was an agent he
had placed in Italy. A man named Correlli. I asked for
the privilege of a personal conversation with this man
to independently evaluate his information. Lepeshkin
told us that Correlli would be attending the Alliance
meetings in Vienna, and that he should not be com
promised."

Voslov gently touched Harry's glass with his own.

"I feared that some accident might befall Signor
Correlli before he left Vienna, so Yuri ran a check of
hotel bookings. I found that Signor Correlli would be
staying at the Sacher. Also, it appeared that a Mr
Harry Lime had been booked into the Imperial. This
of course, was your friend, Mr. . . . ."

"Taradan."

"Yes," Voslov said. "Well, we picked up Correlli upon his arrival. Mr. Taradan, we tracked for a while. I could not help but notice that a charming young couple was tracking him as well."

Harry grinned and shook his head.

"Thanks for the 'young.' We hadn't intended to be quite so conspicuous."

"You were most professional, actually. Your lady as well. But, I'm an old fieldman, as I said, and there are no new tricks. You haven't aged all that much from your school photograph. A compliment, no doubt, to the purity of your living habits."

"No doubt," Harry agreed.

"Well," Voslov smiled, "my calendar of personal interviews was filling up rather smartly. Still, I thought I could squeeze in a Lime or two."

Harry winced.

"Hard," Voslov admitted, "to play words in an alien language."

Harry lifted his glass in a toast.

"Why," Voslov said, "would the SIA have sent their imposter to Vienna?"

"To kill him," Harry said reflexively. And hearing his own voice, he knew that his trust in this little man was now complete. "They sent a man to kill me," Harry added. "I found a notebook on the man's body. Taradan was his next assignment."

Voslov nodded slowly. On the man's body, Harry had said. Difficult to think of Harry besting a professional assassin. Very difficult.

"One wonders," Voslov said, almost whispering to himself. "One wonders why."

Harry shrugged.

"Same reason," Harry offered, "that Lepeshkin would have killed Correlli. Harry Lime had to be unavailable for interrogation. Since they couldn't be certain they

would catch up with me, they set up Taradan as
fall-back. One dead Harry Lime was as good as an
other. Doing it at the Vienna conference just added to
their story."

Voslov's eyelids drooped. Harry thought the old man
must be tired.

"With all respect," Voslov said kindly, "I doubt
that they were concerned about 'catching up' with
you. When those gentlemen send their falcon after a
fieldmouse, the mouse is presumed dead."

Harry smiled.

"No offense intended," Voslov said. "They obvi
ously underestimated their prey. That is why we are
sharing a brandy this early morning. My point is
simply, that Taradan was not a fall-back. They were
going to kill him anyway. They simply wanted to kill
him under the most suitable name in the most suit
able place."

Harry watched the little man's eyelids fall nearly
shut. He decided that he would like to work for this
man someday, in some life. He would like to sit and
sip Rémy and watch.

"The suggestion," Voslov murmured, "is that this
may be a very tight little conspiracy after all. Perhaps
a very few men at the top. Perhaps only one or two on
each side. Most of the errands were run by function
aries who did not understand what they were aiding
Taradan, of course, played the imposter, so that
Lepeshkin could create his little file on Harry Lime
So Taradan knew the conspirators, at least the Ameri
cans. If the conspirators were spread throughout SIA
and the Pentagon, why bother eliminating one man?
No, if he was worth the killing, it might mean that he
was their only spear-carrier. Killing him, they closed
off access to their names."

"Buckley and Longview," Harry said. "And no one else?"

"The smaller the circle," Voslov mused, "the more secure. The more effective. Give us time. Lepeshkin will give us the names."

Harry was silent now. Some men tell the truth under torture, Knowles had said. Some do not. Some just die.

"How did you kill him?" Voslov asked mildly.

Harry's eyes opened wide, startled from his thoughts.

"The falcon," Voslov said.

"I blew his fucking head off," Harry said. "I blew his brains to jelly."

"You sound angry," the little man said. "It wasn't personal, Harry. It wasn't personal at all."

And for the briefest flash, Harry wondered if Reika had turned in the years since Andy's photograph, had turned to work for the opposition. Had been sent by this soft little man to kill him in the snow. Harry shook his shoulders and cursed his goddam paranoid brain. He knew it was not so, but the chill was slow to leave him.

"It was my life," Harry said. "And the girl's. That's as personal as it can get."

"And you want revenge," Voslov said.

The little man's eyes were sad and kind. He was not Harry's killer. He was Harry's friend. Harry felt a stab of guilt for his moment of mistrust.

"That makes you dangerous, Harry. To yourself and to your lady. You are free to go, of course. But I would beg you to accept my protection. Until we have the names for certain. Until we have them all."

It was first light. Harry looked out the double windows to the shapes of the city, beginning to form.

Harry's mind was in the darkness of a void. Below

was the earth, blue and white. And spinning slowly in the blackness, a flat, gleaming rectangle, the sun filling the mirrors along its surface. There was no sound. Only the blinding light of the mirrors, and the lazy turning as the earth passed beneath.

If Harry were to die in the next few days, to whom would he leave this? To whom would he leave the legacy of Norris Steingart, of their afternoon in the garden at Cornell? There was no choice. He would have to leave it with the soft little man. And in simple truth, he could not have chosen better.

Voslow was watching Harry's eyes and waiting patiently.

"The crisis," Harry said finally, "Marco Polo. It goes on."

Voslov pressed his stubby fingers together.

"The threat of violence is over," he said. "But the Alliance exists as an economic cartel. Their power is just as deadly. We have eliminated a wrong solution. We are still searching for the right one."

Harry looked down into the brandy snifter cradled in his fingers. The flat golden rectangle twirled slowly in the amber waters, and Harry smiled. Smiled as if there truly were a God in Heaven, to give him so perfect a moment.

"Do you know," Harry said, "of a man named Norris Steingart?"

Voslov did not.

"He's a physicist," Harry said, "an expert in microwave energy. He told me that the answer has been with us for a long time."

"The answer?" Voslov said.

Harry locked into the older man's eyes. Held them.

"He told me," Harry said, "that only the politics were impossible."

Harry put the snifter back upon the table.

"I'm hungry," he said. "There's a warm little kitchen on the Ring that never closes. Could you eat?"

"Always," Voslov said with a wistful smile.

"I'm buying your breakfast," Harry said. "We'll have a little talk about the impossible."

FORTY-FOUR

Warner Alden thrust his hands deeply into the pockets of his Burbury. Tensing for the blast of wind, he turned onto Fifty-third Street. All the way from Madison to Lex, he cursed his shoes, his clammy socks, the frozen tip of his nose and his dumb-ass secretary.

Turning down Lex, the wind eased a little, and Warner realized that he would make it to Aldo's after all. Why anyone in his right mind would walk five blocks in weather like this for a plate of linguini, and why Jessica couldn't have talked the dumb-ass captain into sending it over to the office in the first place, Warner had no earthly idea.

Once inside, the perfume of the garlic and civilized murmur of uptown corporate law at lunch warmed him somewhat.

Piero helped him with his coat and observed that he had lost a few pounds. Weaving through the tables, Warner had a chance to squeeze the shoulder of asshole Charlie Bates and admire the brunette who was neither Charlie's wife, secretary nor regular girlfriend.

Seated alone near the far corner, Warner managed to mention a vodka gimlet to the captain before his butt hit the chair. He unfolded his napkin, closed his eyes and tried to bid a ghastly morning adieu. There

304

would be two quiet gimlets, alone. Maybe three. Linguini in white, plus a blueberry cheesecake. One sturdy Havana for the road, and the hike back through the wind to that bloodbath of a meeting with Tompkins.

Three gimlets. This was a three-gimlet day, if ever God fashioned one.

A hand touched Warner's shoulder from the rear. Before he could look up, the man had seated himself, unbidden, across the table. The man smiled pleasantly, but said nothing. Warner's annoyance was overtaken by embarrassment. He absolutely knew the face Almost absolutely.

"It's Harry," the man said, reading Warner's mind. "Harry Lime."

Of course it was.

"You're looking terrific," Harry said. "Dropped some weight."

As a matter of fact, he had.

"Sight for sore eyes," Warner chimed in. "Was always sorry we never had a chance to talk after that Washington thing fell through for you."

Harry leaned his chin on his fists. His eyes were merry. "Well, that's the whole point of my looking you up," Harry said. "This is the first chance I've had to thank you. You see, it didn't fall through."

Warner looked very puzzled indeed.

"I know," Harry said, "that's what they told you. Our . . . mutual friend . . . is a demon at playing those cards up against his vest. Took months before he told me it was his idea to have you look me up in the first place."

Warner chuckled knowingly. Of course, he didn't know one goddam thing about the man, but close-to-the-vest sure seemed like his style, all right.

"I'm off the assignment now," Harry said in a confidential murmur. "Waiting for the next one."

"Well, sounds damned exciting," Warner said heart-ily. "Had no idea. Kept me in the dark. I'm glad it worked out so well for you, Harry. Glad to have helped it along."

Harry just kept smiling at him. Just a calm, warm little smile that told Warner something good was wait-ing at the other end of it.

"I'm very grateful," Harry said at last. "I've talked to our mutual friend about you. We need someone who can step in at a high level down at Treasury and knock a few heads together. If you catch my drift."

Warner caught his drift.

The first gimlet arrived, and with it the beginnings of a rosy glow.

FORTY-FIVE

Quiet brick home in Alexandria, Virginia. A man stood in the frosted air of two o'clock in the morning. Gloved fingers picking through the keys. Must have forgotten to leave the porchlight timer on. More likely, the housekeeper screwed it up in her dusting.

Children grown, wife long since discarded, Ross Buckley was accustomed to the gentle inconveniences of the man who has chosen to live alone.

Buckley found the key and let himself in.

The Director of SIA stopped at his hall closet and unburdened himself of overcoat and muffler. He was aware that his right shoulder was still aching, and he began to rub it gingerly as he headed for the kitchen. He didn't really believe in bursitis, but the ache had a nagging way of returning for a couple of days after his weekly racketball.

In the kitchen, he found that Mrs. Dunbar had left some freshly baked brownies. Apparently, she'd cut a few for herself before covering them neatly with plastic wrap. He put four on a plate and, balancing a cold glass of milk, made his way to the den.

At the darkened doorway, he reached with his elbow for the light switch, feeling that twinge again. A thought had begun to rise to consciousness, but the

twinge had cut it off. The thought that Mrs. Dunbar
had never before helped herself to a fresh batch of
brownies.

Before the thought could surface, the light snapped
on.

Buckley did not drop the glass, but the involuntary
convulsion of his arm caused the milk to slosh neatly
over his wrist and his Rolex, splattering onto his right
shoe.

"Hi ya, Buck," said Harry Lime. "Long time, no
see."

Harry was seated in Buckley's overstuffed wing
chair. His overcoat was folded neatly across his lap.
In his left hand, he held a half-eaten genuine Mrs.
Dunbar brownie. The hand itself was encased in a
glove. A clear plastic surgical glove. His right hand
was beneath the overcoat.

"Sit down, Buck," the voice said pleasantly. "Make
yourself at home. Please."

Harry saw Buckley's eyes go once quickly to the
overcoat, then up to meet his own.

Buckley smiled. The strong, confident smile Harry
had not seen for nine years. The eyes had their cool
but merry twinkle. They said, You are my equal. One
of the few. That is our friendship.

"It's good to see you, Harry," he said. "I mean that.
Never thought I'd see you again."

Buckley set down the brownies and what was left
of the milk. He plumped himself down into a chair
and just sat there with his big square smile.

"So whatya think?" Harry said softly. "You think
the Giants'll win the pennant?"

Buckley's smile stayed a little too firmly in place.

"Really," Harry said. "I figure they finally got the
pitching. And they're set at third. Ah, but right field.
What're they gonna do with right?"

Buckley tried an amused shake of the head.

"Come on, Buck. You used to follow this stuff. You used to know."

Buckley folded his thick hands in the center of his lap.

"Harry. It's the twenty-ninth of December."

"Hey, anybody can pick 'em once the season starts."

Buckley tried to chuckle. But no real sound came. A pantomime of a man chuckling.

"It's man talk," Harry said happily. "I just yearn for some good old-fashioned man talk, Buck. About fucking and fishing and shooting a man in the face. I just want some masculine company, Buck. Need I remind you that I'm a guest in your home?"

"I sent a man to kill you, Harry. You probably noticed."

" 'Course you did, Buck. What else could you do? Our friend told you I was a traitor. Showed you the files he'd put together with KGB. He told you I'd sold our country down the river, didn't he, Buck?"

Buckley thought for a moment. With a steady hand, he picked up a brownie and took a huge bite. From somewhere, he found the moisture to chew and swallow.

"How's the golf game, Buck? Playing any stud poker these days?"

Harry's voice was sweet and his eyes were plenty crazy. "Gettin' laid? How're the kids?"

The hand under the overcoat moved slightly, and Buckley could not keep his eyes totally still.

"Who are you talking about, Harry?"

Harry watched him swallow the brownie, reach for the milk.

"Don't protect him, Buck. He lied to you. He's the traitor, Buck. He's working with the Russians. They've spun this web to invade the Gulf. Once they're in there, it's all over for us, Buck. Can you see that?"

Buckley cocked his head to one side. The way he always had.

"I guess," Buckley said, "I don't really know what to believe. That seems to be a chronic condition of this job. Gets worse every year. I do know one thing. I ordered you killed, Harry. That's part of my job, too. If that's your beef, it's with me."

Harry shook his head.

"Can't be," he said.

"Why not?"

"If it was you," Hary said, "you'd have a hole right through the middle of you. About the size of a pack of cigarettes. There'd be blood and little pieces of you all over this room."

Harry's voice dropped a tone.

"But there you sit. Choking down your fucking brownie and trying not to pee in your pants. So it's not you, Buck. Just thank whatever you use for God that it's not you."

Buckley's smile was gone.

"You sound upset, Harry. That's not like you. You are a professional. You always were. From the first day. Rage isn't going to help you, Harry. And you know that."

Harry looked down at the overcoat in his lap. When he looked up, his face was stranger than ever.

"What will help me, Buck? Will you help me?"

Buckley spread his palms.

"I won't lie to you, Harry. I don't know whether I'll help you or not. All I can do is what seems right. If things have been put wrong, you tell me about it. I'll listen. You're in a lot of trouble, Harry."

Harry shook his head. The easy smile returned.

"I'm not in trouble," Harry said. "I just feel bad,

that's all. I feel bad because I'm a dead man, Buck. I sat up there in the snow on some mountain in Switzerland. Freezing my balls off. Waiting for Mr. Reika to stroll up that trail. I knew that I was dead, Buck. Either in five minutes or five days or fifty. That ever happen to you?"

"No, Harry. Never has."

Harry nodded. His eyes were sympathetic. Wanted to help Buckley understand.

"Well," Harry said, "it makes you feel bad. You've seen *Our Town*, haven't you, Buck? Thornton Wilder? 'Good-bye to clocks ticking'? I have a daughter, Buck. I'll never know her as an adult. We were going to take a couple months sometime. The two of us. Drive through Scotland. All the way up to Skye. There are still some things I have to tell her. I've had my last of everything, Buck. Everything in the world. I won't be there when the Marines roll into Riyadh. Won't be around for spring training either. So tell me about the Giants, Buck. I really want to know."

Buck shook his head. "Doesn't have to be that way, Harry."

Harry's eyes narrowed. "You're goddam right it doesn't," Harry said. "Not for me. The only question left, Buck, is whether it has to be that way for you."

The words, the voice, the stone-dead glow of Harry's eyes. Every muscle in Buckley's body twisted into a knot.

"Like I said, Buck, I'm not in trouble. I just feel bad. But I know when I'm going to feel better. When I have him alone with me in a room. Like this. He's going to die so slowly, Buck. It won't even start until all the piss and shit and tears he's got are all over him. And, Buck, then I'm not going to feel bad anymore. Is that professional enough for you, Buck?"

There was no sound. No air to breathe.

"You still have that little place, Buck, down 301? Near King George?"

Buckley barely nodded.

"Nobody's there right now, are they, Buck? And you want very much to tell me the truth."

"Nobody."

"Now, what you want to do, Buck ... what you want to do very, very much ... is take that telephone next to you. You want to squat right down on the floor with it. Right here in front of me. You want to call the man who showed you that file. You tell him to meet us there in three hours. That is five-fifteen. If he's not there on the button, alone, then you're dead, and *The Washington Post* receives a fascinating thirty-two-page document."

Buckley seemed frozen solid.

"I can't do what you want, Harry," he said at last. "You're all twisted around inside. There's no one to call. The file came straight from Lepeshkin to me. We all believed it. We didn't want to, but in the end we did. There's no conspiracy. There just isn't. If the Russians were setting you up, to lead us into this thing in the Gulf, they did it alone. And they did it goddam well."

Harry's face slackened. He was thinking.

"The man I want," Harry said very slowly, "is the man who hired me. They told me my name was recommended by an old school chum. But that wasn't quite the case, was it, Buck? Someone on the inside came up with my name first. Probably had a hell of a time talking you all into it. Am I right? Not exactly an ideal background for a sensitive position. Scandal, treason, coverup. But I was made to order for *him*. He knew I was perfect for this particular fall. There is such a man, isn't there, Buck?"

Buckley licked his lips.

"If there was a man," Buckley said, strength oddly returning to his voice, "who came up with your name. If there was. What the hell would that prove?"

"I'm not trying to prove anything, Buck. I'm just trying to kill someone. If, by coincidence, my little conspiracy theory happens to be not so insane after all, I should think it would be of passing interest to you."

Buckley seemed overtaken by a sudden calm.

"You're asking me to send a man down to King George for you to kill."

Harry slid his overcoat onto the floor. In his gloved right hand he held the tiny pistol Andy Maclennon had given him so long ago.

"I'm asking you, Buck, to save your own life. Because if you won't make this phone call for me now . . . I can never let you make another."

Color slowly drained from Buckley's face.

"With or without you," Harry said, "I'll get him. But you're the only one, Buck, who knows I'm still alive. If you're not part of my solution, as they say, I'm afraid you're part of my problem."

Buckley pressed his fingertips together, brought them to his lips.

"You want him that badly?"

"And if you knew the truth, Buck, so would you. But trusting me is somewhat beside the point. The point is that I know you to be a man whose intelligence overwhelms his courage. Please don't disappoint me."

A clicking sound came from the gun in Harry's hand.

"Let me rephrase that," Harry said. "If you disappoint me for the next sixty seconds, the first bullet will enter your left thigh. You will then have all the time you need to decide not to disappoint me a second time."

Buckley reached slowly for the telephone. He stood and stepped to the center of the Persian throw rug. Harry nodded. Buckley sat, fell, heavily. The telephone in his lap, he punched a number into the touchtone receiver, and a song of seven electronic notes jarred the silence.

Harry straightened his right arm. The gun was held steady at Buckley's face. The distance was less than ten feet.

"This is Ross Buckley. Please wake the General for me. Tell him I have a message that is urgent and private."

There was a pause. Harry guessed it to be not more than thirty seconds.

"Hubert. I'm with Harry Lime. Yes, now."

There was another pause.

"My country place off 301. Yes. Yes. At five-fifteen precisely. You must be completely alone. Harry has something to share with us about our Russian friends. Yes. Of course."

Buckley replaced the receiver.

The gun remained at arm's length. Held steady at its target.

"Who was that?" Harry said quietly.

Buckley blinked. "Hubert, of course. You heard me."

Harry smiled with a most unnerving slowness. "His number plays a different tune on your phone, Buck. I took the trouble to learn it."

Buckley blinked again. Returned the smile.

"He was with his lady friend," Buckley said. "Every Monday, every Thursday."

Harry's arm slowly lowered. The elbow rested on his thigh. The pistol lay flat upon his knee.

"Can I get up?" Buckley asked.

Harry bit his lip, as though he had been asked a most complex question. His thought continued for a long moment.

"You saw Lepeshkin's file yourself?" he said finally.

"Yes. Very thorough, very convincing."

Harry nodded. Buckley stretched his thick legs out in front of him.

"What was the code name by which Lepeshkin referred to me?"

"Harbinger."

Harry nodded again. He began to slowly shift the pistol from one hand to the other. Buckley's eyes followed.

"How did you know it was really me? Any of your people actually see me?"

"No. Only KGB."

"Then what convinced you that it was me? Could have been an imposter. Could have been a complete fabrication."

"Well, the photos, of course."

Harry's eyebrows raised.

"There were photographs?" he said, with mild surprise.

"Harry, we ran them through every chemical and electronic analysis possible. They seemed totally authentic."

Harry nodded. He reached inside the pocket of his jacket and pulled out a scrap of paper.

"A reliable source," Harry said quietly, "advised me that there was a photo of myself in the company of a German General named . . ." Harry glanced down at the paper, "Heinrich Weber. And a Chinese General named Xing Dzu-lin. It was reported that this photo was the single most conclusive piece of evidence condemning me in the eyes of SIA."

Buckley nodded immediately. "As I said, Harry. We ran it through every test in the book."

The slow smile returned to Harry's face. "Good likeness?" he asked.

The sudden twinge at the corners of Buckley's eyes was duly recorded.

Harry reached into the pocket of his overcoat, and tossed a folded manila envelope into Buckley's lap.

Harry looked only at the man's eyes as he tore the envelope and unfolded the photograph.

Buckley shook his head. "It's incredible," Buckley said. "It's the same photo, but this one's obviously been cropped. This is Dave Taradan, of course. The photo I saw was of you."

Harry's brow furrowed.

"Is such a thing really possible, Buck? I mean, look at it. Dave's hands are extended in front of the woman. The shadows. How could it have been spliced together?"

Buckley just kept staring at the picture.

"You're right, of course," he said. "This photo has to be authentic. The shot must have been entirely restaged with the same three people and Taradan. In fact, as I look at it, the positions of all the figures seem slightly different. I don't know what to make of it."

"Imagine my bewilderment," Harry said softly.

"Harry, what the hell does this mean?"

"Could mean almost anything," Harry mused. "Taradan is, after all, Longview's man. Correct?"

Buckley nodded, as if the light were slowly dawning.

"And you're certain," Harry said, "that it was Longview who first suggested I be brought back to the government? You're absolutely positive?"

"Yes, of course."

"Maybe my old school buddy, this guy Warner Alden, maybe he called Longview first. Put the idea in his head."

Buckley shook his head. "No. Hubert called the man from my office. Told this Alden that he could do an important service for his country. Had to be kept very confidential. In fact, Taradan was with us when he called. Then Hubert sent Taradan to New York to instruct this guy on just how to handle you. Now Taradan shows up in this picture. I'm lost here, Harry. What does it mean?"

For the first time, Harry's eyes seemed almost sad.

"It means," Harry said, "that we all get older, Buck. I guess none of us is the man he used to be."

Harry reached into the side pocket of his jacket. He took out two small objects. Slowly, he placed them into the chambers of his pistol.

"Weren't any bullets in this thing," Harry said very softly. "Until now."

Harry was still looking down at the weapon.

"You used to be," he said sadly, "a wonderful liar, Buck."

Harry looked up into the panic spreading across Buckley's face.

"You've made enough mistakes tonight to fill up a lifetime," Harry said. "And, in fact, they have."

Harry's right arm straightened and the gun was leveled squarely at Buckley's eyes. The arm was rock-steady.

"So," Harry said, "it's good-bye to clocks ticking. But I'll fill you in before you go. The Marines aren't going to Riyadh, Buck. And the Giants aren't going anywhere at all."

FORTY-SIX

He would not wait for Harry Lime's appointed hour.

He sped through the dark Virginia countryside, snow-covered fields in the softness of a quarter moon. He knew the way, the shortest way. He would beat Lime there.

It was 4:27 as his high beams caught the outline of the place, far ahead. His lights flicked off and his foot left the accelerator. He coasted nearly to a stop, then pulled the car well off the road.

It was half a mile in bitter cold. He walked the distance slowly, careful not to slip on the icy road. He wore a large coat with deep pockets, and as he walked his right hand touched its pocket more than once, reassuring the rest of him.

As he took his first step up the wooden porch, he stopped. The creak of his own footfall was startlingly loud. The house was dark, the front door slightly ajar.

Three more steps and he was at the landing. As he pushed the door, it clanged into a teakettle placed directly behind. The kettle rolled endlessly across the wooden floor.

He stood in the doorway now, heart pounding loud enough to hear. The house was completely black, and as cold as the night outside. He could see only a few feet into the hallway.

He cleared his throat softly. "Harry?" he called.

There was no answer. He stood for what seemed to be minutes. At the far end of the hall, a light switched on. It came from a room at the left side of the hallway. In four seconds, it switched off again.

Slowly, he started down the hall. Left hand groping blindly before him. Right hand thrust in his pocket. It took forever to find his way to the end of the hall. When he did, the light switched on again. Blinking into the room, he saw a library. An empty reading chair with a lamp standing over it. It was the only light in the room.

"Sit down, Billy," Harry said.

Parkens squinted toward the voice. At the far corner of the room, in only the palest light, sat Harry Lime. Harry was wearing a loose-fitting overcoat, slightly opened. He sat in a relaxed posture, legs stretched out before him. His hands rested lightly on the arms of his chair.

"I said, sit down."

Parkens took his seat in the glare of the lamplight. "Can't see you very well," he said.

"I can see you just fine," Harry said. "Why don't you take off your coat?"

"Cold," Parkens said. "Damn cold."

There was no answer. His eyes were adjusting. He could see Harry now, dimly, see his face. The small smile.

"Where's Buck?" Parkens asked.

"Doesn't seem to be around."

Parkens' eyes were thoughtful. They moved slowly about the room.

"Why the theatrics?" Parkens asked.

"I just want to be not dead," Harry said. "A little while longer."

Parkens' face lost its edge of patrician impatience, became very neutral, thoughtful once again.

"What did Buck tell you about that?" he asked. "Did he tell you that we . . . sent someone for you?"

"Subject never came up."

"You have to understand, Harry. We ordered that before we knew about Hubert."

"Like a drink?" Harry said.

Parkens shook his head. "Too damn cold," he said, and his hands reached well into the pockets of his overcoat. There they stayed.

"Just as well," Harry said, "I'm not really sure where Buck keeps the booze around here. Say, I bring you greetings from New York."

"New York?"

"Warner Alden. The guy you picked to recruit me."

Parkens nodded. He recognized the name.

"Didn't really know him," Parkens said. "I was looking for someone who knew you well. He was your class rep, so I rang him up first. He said he was close to you. I asked him to help."

"You also told him to keep your name out of it," Harry said mildly.

Parkens' face was slightly puzzled. "Did I? Perhaps I did. I was keeping a low profile in the early days. Thought it would make me more effective."

Harry nodded. He understood. It was quiet again.

"Did Buck," Parkens began, "tell you anything about our problem with Hubert?"

"Oh, dear," Harry said softly. "A problem with Hubert."

The twinge of impatience returned to Parkens' eyes. He looked down for a moment. When he looked up, his brow was deeply rutted. This was a serious matter.

"You've been through a lot," Parkens said slowly. "You're entitled to be angry. You're not entitled to be stupid. We sent a man to kill you, Harry. Do you know why?"

Harry sat immobile. Fingers lightly resting on the curved wooden arms of his chair.

"You thought I was the enemy," Harry said. His voice seemed to come from far away. "You thought I was in league with nasty wogs and Chinamen. You thought I was a terrible person."

Parkens squinted. He was trying to see enough of Harry's eyes to read them.

"Thinking as you did, Billy, you did the right thing. Put your faith in the KGB. Why not? They haven't been the enemy for more than fifty years. And it was such an official-looking file, too. With pictures, even."

Parkens cocked his head a little sideways. He was studying Harry now. Thoroughly and with obvious interest.

"File?" he said at last.

"Harbinger file."

Parkens' face showed not the slightest recognition.

"May I smoke?" Parkens asked.

Hands slowly withdrawing from the pockets of the overcoat. Long fingers, exquisitely groomed, reaching to the inside breast pocket of his jacket.

"Each in a different business, you and I," he said.

Fingertips extracted a cigarette case. Flat and gold.

"I'm out of my element here, Harry. You know, I'm not even sure what I do for a living anymore. I'm goddam in the dark about your people."

He held the open case toward Harry. Harry shook his head once.

"What I'm doing here," Parkens said, "at least what I think I'm doing here, is bringing you back in."

Parkens' eyes stayed on the flame as he stopped to

light his cigarette. He was comfortable in delibera-
tion, accustomed to having others submit to his
rhythms.

"Maybe that's not such a good idea," he said. "Harry,
I'm all out of ideas. All out of people to trust."

Harry said nothing.

The golden case returned to its breast pocket.
Parkens drew deeply on the cigarette.

"Why don't I try the unexpected," Parkens said,
"and simply tell you what I know."

His smile was disarming.

"Six days ago," he said, "I was at Camp David. The
President took me on a little stroll. He told me that
Hubert Longview has betrayed our country."

Smoke billowing now around his head. Eyes coolly
peering through. Reading, reaching.

"Hubert and certain members of KGB have con-
spired to send our two nations to war, together, against
the rest of the world. Hubert and Woolly Sharpening
and whomever Woolly has lined up at the Pentagon."

Confiding eyes now. Offering the trust of a man
with no alternative.

"You told Buck to call Hubert," Parkens said. "He
couldn't risk that. So he rang me instead."

Harry nodded.

"So Buck isn't part of the problem," Harry said.

Parkens' thin lips pressed tightly together. The eyes
paused.

"Not according to the President's information."

"In which," Harry said, "you have full confidence."

A small shake of Parkens' head. "I'm scared, Harry.
I've got Buck watching Hubert. But nobody's watching Buck. I don't know these people, Harry. Your
people. I don't understand how they work inside."

The friendly smile returned to Parkens' golden features. "And you," Parkens said, "I don't know, as

they say, from Adam. If I trust you, I've lost my fingerhold on reality."

Manicured finger tapping his knee.

"If I trust you . . ." he said again, almost to himself. "Believe me, Harry. I don't."

Studying Harry's silence. Harry's stillness.

"You have one thing going for you, Harry. The Judas kiss. You were condemned by the traitor. Other than that, I don't have a kind thought for you. But I want to know what you know, what you think."

Harry did not move. "I think," Harry said, "that you are wasting my time."

Parkens' eyes were puzzled once again.

"It was you, Billy."

There was honest concern on Parkens' face. Sympathy for the misdirected.

"Your plan," Harry said. "Your dream. Your operation. Buck told me."

"And . . . you believed him."

"Yes," Harry said. "I'm afraid I do."

Parkens' eyes were now reaching off into distance. Searching for a way to help Harry understand.

"And what," he said at last, "what if it were true? Do you know, Harry, what we are really facing? Deprivation. Strangulation, anarchy. We are the strongest people on earth, Harry. And we're helping these piss-ants castrate us."

His shoulders hunched, perhaps against the cold. His hands slid quietly into the pockets of the overcoat.

"They're goddanm smug, Harry. They've got the oil. They've got the cash. They come into Manhattan and L.A. and Houston and they buy up the best of everything. They drive our industries into bankruptcy. They hold our life's blood for ransom and then buy what's left of us with our own money. And we, well, we kiss their ass."

There was no anger in his eyes. They were clear and flat and open.

"Saddest of all, Harry, we have the muscle. Only we're sitting on it. Afraid of it. Stalemated by our fear of the Soviet Union, whom we call enemy. Well, if we sit on it any longer, Harry, we're going to find out who the real enemy is, who's been bleeding our soul for the past twenty years."

His lips were pulled back now. His teeth seemed to gleam in the lamplight.

"Allied with the Soviets," he said, "we have a monopoly of our own, Harry. A two-nation cartel of conventional and nuclear military supremacy. It won't last forever, Harry, but thank God it's still there. They've used their monopoly to the hilt, Harry, and we goddam better well use ours."

There was a change in the eyes now. Harry could see it. They were under control, but flashing and snarling just the same.

"We're going to roll in, Harry. Roll in. Roll. Roll into that pathetic little sandbox they call a country. We're going to beat the living shit out of those bastards. Beat them, Harry, beat them bad. Then we're going to turn to the East and to the West and say, 'Who's next? Who wants a taste?' "

Harry nodded.

"Bear's in the Gulf," Harry said. "Seems like he'll have more than a taste."

Parkens' left hand came out of its pocket, fingers spread, palm out.

"We'll handle the Soviets. We've stalemated them for fifty years. We can do it forever."

"Oh," Harry said.

There was a long silence.

Parkens' beautiful features gathered in disbelief. "You can't tell me," he said, "that you don't really see it. Down there past whatever you use to tell yourself that you're who you'd like to be. Down there past all the easy lies. I'm going to save this country, Harry. Save our people."

Harry shook his head. "You're going to start a war, Billy." His voice was very soft. "Maybe a nuclear war."

"Won't be a shot fired outside of that sandy little anthill."

"Unless . . ." Harry said, "unless, of course, you're wrong. If you are, I know that we can all expect an immediate apology. It's all in the breeding, isn't it, Billy? Princeton, I believe?"

"The fact of the matter," Parkens said, "is that I'm not wrong."

"Sure hope not. When you take unto yourself guessing about life or death for a few hundred million people, I know you'd feel just awful if something didn't go according to your analysis of the situation."

Harry smiled. "Come to think," he went on, "they elected a guy named Cole to make some of those decisions. Why wasn't he taken into your confidence, Billy? Too blind, too gutless?"

Harry stopped and looked at the man. "Sorry, Billy, now I'm wasting *your* time. You want to hear it from Darwin, not Jefferson."

The puzzled look slowly returned to Parkens.

"Forget right and wrong," Harry said. "Go straight to the bottom line. You got beat. I beat Reika. I beat Buck. I beat you."

Parkens' smile came very slowly. Slow and thin, it split his face in two. Slower still, almost as an afterthought, his right hand left its pocket, and in it was what looked to be a .45. Huge and black.

"Tell me everything," Parkens said. "Slowly and in magnificent detail."

Harry's hands still rested lightly on the arms of his chair. He pressed his elbow against Andy Maclennon's spring. His hand raised slightly, and the pistol leapt down his arm toward his palm. All he had to do was catch it.

He did.

Harry's fingers closed and the gun was there. Tiny, silver. Aimed at Parkens' chest.

Parkens' smile never wavered.

"Parity," said Parkens. "Time to negotiate."

Harry shook his head. His left hand slowly pulled his coat open.

"Ever seen flack apparel, Billy? Standard issue. It would take a small cannon to get through this. Billy, you're gonna have to hit me in the face. With your first shot. At this distance, in this light, I don't think you have one chance in hell of doing it."

Harry took a deep breath of pure satisfaction. "Now I want you to take a deep breath, Billy. I want you to suck up your balls and give it one good try for Princeton."

There was no sound. Only the terrible cold and Parkens rigid in the lamplight.

"You asked about my people, Billy. How we work inside. There's a silly old code of honor. You see, I can't kill you unless you take that first shot. And I want very much to kill you, Billy. Gonna be the high point of my young life. Let me smile for you, Billy. Give you some teeth to aim at. Just squeeze one off and let me empty this thing in your belly."

But Parkens did not move. Did not breathe.

Harry shook his head again. This time in disgust. "Turn the barrel toward yourself," Harry said wearily. "Slowly. Lay the thing on the floor. Slide it to me, butt first."

One more frozen moment. Then Parkens did as he was told.

The .45 lay at Harry's feet. Harry shifted his own gun to his left hand. From his coat pocket, he pulled a single rubber glove. Carefully, he slipped it on. Not a word was said.

Harry bent and picked up the .45 in his gloved hand. He held it steady at Parkens' chest.

"Flack jacket," Harry said, shaking his head. "A guy who believes in flack jackets would believe in Santa Claus. Or codes of honor."

Terror was now beginning to radiate from Parkens' eyes. The mask was starting to shatter.

"You know why I believed Buck?" Harry said. "I always believe what a man tells me between the screams."

And now Harry's smile shone through the dim.

"Not the first screams," he said. "Not the first hour. No. You wait for the real screams. The ones they can't catch their breath between. So it's just one long scream, with some words between. Ah, but those are the words you listen to, Billy. Those words are the truth."

FORTY-SEVEN

It must have dawned. It was light. There was no hint of where the sun might be, however. The sky was gray and darker gray above the snow.

Harry watched them drive up. A modest sedan. Three black and whites. They stopped a little way up the road. No one got out.

Harry stepped through the doorway and onto the covered porch. There was a wind, but somehow to Harry it seemed warmer on the landing than it had inside.

The passenger door of the sedan opened. Longview stepped out into the cold, clapping his bare hands together, blowing on them as he walked toward the house. Then his open hands raised to shoulder height, palms toward Harry.

"Friend of yours asked to be remembered," Longview said, squinting into the haze. Longview took a few more steps. "He said to tell you his name was Andy," Longview said. "The 'other Andy,' he said to tell you."

Inside the pocket of Harry's coat, his right hand released its grip. "Little fat guy?" Harry grinned. "Talks with an accent?"

"Never saw him," Longview grinned back. "With a British accent."

Slowly, Harry walked down the steps. Longview came to him and threw an arm around his shoulders.

"Let's take a walk," he said.

They set out across a field, snow rising well above their ankles. They walked very slowly, and four cars sat in the road in silence.

"Your friend Andy," Longview said at last, "told us you should have had more patience. His friend Comrade Lepeshkin has given him two names. I dropped by this morning to visit these gentlemen. They were nowhere to be found. Foul play is suspected."

They walked on through the snow. The black and whites seemed a million miles behind them now. Longview's arm firmly clasping Harry's shoulder.

"You like old movies, don't you Harry? Jesus, you should. You were named after one of them."

Harry looked over at the General's leathery face, clenched tight against the glare of the snow.

"Don't be so surprised," Longview said. "I'm a damned old guy. Thirteen years old when I saw *The Third Man*. Never forget it. Wonderful old film."

They walked on.

"My favorite was *Casablanca*. You remember *Casablanca*, Harry?"

Harry did.

"I mean," Longview said, "that part at the end. Bogie shoots the German. Claude Rains arrives on the scene. He takes one look at the situation, and he understands it all. He turns to his men and he says, 'The Major's been shot. Round up the usual suspects.'"

The hand on Harry's shoulder squeezed firmly. He was an old man walking with his only son, a son who had made him very proud.

"So I said to the boys as we motored down here this

fine morning. I said, I think we're just gonna have to round up the usual suspects."

Harry looked at him again. Longview's eyes were damp.

"Not one of them," Longview said, "knew what the hell I was talking about. Pups. Just pups."

Harry smiled. "Anyway," Harry said, "it's the thought that counts."

Longview did not understand.

"Buck's in the basement," Harry said. "Parkens in a closet in the back. They're tied up. Gagged. That's all. Not a mark on them."

Longview's smile just got bigger and bigger.

" 'Course they're not real men like you and me, Hubert."

Longview shook his head. " 'Course not," Longview said, tongue firmly in cheek. "Pansies."

"High-strung," Harry agreed.

Harry reached under his jacket, fumbled for a moment, then ripped out the recording device which had been taped to his belly. His fingers felt frozen solid, and by the time he popped the cassette loose, it fell to the fresh snow. He bent down to retrieve it.

"Something inadmissible for your listening pleasure," he said, and handed the cassette up to Longview.

"Much fascinating detail," Harry said, "arguably obtained, I'm afraid, under what might technically pass for psychological duress."

"Tape?" Longview said. "What tape?" And put the cassette in his pocket.

They walked on. Side by side now. Hands stuffed in their pockets. Heads bowed to the wind which was whipping around again from the south. They were quiet for a time. The road, the house, the black and whites, had disappeared. They were alone in the world.

"See," the General said at last, "I had this sort of

disagreement with Bobby Cole. He thinks there are more important things he can squeeze out of you than just running the Agency. I, of course, mentioned politely that he was full of shit."

They walked on.

"So whatya think?" Longview said at last.

"I think I'm in retirement," Harry said. "Starting very soon. Soon as my friend Andy and I keep one little date."

FORTY-EIGHT

High in the uplands of the Central Hijaz is the city of Ta'if, built of stone, five thousand feet above the sea. Its cooling breezes have made Ta'if a summer haven for the royal family of Saudi Arabia, and for its court and cabinet.

Now, in Saudi winter, the palace and courtyard seem almost deserted. Three men sit in a cool garden, looking down into the valley. They sit and are served the most elegant of luncheons. Gold and crystal and finest linen. And then the servants are gone, and the three men are left to their chat.

The Arab adjusts his mishlah about him as it billows in the breeze. His face and his hands are utterly serene. The black eyes now stare straight before him, now flick to the faces of his guests.

An hour slips past. Then another. The youngest, the American, speaks his monologue in soft and respectful tones. Every courtesy, every delicacy, is observed.

The Russian sits with fingers folded across his abdomen, his eyes half closed as if barely attending to the American's words. But now and again, gently, a guiding thought is offered. And when he speaks, the Arab listens most carefully of all.

The third hour passes, and the air is liquid with the freshness of the highlands.

At last the American has finished. There is a lingering stillness in the garden.

"Please know," began Majid ibn Fawwaz, "my gratitude. The gratitude of my King and my people. That we would be offered an opportunity to participate in an undertaking so auspicious and enterprising, is more than proof of the great bond between each of your nations and my own."

Silence.

"I can only admire in wonderment," Majid said, "the genius and the ambition of such a plan. I know that the prayers of my people, and of the entire world, will go with you in this effort."

With *you,* was the operative phrase. Voslov's eyelids drooped a bit lower.

"Of course," Majid continued, "I will report your gracious offer to the King and cabinet with the utmost enthusiasm."

Utmost.

"I only hope," Majid added, his eyes now finding Harry's, "that we will not be forced to conclude that . . . the cost . . . the very scope of what you are considering . . . may be somewhat beyond our available resources."

Harry nodded in total sympathy.

"Then, too," Harry said, "the sacrifice required in terms of our request concerning petroleum production. It seems, on reflection, more than even a people as great as yours should be asked to bear in any cause, however noble."

This thought was dismissed by Majid with the slightest motion of his hand. No sacrifice too great for friendship, the gesture said. The silence remained for a long moment.

"Being so near to Mecca," Harry said, "as we are now, makes one think of embracing Islam for himself. If only to be admitted for a single day to the Holy City."

Majid's head nodded slightly in agreement.

"So glorious," Majid said, "as to be without description. For myself, I regret the laws barring infidels from the city. So many of our dearest friends who will never know the surge of feeling that consumes one while in Mecca."

Harry nodded. "The jewel of the world," Harry said.

The silence again. Harry and Voslov would leave it there as long as needed. Sit carved in stone until the Arab spoke.

At long last, Majid cleared his throat. "Your mention of Mecca . . ." he said.

Harry looked straight at his eyes. "Only a stray thought."

The Arab forced a smile. "Please," he said, "share your thought with me."

"How precious Mecca is to the world," Harry said. "How important that she always stand."

Majid's face did not move. The cloud was unmistakable, nonetheless.

"There are," Harry said so softly, "sick and evil men in the world, my Prince. Some within the councils of the strongest of nations."

The air had disappeared from the garden. What was silence was now vacuum.

"I have heard," Harry went on, "such men say the most terrible things. Things I could never repeat to you."

Majid's eyes were now very hard. But his voice still the kindest of whispers. "I think, my friend, that you must."

Harry's eyes carried the weight of inexpressible sadness. "These men say if Arabia is ever to be threatened, that death is not the answer. For honorable death in defense of his faith is faced by every Arab without fear. So great is your people. So great their honor, their courage."

Majid's face was changing now, against his will.

"These men," Harry said softly, "say that to destroy Arabia would be without purpose, without effect. Rather, they would make a fiery crater of Mecca only, and leave all else untouched. Leave each Arab mercilessly alive to bear his grief without the release of honorable death."

It had been said. Voslov drew a heavy breath. "Shocking," Voslov said in quiet agreement.

Majid's face turned fully toward him. Voslov offered the Arab a small, pleasant smile. A smile terrible in its ease.

"Desperate men," Voslov said, "think desperate thoughts, my Prince. And what is diplomacy, if not the honest effort of the calm and wise to save the world from desperation?"

FORTY-NINE

Glass tubes. Above, below, in all directions. Still figures passing through space on moving belts.

A musical tone. A woman's voice in three languages. Swissair to Teheran. Air France to Helsinki. Another tone, another voice. Silent figures, moving silently toward Frankfurt and Milan.

She held his hand. Her fingers pressing too tightly. The fingers were saying what had already been said. The same lies. She accepted—she understood. She was all right. He wasn't to worry about her.

The ticket exchanged for boarding pass, the bag collected, the passport stamped. There were twenty minutes and nothing to say.

They stood. A toddler wobbled about, spouting baby-French, under the watchful eye of her mother. The father sat to one side, eating chocolate and oranges.

They stood. Three nuns bustled by with handsome leather bags, vows of poverty notwithstanding. They spoke in German and their faces were very white, with perfect pink circles at their cheeks.

It was time.

Cassie's tears came so quickly, so openly, that Harry could not stop his own.

Her hands were loosely in his now. Staring at each

other's tears. Smiling, squeezing fingertips. She looked
so lovely, just now. Lime's Crisis. In all the textbooks.
He touched her face. He kissed her.
He was gone.

FIFTY

The din was enormous, the electricity undeniable. They had been summoned to State 405, the huge, oak-paneled theater deep within the State Department. Not only diplomats and congressional leadership, but hundreds of invitations to a press corps more accustomed to after-the-fact table scraps from second assistant press secretaries. Black tie, please. Open bar at 5:30 o'clock. From Bobby Cole, no less. The Prince Hamlet of silent, brooding frustration. Buffet to follow.

Six fifty-six, Eastern Standard Time. Television technicians swarmed at the apron of the stage. Each cameraman and boom operator, each nervous fellow with his clipboard, in full evening dress.

If it were possible, the noise level moved up still another notch. Excitement had been extinct in this city for years. They were chattering and beaming and pressing flesh in their joyous amazement at finding themselves still able to feel alive. The bar had been open for ninety minutes, for godsake, and they were juiced and ready as they would ever be.

Howard Dougherty, fat and red-faced, mike in one hand, drink in the other, grinned his way to the center of the stage. Jovial would be selling it short. The

Press Secretary had swallowed a canary the size of an ostrich. Reporters who had hated his guts now called his name and waved. Howard waved back, spilling a drop or two in the process.

"There are two minutes to network air," he said into the microphone. "Find your seats, folks. Help each other out. Settle down now, for chrissake. One minute forty-five to air."

There was good-natured grumbling, bodies jostling past one another in the scramble for seats. On the stage, overseeing it all, was Dougherty's benign grin.

"Sixty seconds," he said. "Buy you all another round at the buffet." He turned and walked smartly to the wings.

An unseen voice, "Thirty seconds, please. Thirty seconds to air. Everyone very quiet now."

And, miraculously, within ten seconds, they were.

Silence hovering. Curtain up. Single podium. The Seal.

Camera two, red light on.

"Ladies and gentlemen, the President of the United States."

Hail to the Chief. Suddenly they were on their goddam feet, bless their hearts.

Cole appeared at the back of the hall, handsome, nearly gorgeous, in crisp evening jacket. He walked slowly up the center aisle and they pumped his hand and they reached to touch him and Sonja Barnet actually gave him a big wet kiss on the cheek.

It was a victory march. And no one knew what the hell it was he had to say.

He stood at the podium, above the Seal. He waved and they applauded and *Hail to the Chief* kept the gooseflesh in place.

There was no doubt from the third row. There was no doubt from the monitors in the control booth. Two hundred million Americans were seeing some good honest mist in their President's eyes tonight.

The strong, square hands raised above his head at last.

"My fellow Americans . . ."

He paused. Looked around the hall.

"If those of you at home sense an air of celebration in this hall tonight, I must tell you that this reception is a glorious mystery to me."

He looked around the hall again.

"Glorious. Because it *is* a celebration. Mysterious, because I don't think that any of these good people know what the heck we're celebrating."

Laughter.

"I was so committed to preventing a leak, I haven't even told Howard yet."

More laughter. Cole joined them.

"You know," he said, "a President, a part of a President, is still a politician. And a politician learns early on that it's a big mistake to make a sweeping, optimistic prediction of any kind."

He leaned forward on the podium for emphasis.

"It's a mistake because if you happen by accident to be right, well, the good news is old hat by the time it gets here."

His voice became richer, deeper.

"It's a mistake because when you're wrong, you've let the people down. Built up their hopes and not delivered."

Right arm forward, finger thrusting at the air.

"It's a cruel thing to let your people down in that way. So it's a risk not many politicians take."

Hands flat on the podium before him.

"You've got to be pretty darn sure you can deliver the goods."

His smile could not be suppressed any longer.

"Well, tonight we celebrate a most extraordinary international partnership. A breakthrough in meeting the energy needs of this nation, both now and for the future."

Sharp, strong applause. Houselights down. From behind the podium, a large screen is lowered.

"Future first," Cole said into the microphone.

The hall was dark now. The screen lit with a detailed animation. A flat golden rectangle was spinning in the blackness of space. Brilliant blue earth beneath. The room was deadly still.

"The Saudis," came the President's voice through the darkness, "and our other good friends among the nations of OPEC, how did they come by their dominant position in the economy of our planet? And let us not mince words as to the extent of their power."

Silence. The rectangle twisted slowly, soundlessly.

"Any American schoolchild can answer that question. These people were able to monopolize something that everyone needs. Energy. And the stronger, the more advanced the nation, like our own, the more we need it."

Silence again.

"What a miracle it would be to assume such a monopoly position for ourselves. To control a major source of world energy, use all we need for our own purposes, and sell the rest to our friends at prices of our choosing."

Silence once more.

"What is our monopoly? Where is our cartel? The answer is obvious. Together with the Soviet Union, we share a practical monopoly on the technology of space."

And now camera three picked up the President's profile. In the booth, this image was superimposed on the spinning rectangle.

"Energy from space? You will be as amazed as I was to learn that most of the elements of the necessary technology have long been in place."

The voice gained still more resonance.

"It was the politics that were impossible, the politics that kept us prisoner. How could we join together in partnership with a nation whose political ideology is so opposite to our own? How could such a partnership work? What would it mean?"

Brilliant light shone from the mirrored reflectors of the spinning rectangle. Like a leaf, the flat mirrors turned soundlessly to the sun.

"What it will mean is new life, new prosperity, for both our nations. It will work because the leadership of the Soviet Union, despite our long-standing irreconcilable differences, wants that new life and new prosperity for its people. I have spoken directly with Secretary Cherny, and I have found him to be a brilliant man, a realistic man, a man who understands and is dedicated to being responsive to the needs of his people."

The pause was the longest thus far.

"You are looking at a power satellite. Only one design. There are many others. Why in space? Sunlight is the ultimate, inexhaustible, source of energy. Above the atmosphere, the sun is many times more intense than on the Sahara Desert at high noon. There is no night, no cloud, no question of angle or filter. The collectors always face the sun. The transmitter always faces its receiver on the earth."

The screen filled now with the detailed image of the collector panels. Camera slowly moving across solar cells and mirrors.

"The size is potentially unlimited. The panels on the model we are watching would be eleven miles long. The large figure you see there in the center is the transmitting antenna. The energy collected by the panels is converted into microwaves and beamed to its receiver on earth."

Detail of the transmitter. Artistic license showing the earthbound beam of microwaves as one would see a beam of light.

"Microwave energy beamed continuously would be safe, quite unlike the pulsed radiation we find in our kitchen ovens. Let me stress this again, for all who share my concern for our environment. Microwave is simply a warming ray, it is neither ionizing nor radioactive. Safer, actually, than the sun itself."

The image on the screen has suddenly shifted to rows and rows of flat rectangular panels. Incredibly long, stretching endlessly, each tilted slightly from the upright, toward the sky. The panels that Norris Steingart had carefully described to Harry as they strolled through a quiet garden. The camera pulls back sharply to reveal that the rows of panels are bobbing slightly. They are on the sea.

"These panels form the rectenna, the receiving antenna. Again, size is virtually limitless. This model is sixteen miles in diameter. It generates sufficient electricity to fully service twelve cities the size of Washington, D.C. We can put these out to sea, in the middle of deserts, wasteland, anywhere most convenient and economic."

Once again, we are out in space. Now a wafer-thin silver rectangle hovers motionless above the earth. Artistic license shows a beam of light from earth bouncing off the rectangle and back to a different point.

"This is a relay satellite. When we've stored up all the energy we wish to use, we can beam the excess to our overseas customers."

At the word "customers," an appreciative giggle tinkled through the crowd.

"Again, transmitters sending microwave beams to receivers. The satellite is in geosynchronous orbit, always remaining at the same point above the earth. Of course, this also means that we can have our own receivers anywhere and everywhere in the world."

House lights up. The President once again at his podium. Outstretched palms stifling applause before it can begin.

"How much of the world's energy needs can ultimately be supplied in this way?"

Smiling, making eye contact with the first row.

"How high is up?"

Instant, thunderous applause.

"What a dream for our children's future. Limitless, clean, safe energy for all the world's needs and plans and dreams. Industry, transportation, a world of tools that do not pollute our world, tools that work only *for* man, not against him."

More applause. And this time Bobby Cole let it run its course. More than two minutes.

"Worth working for?" he asked, and had to stand silent for another minute.

"Then roll up your sleeves. It is not a dream. But it is in the future. And don't look at your watch. Don't reach for a calendar. It hasn't been printed yet. Start thinking in terms of decades. Thirty years. Fifty years."

The room was quiet now.

"Part of the time is technology. Better and cheaper solar cells. But mostly, we're talking about money. Each one of these golden birds has to be carted to space in pieces and assembled on the job. They are expensive, ladies and gentlemen. They go up one at a time. Each one, precious as life itself. That is what we are investing in. Our life, our planet, our future."

Very quiet.

"Where does the money come from? Can the peoples of two great nations alone finance such a dream in half a century? And how are today's energy needs met, while we are waiting?"

And the smile returned to the broad, strong features.

"Well, like any experienced politician, I've saved a little of the best news for last."

Hands flat on the podium. Grin as wide as the Potomac.

"Our venture has a third partner. Our good friends of OPEC, spearheaded by the Kingdom of Saudi Arabia, have offered the major portion of the capital needed for our enterprise. They realize, responsibly and wisely, that the energy source they monopolize is finite. To our undying gratitude, they have chosen to invest in the infinite."

Vigorous applause.

"The return on their investment will be handsome. And it will continue for centuries after fossil fuels have passed into history."

Cole took a breath. He was in the home stretch now.

"This new partnership and the coming of the power satellite means that Saudi Arabia and other OPEC nations need no longer be as self-protective in conserving their own petroleum resources. Generously, they have offered to step forward to meet our current and, God willing, temporary, petroleum needs."

Applause became the crackle of thunder as the final piece fell into place.

"Saudi Arabia alone has volunteered an immediate and substantial increase of petroleum export to this country ... and by 'substantial,' I am speaking of millions of barrels per day."

His hands shot up to hold back the crowd, for the final words were too sweet to miss.

"This to be accompanied by an immediate reduction in the price of Arabian crude . . . a reduction of slightly more than forty percent . . ."

Nothing further could be heard. V-E Day, V-J Day. The war was over.

FIFTY-ONE

His legs were heavy. Halfway up Russian Hill and he was slowing down already. By Jones Street, he thought, I'll be going backward.

The gate. Macondray Lane. That hunk of nicely simmering lead had moved from where his ribs came together, right up to the base of his throat. This, of course, was a lucky break. If he could just asphixiate or prompt a coronary, maybe even just throw up on his nice new tan suit, they would all let him turn around and go back down Russian Hill.

One shallow, gulping breath. Harry's First Rule, the one he never used enough: You don't ask, you don't get.

Through the gate. Never find the goddam place anyway in this jungle. To his horror, he walked straight to it. He watched his hand, as if it were an alien insect, reach up and press the doorbell.

Before he could pray for a short circuit, he heard the song of Stu Hagen's cutesy-pie chimes.

Properly viewed, of course, he had simply come to ask one small question.

The door opened.

Jennylime appeared, a vision in pale yellow. Her ski tan was dark and creamy and altogether ravishing.

Her arms were folded across her breasts. She was a
little nervous. Her eyes said more good-nervous than
bad-nervous. His call had been so cryptic and strangled.

"Hi," he said. Once again, wizard of words. Master
of the bon mot. Never ceased to amaze himself.

"Hi," she said back, and the gray eyes really siz-
zled. There was some pop there tonight that shot
right to the base of the old medula oblongata.

"I sent Lissa to her girlfriend's," she said as they
walked to the den. "You said not to tell her you were
flying in. So, we're all alone."

Harry heard applause. Two rooms away, the television was playing Bobby Cole's address to an empty
sofa. No problem. Harry figured even the furniture
would give Bobby a standing ovation on this one.

"Stu's out?" he asked redundantly.

"Stuart's out," she said, sitting across from him. In
the interests of avoiding her breasts, Harry's eyes
wandered to Stu's shameless golf trophy, still promi-
nently displayed as a stupefying confession of egoma-
nia and gaucherie. Nice to know that some things
never change. Gives one a feeling of continuity with
the past.

"Stuart's out a lot lately," she added with a firm
smile.

"I think I'm supposed to say that I'm sorry to hear
that." His voice was very gentle.

"Everything ends," she said. Said with the immuta-
bility of $E = mc^2$. "Maybe this is that time."

Everything ends? For Harry, it was a question. The
only really worthwhile question in all the world. The
greatest truth. Greatest lie. Everything ends. It di-
vided the world into two religions.

"Small talk first?" she said. Smile of dazzling
honesty.

"First before what?" he said.

The smile became genuine amusement.

"You telephoned from Paris. You said you were flying to San Francisco so that you could ask me a question."

Harry remembered.

"Should have just asked you over the phone, huh?" he said. Certainly would have made one person in particular very happy. He should have done it that way. In fact, he had temporarily forgotten why he hadn't. Something about the right way to ask a question. Something just about that stupid.

She hugged one knee. "It's very good to see you," she said.

Harry just looked at the gray eyes and said nothing at all, because, suddenly, the gray eyes were telling him that he could say anything he wanted to.

"I'm growing up," she said.

"What's that mean?" he said. Once again, that majestic flow of rhetoric. The magic that was his alone. He sure hoped somebody was getting all this down.

Her smile grew very tight.

"Growing up," she said, "is learning the difference between what you think you want and what you really want."

Who the hell told her that?

"You told me that," she said, reading his face more than his mind. "On our second date. I thought it was the wisest, the truest thing, anyone had ever said."

Spellbinding. No other word for it.

"That was," he nodded, "before I outgrew the gift of articulate speech."

"The best people, you always said, are the ones who never let go of their dream. Once they find out what their heart really wants, they chase it and chase it and never give it up. Never till they die."

And now Harry was more than uncomfortable. He was starting to feel a little sick.

"The only thing is . . ." Harry said, and realized he was looking away from her. He looked up to her eyes.

"The thing is," he said softly, "that sometimes chasing your dream turns out to be . . . just . . . hanging on to your fantasy of the way things were supposed to be."

The light went out behind her eyes and he fought like crazy to keep from looking away again.

"The way things were supposed to be," he said with the saddest smile. "The place no one ever finds his way back to, because he was never there."

Not a dry eye in the house. He never thought it would be this way.

"We can't help but cry when we think about that place," he said, hearing his own voice. "Because it's the most wonderful place there is, the place where everything is finally right."

He had to reach over and take her hand. She squeezed with all her strength. Jennylime. Nothing ends.

"What I came to ask," he said, "is that I want Lissa with me now. I'm living in Paris. I'm with a woman I love very much. Her name is Cassie. We're . . . going to wind up married. We're the marrying kind. That's us. I want Lissa to live with us for a while, so that the three of us can love each other."

And two rooms away, the television was still speaking to its empty sofa. The President had finished his little chat. The anchorman was mopping up.

"And so the beautiful city of Ta'if, mountaintop retreat of Arabian royalty, finds its way into our language forever with the Ta'if Accord. Speculation, authoritative speculation, now is that this document was basically the handiwork of three statesmen. Three men who met, we are told, in the lonely splendor of a windswept garden and hammered out the principles that may change our world. Three men. Saudi, Russian, American.

"The Saudi was almost certainly Prince Majid ibn Fawwaz, Minister of Petroleum and Mineral Resources, thought perhaps to be the most powerful figure in his nation's government.

"The Russian may well have been Andrei Ilyich Voslov, an obscure but influential member of the Politburo and his country's ruling Presidium."

The anchorman paused. He actually turned his copy slip over, as if looking for hidden information. Apparently, there was none.

"The third man," he said simply, "remains unidentified."